PHOEBE'S SECRET

Phoebe's First Mystery

Sydney Tooman Betts

ISBN 978-1-7329079-3-5

For

Lincoln Arrow Schrock

2014-2019

"All I want is love
Love is the best
I love love"

Other series by
Sydney Tooman Betts

The People of the Book
A River Too Deep
Light Bird's Song
Straight Flies the Arrow

Phoebe's Mysteries
Phoebe's Secret

Chapter 1

April 26, 1843

"A MURDER?" squealed Augie. "A real murder?"

The errand boy bobbed his head like a straw-haired puppet. "Asa Kiker's foreman. My pop got a wire from Winchester this morning. Gash in his head as big as an ear of corn. Oh, and this came for you, Mrs. Farrel."

"Uh, thank you, young man." Reverend Farrell placed a Liberty dime in the small, outstretched hand and handed the folded paper to his wife.

Flashing a grateful grin, the youngster pocketed the coin and began trotting down the center aisle, but he paused when he reached the compartment's exit. "Be careful when y'all drive past The Lilacs, Kiker's plantation. They ain't caught the killer, so no tellin' where he's hidin'." Jumping onto the platform, he turned to wave as the train started rolling.

Only Phoebe noticed. Her father was watching her mother clutch the telegram to her heart; and Augie, eager to gain their attention, was bouncing up and down.

The reverend knit his salt and pepper eyebrows, leaning toward the seat opposite his own. "What does it say, Amelia?"

"Oh, Ernest, it's my mother. She's had an apoplectic seizure. The entire right side of her body refuses to function. My father begs me to return to Baltimore—I must get off the train."

"Slow down, darling, and hand me Lucy. You can't get off now, the engine's already picked up speed. Anyway, you would just have to wait at the station until this train returned."

"But my ticket. Father said I am to pick it up." Mrs. Farrell wadded up the telegram but thought better of it and thrust the

1

dispatch, instead of the baby, toward her husband. "Here, dear. Read it for yourself."

Smoothing out the wrinkled paper, Reverend Farrell softened his frown. "You've no need for concern. The stationmaster will issue it to you once you return to Winchester."

Augie began tugging his mother's sleeve. "Can we see the body?"

"She's ill, August, not dead."

"Not Grandma Ada, the man."

"What man?"

"The one who was murdered."

"Ernest, what *is* Augie going on about?"

"The lad who brought the telegram told us a man was found murdered this morning."

"Murdered? How dreadful. Somewhere nearby?"

"A local plantation, I gather. Dreadful indeed, however, at this moment, we have more pressing issues to discuss."

Mrs. Farrell sighed. "I don't relish the thought of another train trip, but it can't be helped. Ernest—the new parsonage. How can I leave you to sort everything out yourself?"

"I won't be alone." He slid their daughter a warm look. "Phoebe has become a responsible young woman, and most of what we need to function will already be in order. Besides, she will have Augie to help her."

"That's what I'm afraid of." As Amelia spread her shawl across her blouse to nurse Lucy, she flicked him a troubled glance. "You will be busy meeting your congregation, and…"

"Mama, I'll manage." Phoebe injected her voice with as much enthusiasm as she could. "I have often helped you in the kitchen."

"I know. Still, I dislike placing such a heavy burden on your young shoulders. Of course, I will bring the baby with me, but I will dearly miss the three of you."

"Well, my love, you won't be able to miss us for at least a few more hours. The train has just begun its southern descent. We won't reach Winchester until midday."

ONCE EVERYTHING WAS decided, Phoebe again stared out the window. Late April felt surprisingly chilly, though the rest of her

2

family did not seem to notice. Perhaps it simply reflected her frame of mind.

She did not understand why Papa wanted to leave Princeton, the only home she or Augie had ever known, so he could pastor a church in a tiny town hardly worthy of the label. He still loved teaching antiquities at the college and, even more, theology at the seminary next door. She already missed her old friends, and without Mama's company, the task of meeting new ones seemed daunting.

While the rough track rattled the window, she gazed across the verdant Shenandoah Valley, named for the sparkling river winding through its length. According to Papa, the first Englishmen to reach the river's banks were so astounded by its depth and width they dubbed it The Euphrates. The name had not stuck.

"Look!" Augie pressed his nose against the cold glass. "What is that?"

Leaning forward in his seat, Papa gazed past her at the sizeable cloth-covered wagon. "I believe they call it a Conestoga, and it's hauling locally grown food to Pennsylvania. The road is the old King's Highway, now the Valley Pike."

"Why's the driver's skin so brown?"

As Papa cleared his throat, Phoebe watched Mama press her lips into a frown.

"Because his parents' skin was brown, just as Phoebe inherited my dark eyes and you inherited your Mama's light ones. You've brought up a subject, though, I'd like to talk about. We aren't used to seeing people kept in bondage. It's the custom here, and one we are going to have to live with if we are going to reach our neighbors with the gospel."

"But how can it be right?" asked Phoebe.

"I don't believe it is. Legal, yes, though legal and moral don't always travel hand in hand."

"Ernest, how can I sip tea served by an enslaved housemaid?"

"I feel as you do, but what is our alternative? We can't reject a whole commonwealth of people. What if Paul never ventured into the greater Roman world? More people were slaves than citizens during the reign of the Caesars. Until Congress enacts a change in the law, the best way we can help that driver is to share the gospel with his owner. Only changed hearts change habits."

3

Phoebe shivered. Before she had made even one new acquaintance, she already felt at odds with the lot of them. Why, she wondered, did the Bible address so many more passages to slaves than their masters? She was just about to ask when her tiny sister started fussing so loudly all conversation ceased.

While Mama held Lucy upright, Phoebe's dimples began to twitch. Augie was scrunching himself tightly against the window to avoid a stream of curdled milk that barely missed his hair. Although she could not envy his present seat, she certainly envied his ringlets. Grandmother claimed they were the result of his love for bread crusts, but Phoebe was not convinced. One week, she had eaten every crust she could get her hands on to no avail. Her hair remained as straight as the curtains hanging beside their compartment's window. At least it was a richer color than her brother's mud-brown.

Glancing from him to Mama, she saw his antics had brought laughter to her eyes. They were similar to Augie's in size and shape, but though hers were a grayish-green, his were the color of the hazy blue mountains to the east. As he turned them toward Lucy, wary of the white dribble Mama had missed while cleaning the puffy rose-bud lips, Phoebe's dimples deepened. She had been thrilled when he was born and claimed credit for his existence. After all, as she had often reminded her parents, he was the answer to *her* prayer. Their little sister was another story. At the advanced age of seventeen, Phoebe grew downright embarrassed when she considered all the baby's existence implied.

Mama looked lovely in her dove gray frock and matching small-brimmed bonnet. Once, Phoebe heard two gossips say they thought her unfashionably plump. Augie and she disagreed, and she suspected Papa did also. He regularly claimed Mama's ample cushioning gave him more to hold. Phoebe heartily concurred. When she hugged her friend Samuel's petite mother, she felt like she was embracing a broom handle.

Samuel...

Would she ever see him again? Although Papa had frequently brought home students, she had found none so attractive. Several had better-formed noses or jaws, but Samuel had a certain something she found hard to put into words. It may have resulted from the summers spent in an Indian village. They not only lent him a sense of

4

intrigue and maturity that outstripped his classmates, but they also fostered his ability to entertain on days too wet and dreary to venture outside. After listening to so many of his fascinating stories, Augie grew severely disappointed when Papa informed him the family was not moving *that far* west.

Phoebe withdrew the letter of introduction Samuel had written on her behalf to his relations. For the thousandth time, or so it seemed, she searched his words for any hint of his regard; and for the thousandth time, she was disappointed. In truth, he had written nothing more than she would have expected from any polite acquaintance.

Papa elbowed her arm and nodded toward the window. "It seems we are slowing down. Ah—yes. Here's the depot. August, grab your mother's purse while I pull down our bags."

Augie looked as if he might protest until he saw Mama struggling to stand while holding Lucy.

"Here. I will take it," Phoebe offered Augie. "You might spill its contents."

As she reached for the purse, he stuck out his tongue, earning a censorious glance from Papa; and as the train pulled to a full stop, they all gratefully joined their unloaded trunks on the platform.

Reverend Farrell craned his neck, searching for Colonel Nelson, the head deacon the church board had sent to collect them. Spotting a man of proper description standing next to a black-wheeled wagon, he waved him over, made their introductions, and appraised him of his wife's situation. Minutes later, the colonel had returned with the appropriate ticket and excused himself so they could enjoy private farewells.

"Oh, I hate to leave you," crooned Mama, her affectionate gaze encompassing them all. After hugging Phoebe, she pulled Augie close and cupped his face in her hand. "Do not give your father or sister any trouble. And Phoebe, make sure your father has enough to eat. You know how distracted he becomes."

"I will."

As Augie echoed her words, their father slipped an arm about their mother's waist and leaned in for a kiss; then, drawing them all into his embrace, he uttered a parting prayer.

"You'd better hop back on, Amelia." When he released them, he noticed the engine was puffing. "The conductor is staring a hole through us. We will be counting the days until you return."

Chapter 2

ONCE AUGIE HAD climbed into the wagon, he tugged his father's sleeve. "Now can we go see the dead man?"

Colonel Nelson arched a brow above one of his round, blue eyes.

"No, son," replied the reverend, noting his deacon's reaction. "We will leave the investigation to the local authorities. I'm sure Colonel Nelson is eager to take us to the parsonage."

The colonel nodded. "It's a good way down the Pike. We'd better hurry if you want to get home before supper."

"Deacon Nelson, are there many young women around my age in the congregation?"

"Oh, I'd say about four girls, including my granddaughter, Emily. She is very eager to meet you. Five if you count the Kiker girl. She's a little older: nineteen, maybe twenty."

"Kiker?" asked Reverend Farrell. "Isn't that the name of the man whose foreman they found dead?"

"Yes. A bad business and not a particularly pleasant welcome. His funeral is tomorrow morning, and as you are his family's pastor..."

"Of course," replied the reverend, frowning at Augie, who was nearly bouncing out of his seat.

"Who did it?" asked the boy. "A robber?"

The deacon glanced from him to the reverend, raising yet another brow.

"Son." Reverend Farrell cleared his throat. "The man's family—who you just heard are part of my new congregation—are sure to be hurting, so I'd appreciate it if you keep your questions within our family. Colonel, you might as well answer. My children are bound to hear details from someone or another, and I'd rather they hear them from a source we trust."

"Mr. Simmons was found out back of a slave named Kitch's cabin, so I imagine the sheriff will search no further."

"But if this enslaved man killed him," reasoned Phoebe, "wouldn't he have hidden the body? Leaving it behind his home pointed straight to him."

The colonel stared down at the reins a moment before answering. "He may not have had time. A crowd came running fairly fast, and no telling what a man will do to protect his children."

"He has children? What will happen…"

As the wagon hit a rut, Augie barreled in. "Did you see the gash? The errand boy told us it was as big as…"

His father shot him another warning. "When will I be able to meet with the family, Deacon?"

"It'll have to be this evening after you become acquainted with the church board. The man's widow and children are pretty shaken up. Simmons was not an easy man to like, but no one expects this sort of thing."

As Colonel Nelson guided his horses onto a well-worn lane, he tilted his head toward a tawny stone building perched on a small rise a few hundred feet from The Pike. "The church's over yonder and the parsonage's up on the ridge, peeking through the maples."

Phoebe craned her neck, first toward the church and then at their new home. "They are both the most interesting color."

"River rock pulled from the Shenandoah. The South Branch cuts a channel a ways beyond the house down the other side of the hill."

While the wagon ascended, Augie began pointing to two small windows set into the roof. "Can I live up there?"

"I'm afraid they're just for show. I don't think they even shed light into the attic. The wife of the original pastor, way back when I was your age, was mighty taken with the looks of an old manor and added them to raise the profile."

"Is someone still living in it?" asked Phoebe. "A lovely quilt is hanging on the line."

Colonel Nelson spun his head toward the left side of the house. "Um…likely Mr. Foster, the church's caretaker, is airing out the linens."

"The pattern's lovely. It appears to be masses of colorful little boxes. What is it called?"

The deacon's blue eyes crinkled. "I don't do a great deal of quilting. You'll have to ask Mary—Mrs. Nelson."

8

As Phoebe smiled, he pulled to a halt beside a modest-sized two-story house topped by a deeply-pitched roof. Chimneys flanked it on either side. All around and behind stood budding maples and blossoming dogwoods, and on the northeastern face grew an engulfing mass of vines.

"Here comes Foster now."

"Look!" cried Augie. "A treehouse. May I climb it?"

"I don't see why not," answered his father, though the colonel's cautious glance at its wooden rungs made Phoebe wonder if it were safe.

Augie leaped from his perch while Pastor Farrell scrambled down from the wagon. Once he set Phoebe on the gravel, he offered to help the grizzled caretaker heft out their heavy bags.

"No need. Might be slight o' stature, but I been totin' sacks filled with all manner o' goods all my life. Sometimes rocks from the riverbed." He glanced from the church to Augie, who had torn past him toward the largest maple and was already halfway up the tree.

Before the deacon had a chance to introduce them, Reverend Farrell held out his hand. "It's a pleasure to meet you, Mr. Foster. Please excuse my son. He has been cooped up in a train far too long for a boy of nine. This is my daughter, Phoebe. My wife has been delayed. On our way, she learned her mother has fallen ill and took the train back to Maryland to help tend to her."

"It's nice to meet you, sir," said Phoebe. Although the caretaker shook her hand, she could not tell if he was peering at her or the parsonage. One eye gazed in her direction and the other over her head and off to her right.

"Missy, you be watchin' yer brother, an' don't come runnin' to me if he breaks a leg.

"Come on, Phebes, climb on up," yelled Augie. "I can see for miles."

"You'd better come down, son," answered his father. "Mr. Foster would like to show us our new home."

The caretaker frowned, picked up the bags he had just set down, and turned toward the parsonage. Papa did likewise, following him through the open door with the family's other parcels.

"Stop pushing!" whispered Phoebe. Augie was forcing his way between her and the doorframe. "And wash your face."

"You're not my boss."

"August." Papa's voice dropped low and deep. "You will listen to and obey your sister as if she were your mother. Now, go wash off that streak of dirt as she told you. And I trust," he added, pinning his daughter with a stern glance, "you will not misuse your new-found power."

"Yes, sir," both answered. While Phoebe waited for Colonel Nelson and Mr. Foster to lead them onward, Augie squeezed between them. "Where's the spigot?"

"Yonder through the kitchen. Y'all find the pump in the back."

"In the back?" Rolling his eyes, Augie tromped out the way he had come in while the deacon peered around the sparse parlor.

"I'm afraid, Pastor Farrell, you and your wife—or Miss Phoebe—won't find as many niceties as you were accustomed to in Princeton. There's a good little kitchen with a long work table and a stove attached to the rear of the house, but you'll have to fetch in your water."

"We'll manage just fine, Deacon. It'll do Augie good to build more muscle."

"Well, this here's the parlor," the caretaker informed them. "Up them stairs are the bedrooms and through there is the dining… "

While Mr. Foster pointed out the rather obvious layout, Phoebe barely listened. She was already missing her mother, and with their journey over, she was feeling overwhelmed by the thought of setting up home alone. Besides, wheels were crunching the gravel outside. Glancing around the parlor and out a window, she noticed someone—likely the ladies of the church—had cleaned the house until it shone.

"Hello?" Knocking her straw bonnet sideways, a young woman with a toddler on her hip stuck her head through the front door. "Is anyone home?"

"We're in the dining room." Colonel Nelson peeked his head around the pocket door. "Lisa, come in. I'm showing the new pastor and his family around."

"Good afternoon." The young woman radiated genuine welcome. Holding out her hand to Pastor Farrell and then Phoebe, she said, "I'm Lisa White. And you must be Samuel's friends. My parents received a letter from him yesterday." The glint in her brown eyes set Phoebe to wondering exactly what he had written.

"Oh, yes. I have his letter of introduction."

"I don't need it. No doubt it is lovely. Sam has a way with words, but I already know we'll be great friends. Where is your mother?"

"On her way to Baltimore. My grandmother has taken ill."

"Oh no. I hope it is not serious."

Before Phoebe replied, Augie tromped back into the house and stared at his sister. "What happened to you—your neck is all red."

Papa sidled over and gripped his shoulder so tightly he fell silent. "Mrs. White, this wet-headed boy is my son, August. We'll leave you to get acquainted with Phoebe while we wipe up the trail of water he's dripped in. I'm sure we can find a rag."

"Aw," groaned Augie as Papa steered him back toward the kitchen. "Mama told Phoebe to…"

"I'll see you at the church at seven, Reverend Farrell," Colonel Nelson called after him. "Mary will be waiting for me to eat."

"Alright," answered Pastor Farrell, leaning around the doorframe. "And please call me Ernest."

"If you will call me Gary."

"I will, Gary. We appreciate you picking us up."

"My pleasure."

As the deacon departed in one direction and the reverend and his son in the other, Lisa guided Phoebe toward the parlor's settee. "How is dear Samuel? His letter said he spent hours at the table talking with you."

"With our whole family." Phoebe dropped her gaze. "He told us such fascinating tales about his…what did his sister call it?"

"Life among the savages?"

"Yes. If he had not told them so earnestly, I'd have thought he made them up."

"They are all true. I'm sure he told you his sister married my brother. He was her father's adjunct, and his godmother is Samuel's aunt of sorts."

"Of sorts?"

"The connections are complicated and I cannot stay long, but I promise to tell you someday. Will you be attending Mr. Simmons' funeral?"

"I'm not sure what Father has planned."

"Please do if you may. Everyone will share a meal afterward at the Simmons' house, and while the occasion is not a happy one, the ladies of the church are looking forward to meeting you."

"I'm sure he will—oh, there you are, Papa. May I go with you to Mr. Simmons' funeral tomorrow?"

"I don't see why not. You will need to keep an eye on Augie for me. I would like to make myself available to Mr. Simmons' family. Mrs. White, please tell the other women in the church thank you for all you have done to welcome us. I've never seen a cleaner parsonage. I only wish my Amelia could be here to meet you."

"Yes, I hope her mother will recover soon. My mother is eager to meet her—your wife, I mean. Do you know how long she will be away?"

Pastor Farrell shook his head. "Likely for some time. And who is this handsome fellow?" The toddler Lisa held offered a wide, if somewhat toothless, grin as he grabbed one of Pastor Farrell's outstretched fingers.

"This is Jack." As Lisa ruffled her son's sandy-colored hair, he turned his face up toward her. Phoebe thought him the most adorable little boy she had ever seen. "In light of Mr. Simmons…parting…my mother postponed a tea she had planned for tomorrow for your wife and daughter; but though Mrs. Farrell is away, we hoped we could still hold it Sunday afternoon in honor of Phoebe."

"I'm sure she will enjoy it. Your mother is very thoughtful."

"It won't be anything fancy, Phoebe. Just a few of the local girls about your age and their mothers. I will swing by to pick you up Sunday at two."

"Thank you. I will be ready and am excited to meet your family."

AFTER EATING A fine meal the Ladies Hospitality League had provided, Reverend Farrell walked down the small slope to the church. Phoebe began unpacking the trunks Mr. Foster had hauled up the staircase and deposited in each of their rooms on the second floor. Beginning with Papa's, she propped the lid against a windowsill.

She was hanging his best suit to air on a hook attached to the wardrobe when she was startled by an unexpected thump above the window.

"Augie, what are you doing?" He was supposed to be in his room putting away his clothing, not exploring the house.

"What do you care?" he called from across the hall.

Darting her eyes to the thick curtains, the hair on her neck began to prickle. She saw—or thought she saw—a moving shadow.

I am being ridiculous, she assured herself. Reaching to pull aside one of the heavy panels, another thud—louder and quite close— nearly catapulted her from her skin. Without glancing down, she knew what had caused it. She had felt the breeze the heavy lid created while falling. I must have bumped it with the curtains.

"Phoebe," Augie called. "Come here."

"What?"

"Just come—hurry!"

Crossing the hall to Augie's bedroom, she saw his nose pressed against the window.

"Look—beneath the trees. What is he pushing in his hand-cart?"

"Who?" In the dim moonlight, Phoebe had trouble locating anything through the budding canopy. "I don't see anyone."

"The caretaker—Foster. There, down the lane. Something's in it."

"Of course something's in it, silly. Why else would he be pushing it?"

"It was moving. Maybe it's a dead body."

"Dead bodies don't move."

"Then a wounded one."

"It's probably an animal he caught in one of the outbuildings— like a skunk."

Augie pulled back from the window and gaped at Phoebe. "A skunk? Even I know not to give a skunk a ride."

"Then a dog or a cat—or more likely nothing but dirt. He is our caretaker. Anyway, it's too dark to see a thing."

"What would he be taking care of at night?"

"I don't know. He could just be hauling away a broken stool or something from the garden."

"He gives me the creeps. He has hair growing out of his ears, and I can't tell which way his eyes are looking."

"I know, though he can't help that. How would you like it if he thought badly of you just because your curls won't lay flat?"

Augie shrugged. "Why would I care?"

"You know what I mean. Be all the kinder to him." Among her brother's things, she spotted the small wooden train engine Samuel had crafted as a gift just before they left. It was like all his work: exactingly intricate and precise. It even had moving wheels. Rubbing her thumb over the carved window, complete with a tiny conductor, she wondered if there was anything he did poorly.

"I'm going back to Papa's room, but when I come back, I expect your stuff to be put away."

"You're not my boss."

Phoebe shook her head and left. Arguing the point would be a waste of time. Once she finished her father's cases, she moved down the hall to her room and unpacked her favorite day dress and attempted to smooth the wrinkles from its moss green folds. It was simple, serviceable, and of a color that brought out the faint golden flecks and the dark green encircling her otherwise brown eyes. Wearing it to the tea might lend her some much-needed confidence.

As she held it up before the mirror, she distinctly heard a door quietly shutting. Trotting to the upstairs' landing, she held out a candlestick to illumine Papa's way, but he was not there. Instead, she found Mr. Foster wiping the dirt off his hands and onto his trousers.

"You still up, Missy? I see'd a light and came to check on you and the little boy."

"Yes," answered Phoebe, descending the stairs. "Is it much past eight?"

"Can't say for sure. Don't own a watch—just judgin' from when the sun went down." The man stared at her in the same disconcerting way Augie had described, only this time one eye was looking directly into hers and the other up the stairs.

Ashamed of her aversion, she attempted what she hoped would be a welcoming smile. "Thank you for making sure we are alright. So far out in the country, this house stays very quiet."

"Quiet, eh? I'm glad o' that. Some says they hear things in here they oughtn't."

"What sort of things?"

"I don't want t' go scarin' yuh now, do I? 'Tain't nuthin more 'an the wind, I reckon. The last Missus said she heard shufflin' about and thought she heard doors 'n windas closin'.""

"Perhaps she heard squirrels dropping nuts from the trees. I've heard a few this evening."

"Sure 'nuff. We got a heap o' squirrels and such. I once looked out my winda and see'd two glowin' red circles starin' back at me." He chuckled at Phoebe's widening eyes. "Tweren't nuthin' to be scared of, Miss. Just a possum. Ugly creatures. Like to climb trees, an' if yuh shine a light on 'em in the dark, their eyes seem like they's aglowin'.""

One of Phoebe's cheeks dimpled. "I appreciate the warning."

Chapter 3

"HOW WERE THE Simmonses?" asked Phoebe the next morning. Her father, brother, and she were leaving the parsonage to walk to the graveyard. "You were so tired when you came home last night, I didn't ask."

"About as you would expect: still stunned and groping for answers. They will never be the same. How does a person recover from such calamity?"

Augie cut in, "Did you see the body?"

Phoebe tossed her eyes toward the clouds and shook her head.

"Yes, son, and he will be on display in his casket this morning, but while we are at the funeral—or anywhere outside our home—please refrain from speaking of his murder."

"Papa, how many children did he have?"

"Six. The oldest two are men now, and the youngest is about Augie's age."

"Will the plantation owners turn them out of their home?"

"No, I don't think so. I believe they own it, and if not, Mr. Kiker seems like a fair man. Colonel Nelson said he also employs Simmons' oldest son."

"Mrs. Simmons must be devastated. I know Mama would be."

Slowing to a stop, Reverend Farrell began stroking his mustache. "You know, Phoebe, you've just put a finger on something that's been niggling me. Mrs. Simmons seemed overly calm, as if she felt more relief than grief, and the eldest son appeared the opposite: agitated."

"Surely, his anger is natural. He's likely eager to bring his father's murderer to justice."

"I agree, though that's not what I mean. He showed little emotion while talking about the crime, but when his mother began to speak about his father, he began to…the only word I can use to describe it

16

is seethe. Although he kept his face devoid of expression, the anger in his eyes was palpable."

"Perhaps Mr. Simmons was not the sort of father you are—or the sort of husband."

Augie cast her an incredulous look. "How would you know anything about husbands?"

"Mama talks with me—and she tells me she has the best husband in the world."

Eyes a twinkle, her father waved to a board member in the churchyard down the hill, but while he picked up his pace, Phoebe caught hold of her brother's arm. "Don't go blabbering what Papa told us to anyone. As he said, what we discuss at home stays at home."

"We're not at home, Phoebe. The church is right there."

"Ohhh!" She threw her eyes up. "Must you take everything *so* literally? He meant whatever the four of us discuss should never be repeated. Do you understand?"

"I'm not a baby—let go of me."

"Hold still." Tightening her grip, she moistened her fingers. "Your cowlick is sticking up again."

Augie jerked back. "I don't want your spit in my hair!"

Twisting free, he trotted down the hill to catch up with his father. Phoebe stood where she was, asking the Lord to increase her patience and to give her the right words for the grieving family. She watched a rather fine carriage pull to a halt beside the sanctuary doors, followed closely by a wagon bearing a black-draped box.

As she counted the emerging family—six, not seven, including the widow—she noticed several girls who might be close to her age. The widow was a heavy woman nearly a foot shorter than her tallest son, but the veil she wore covered so much of her face, Phoebe could not tell if her father's assessment had been accurate. She stood motionless, grasping the hands of a young boy and girl.

Walking down the hill, Phoebe soon found Mrs. White with two men. One, about her father's age, was avidly listening to a petite dark-haired woman a tad older than Phoebe's mother. The other was holding little Jack. "Good morning, Phoebe. This is my husband, Jordan, and my father and mother, John and Allison Wilson."

Lisa's mother warmly clasped both of Phoebe's hands. "Well, look at you. Aren't you the sweetest little thing? I was so sorry to learn your grandmother fell ill. I've been so impatient to meet your mother."

"She is eager to meet you also. You are just as Samuel described."

"I was thinking the same of you. I told Samuel he should turn his letters into a story and give that gloomy Mr. Dickens some stiff competition."

Phoebe had never seen eyes more full of sparkle, however, since Colonel Nelson was beginning to call everyone inside the church, she smiled and slipped willingly into the space mother and daughter made for her between them.

AFTER THE INTERNMENT, Allison Wilson wound her arm through Phoebe's. "The Simmonses have invited everyone to their home for a meal. Your father said I may ask you to ride with John and me. It will give us a chance to talk privately—the Simmonses live a quarter-hour away—and our carriage will be far less jolting than the parsonage wagon."

"I would like it very much."

"Good, it's all settled. I see our coachman bringing it up now, and John will only be a minute."

As Mr. Wilson made his way over and climbed into the opposite seat, she almost regretted her compliance. Even after removing his hat, his head nearly grazed the carriage ceiling, and his shoulders took up more than half of its width. His earnest hazel eyes and affable manner soon put her at ease.

Mrs. Wilson could not have been kinder. "I am so happy your family decided to move here. As you likely know, our son, Joshua, traveled four years ago with Senator Anderson, Samuel's father, through the Wisconsin and Iowa Territories. That's how he met his wife, Abigail, Samuel's sister. Two years later, Jordan married Lisa, so though we couldn't be happier to include him in our family, I miss the companionship of a daughter. I hope you will visit me often, perhaps even stay for several days."

Phoebe could not keep her dimples from twitching. Not only had she taken immediately to Lisa's mother, but she also cherished the connection to Samuel. "I would be delighted; however, until my mother arrives it will be out of the question. I am needed to care for my father and Augie."

"Of course you are, and I wouldn't dream of taking you away from them, but you are always welcome anytime you become homesick for a mother's particular..."

Just then, they felt the coachman pull the horses to a halt. Jumping off his box, he swung open the door.

"Well, here we are," observed Mr. Wilson.

Once they had entered the Simmons' home, Mrs. Wilson conducted the two of them to empty seats beside the widow. Behind them, Phoebe noticed a tall dark-haired man with intensely blue eyes walking in with her father, Colonel Nelson, and John Wilson. He rivaled Mr. Wilson for height, making the reverend and colonel look short by comparison.

"Hello, Asa." Phoebe overheard the colonel say. "Where's Lavinia? I haven't seen her all morning."

The man pulled down the corners of his mouth. "She asked me to convey her regrets. She has a debilitating headache."

"Reverend Farrell," John Wilson chimed in, "this is Asa Kiker."

"Pleasure to meet you, sir. I'm sorry to hear your wife is unwell. Does she get these headaches often?"

"She used to. This is the first she's had in years."

While they continued conversing, Mrs. Wilson laid her hand over the widow's. "Mahala, I cannot express deeply enough how sorry I am about...all of this. Not only Edward's passing but also the horrible circumstances."

"Oh, Allison." Mahala Simmons pressed her lips down severely. "Never, in my entire life, have I heard of such a thing. Men die in their beds or on the battlefield. They are never struck down while attending to their duties." Her eyes landed on Phoebe as if seeing her for the first time. "You must be the new pastor's daughter. Please pardon me for not introducing myself to you at the service. I cannot seem to keep my wits about me."

"That's understandable, Mrs. Simmons. I'm sorry for your loss. My father said your husband was well-known in this valley, and by the crowd gathered, I can see he was correct." All through Papa's graveside comments, she had been practicing the line. The dead man *was* well known, however, neither her father nor she had heard anything to convince them he was liked. "I imagine it's difficult to lose a husband, let alone the father of five."

"Six. Yes, I am certain many people will keenly feel my husband's absence, however, we are more fortunate than most. Edward did not leave us without means, and my oldest two will do what they can. They care deeply for me and their sisters and brother." Smiling up at a young man talking with Lisa's husband, she took hold of his hand. "Don't you dear?"

"Don't I what, Ma? I'm sorry, I was listening to Jordan."

"Care for your family."

"Yes, deeply." While the young Mr. Simmons returned his mother's affectionate gaze, Phoebe studied his features. They bore scant resemblance to the body she had passed within the line of mourners in the sanctuary, but he was the image of his mother in the masculine form: blond wavy hair, pale eyes of a color she could not determine at her distance, a sharp upturned nose, and a chin some might consider slightly weak. "I am sorry for your loss, Mr. Simmons."

"Thank you, Miss Farrell. My father's absence, as my mother said, will be keenly felt."

Knowing nothing more to say, Phoebe fell silent. All the faces of his siblings, she noticed, were as unreadable as his and his mother's, setting her to wonder how she might look if they just laid her father in the grave. She concluded she too might appear devoid of emotion. She often preferred to keep her feelings to herself; and if she had been offered a nickel—as the old saying went—for each time someone mistook her concentration for unhappiness, her mother would not need to work so hard to stretch her father's income.

When Mrs. Wilson and the widow had begun to speak of things she knew nothing about, Phoebe offered to fetch them food from the long table. She felt blessedly invisible as she loaded up their plates. As a pastor's daughter, she was often forced to act more sociably than inclined and welcomed the reprieve. While slipping into the pantry to find more fried chicken, a reverberating clang drew her toward the kitchen out back.

"What's wrong wit' you today?" A sharp voice muttered. "You seem plum shakin' up."

"Just don't like funerals none, 'specially this one."

"I'm glad for yer help, but yer Master got some nerve comin' here to comfort the widda…"

"…an' with Mr. Simmons barely in his grave."

"What d'ya expect? They's been passing off his son as Mr. Simmons' all these years. Mr. Charles took one look at 'im an' took off. You reckon that's why they's so set on keepin' him on up there?"

"Yes'm. I 'spect Simmons found out an' was holdin' Massa Asa by the short hairs o' his neck."

"He was nastier than a wild boar. Who you reckon done 'im in?"

"No tellin'. Ms. Lavinia done had one o' them spells, like she used to, and took to bed."

"Why she care? What's he to her?"

"She found 'im. Started screamin' like one o' them banshees."

"Sorry 'scuse of a man. Ain't nobody gonna miss 'im, least o' all under this roof."

"Don't know how yer Missus stood 'im."

"Guess she ain't had no choice. Soon as I heared his voice each evenin', I took off to my kitchen. Mr. Charles'll be a sight better on you folks."

"Don't we know it?"

Without warning, a middle-aged woman rounded the doorway carrying a platter piled high with freshly fried chicken. She froze when she spotted Phoebe, her dark skin gleaming from perspiration. "Folks is gathered yonder in the house, Miss." The ends of her kerchief bobbed above her eyebrows as she nodded toward the parlor.

"May I take that for you? I'm the new pastor's daughter."

Drawing the platter closer to her chest, the woman stared as if Phoebe had food caught in her teeth. "Mitilde an' me be doin' the servin', Miss. You go back now, right through that door, an' sit with the other guests."

Dropping her smile along with her hands, Phoebe slunk out of the pantry and glanced around the parlor. Young Mr. Simmons was, as she had overheard, nowhere to be seen. Phoebe kept her eyes to the table as the taciturn servant set down her fried chicken, however, when she went back to the sofa, Mrs. Wilson was not there. The widow and the tall man John Wilson had introduced as Mr. Kiker were deep in conversation.

"Asa, I am deeply disappointed—Lavinia deserting me at a time like this. Even if she *is* having one of her spells, we've been close friends for decades."

Phoebe felt like she was eavesdropping. Still embarrassed by her gaffe in the pantry, she wordlessly slipped Mrs. Simmons her plateful and searched the room for Allison Wilson. She found her talking with her daughter, who was trying to keep Jack from making a mess while eating a drumstick, and Clara Kiker, a willowy brunette Lisa had pointed out while they walked back from the graveside. As Clara lifted her eyes, Phoebe felt taken aback by their similarity to Asa Kiker's. It was only natural, considering he was her father; yet in addition to color, hers were a replica in shape and size. Whether they shared the same expression, Phoebe could not say. She had yet to engage Mr. Kiker's eyes directly, but as Clara's gaze traveled from her face to her attire and back to Lisa's mother, she was not sure she wanted to.

Once Phoebe handed the plate of food to Mrs. Wilson, she took the empty one Lisa was holding away from Jack while balancing him on her lap. She was stooping to retrieve another laying on the table when Clara laid a gloved hand over her wrist.

"No need for you to wait on us, honey. Ruby'll pick them up—or Mitilde. Father has loaned her to the Simmonses for the day."

Phoebe set down the plate and fell silent. Members of her family had loaned out tools, gowns, and trunks for traveling—just never another person.

"Why, you must be the new preacher's daughter. Mitilde is our house slave. My father brought her over this morning so she could help her sister with the cooking and serving."

"I'm sorry," Lisa interposed. "I should have introduced you. Clara Kiker, this is Phoebe Farrell. Phoebe, this is Miss Kiker." While the two exchanged the expected niceties, Lisa wiped the grease from her son's tiny fingers.

"I'm glad your father arrived in time to perform the service," Miss Kiker continued. "This has all been so upsetting."

"Clara," asked Mrs. Wilson, "where is your mother?" I haven't seen her or your brother all day. Mr. Simmons seemed very fond of him."

As Miss Kiker gave her mother's excuses, Phoebe watched the two brown-skinned women filling empty bowls and platters on the table. She now knew both of their names but not which one belonged to the woman she had offended. While she was considering how she might make amends, Clara dropped her voice so low, she drew Phoebe's attention.

"…could not abide him, though why, I've never understood. Mr. Simmons took every possible opportunity to ingratiate himself, nonetheless, my brother avoided him like one of those lepers from the Bible."

"Perhaps he had a reason," offered Lisa.

"It embarrassed Father to no end, still when he finally insisted Hugh at least offer him respect, Mother responded as if her bloomers were twisted in a knot. She said Hugh needed to make his own choices. Do you remember that pup Simmons gave him?"

"Yes, a fine, well-bred retriever."

"Hugh would have refused it had Father not insisted. And Charles—those two have always been inseparable—you should have seen the expression on his face while he watched him give it away."

"Charles may have hoped to keep the puppy himself."

"I wouldn't doubt it. Charles doted on the little thing. I always thought it odd. You'd think you'd give your own boy first pick."

"Phoebe," Reverend Farrell whispered. "I think it's time we excuse ourselves. Augie has behaved better than I might have at his age, but I can tell he is getting antsy. Besides, I still have a lot of books to unpack if I am to prepare my message for Sunday."

Augie—she had entirely forgotten to watch him. "Yes, Father." As she stood up, Lisa put out her hand.

"Don't forget about Sunday. Mother is lending me her curricle. I will pick you up at two."

"Thank you, and you also, Mrs. Wilson. I will look forward to seeing you both—and you too, Miss Kiker. I am pleased to have made your acquaintance."

ONCE THE REVEREND assured the widow he would be available if she wanted anything, the three Farrells bid their new acquaintances farewell and climbed into the church's wagon.

"Now you have met Mr. Simmons' family, Phoebe, do your impressions match my own?"

"I'm honestly not sure. I spent little time with any of them beyond introductions."

"What are your impressions of our new congregation? Most were present today. Did you meet anyone you think might become your friend?"

Phoebe flicked her eyes over to a field they were passing. "Samuel's friends, Mrs. White and Mrs. Wilson. I also liked Colonel Nelson's wife and granddaughter, though I hardly had a chance to speak with either."

"I think your mother will like Allison—Mrs. Wilson—very much, and Mary Nelson, still, you seem as if something's bothering you."

"I believe I upset someone."

"Who?"

"A servant."

Augie looked at her as if she had sprouted an extra head. "How could you upset a servant?"

Phoebe shrugged. "Servants are just as human as we are. Well—maybe more human than you."

Augie crumpled his forehead. "Jeremiah Simmons said his father used to whip the Kiker's slaves. What if the Kiker's new foreman whips one on a day we are visiting?"

"Well…" Father took in a deep breath and let it out again. "You won't like my answer."

Both heads swiveled toward him.

"I hope I'd do exactly what Jesus did—offer my own back for the whipping."

Augie's eyes grew large as saucers. "Why? You aren't a slave."

"Jesus wasn't a sinner, but He gave Himself to pay for our sins."

"Wouldn't you be scared?"

"Horribly, so imagine how the slave would feel. I'm also afraid, though, I might prove a coward, so I would need you to cry out to the Lord with all your might and plead for Him to grant me courage. Do you think you could do that, son?"

24

"Yes, sir! I'll pray so loud, they'll hear me in Princeton."

Phoebe began toying with her bottom lip. "Papa, I heard some things while I was in the Simmons' pantry."

"What sort of things?"

"Awful things—from two servants talking in the kitchen. They said Mr. Kiker and Mrs. Sim...."

"Now Phoebe." Her father did not let her finish. "Your mother and I have taught you better than to repeat things you overhear. Why were you eavesdropping?"

Phoebe grew pink. "The way they were whispering, I couldn't help..."

"Phoebe, you know better than using 'I couldn't help' as an excuse, and you know what you must do."

"Yes, Father—keep what I heard to myself."

Reverend Farrell put his arm around her shoulders and pulled her close. "That's my girl."

Chapter 4

AS PHOEBE SET another pie to cool in the kitchen window, she wiped away the moisture clinging to her hairline. Spring had raced straight into summer, leaping from chilly to stifling in the space of days. Beneath her workaday dress, her chemise felt as wilted as the dogwood blossoms outside the window, and removing her pinafore had barely helped. Rivulets of perspiration ran down her bodice.

"Oh," she groaned, filling a bucket of water at the pump. "What I wouldn't do for a dip in the old swimming hole."

"There's a river a ways down the hill, Missy."

Whirling about, Phoebe found Foster clipping the spent forsythias a few feet beyond the kitchen garden.

"Just watch for them cottonmouths. They like to hide in the grasses toward the edge."

"Thank you, Mr. Foster."

"Just call me Foster. Everyone does."

Alright, Foster," answered Phoebe, narrowing her eyes in the direction of the river. "What about visitors? Is anyone likely to walk by?"

"Nah. Wouldn't make no sense. Church folks'll come up by the path. Ain't no others 'cept maybe that brother o' yers. He was catchin' frogs down there this mornin'."

Phoebe dimpled. "You are getting to know us all well. Augie rode to town with Papa."

"That right? I seed yer pa roll out 'bout an hour ago, so if you hurry like, you'll have plenty o' time. 'Member what I said, though, 'bout them snakes."

"I will."

"An' don't worry 'bout me none. I'm headin' 'round the front o' the house to clear up the branches the storm blew down, an' then I'll be tendin' the weeds a growin' in the cemetery."

"Thank you—not just for the privacy but also for all the ways you've helped me since we arrived."

"'Tweren't nothin'. A caretaker's fer taking care."

Running down the slope, Phoebe felt like a little girl again until she thought of Augie. "He is becoming incorrigible," she muttered to herself, unbuttoning her bodice and her skirt. "And he's developing horrible habits."

Just this morning, an entire rhubarb pie had gone missing from the kitchen sill. He had sworn so convincingly he had not touched it, she might have believed him had she not spotted pink stains among the others on his shirt.

"I won't tell Papa *this* time," she had promised. "At least you had the grace to take only one. The other was for the Wilsons. They invited me to tea tomorrow afternoon, and I don't want to show up empty-handed."

"Why would I want to steal one of your old pies? They are always too tart—bleh!"

She turned away, refusing to let him see her stinging tears. "Well, don't' you dare snatch another or I'll tell Papa, and he'll take you to the woodshed!"

"We don't have a woodshed." Hands on his hips, he had waggled his head and stuck out his tongue at her retreating form; but before she could shake a skillet at him, he had scampered up the maple to the treehouse.

"A good clobbering would have done him good. Mama cannot come back soon enough." Neatly folding her frock, she laid it atop her discarded boots and threw a cautious glance at a large clump of grass by the river's edge. The water felt gloriously cool as she tested it with her toe, so she waded out just deep enough to float. Lying back, she allowed her tightly coiled bun to sink beneath the gently undulating waves, righting herself when they had carried her too close to a clump of tall grass.

A brief movement sent her hand to her mouth. Two dark eyes peered at her above the surface looking as full of fear as she felt. Phoebe breathed a relieved sigh. They belonged to a girl, about her age and brown as a mink.

"Don't be afraid." Phoebe slowly tipped up her lips. "I live up in the stone house." As she glanced in the parsonage's direction, the girl

27

followed, although Phoebe doubted she could see anything from her hiding place. "I'm Phoebe, the new pastor's daughter."

The young woman only blinked, but before Phoebe thought how she might put her at ease, a masculine voice hurled her stomach into her chest.

"Well, who do we have here?"

Spinning around, she flung her arms across her chemise. A rush of red spread up her throat. Not only was the man a mere arm's length away, but he was also strikingly handsome. His dark eyes were thickly fringed, and his black hair curled around the nape of his neck, grazing the open collar of a sparkling white shirt. As he crouched down on the bank, she sunk deeper.

"I'm Hugh Kiker. My father and I own some land a bit north of the church. Would you care to come out so we can make more proper introductions?"

As he reached out his hand, she shook her head and peeked beyond him at her folded garments. "I am…I am Phoebe Farrell, the new…new pastor's daughter."

"It's a pleasure to meet you, Miss Farrell." Hugh fought mightily to rid his face of laughter until hurried footfalls drew his attention. A second man came running down the slope, and from his coloring and stature, Phoebe guessed he was another Kiker.

"Find him?" asked the stranger. "Foster said he might have seen him earlier, sneaking through the graveyard toward The Pike." The stranger nodded in the direction of the church. "But I'm not sure I trust him. He kept looking around like he didn't want me coming down here."

"Foster's okay." Hugh rose to his feet and clapped the other man on the shoulder. "He's just protecting his new mistress. Charles, meet our new pastor's daughter."

The stranger startled, giving Phoebe a chance to take in his features. They bore out her earlier conclusion. Though he appeared a tad younger and possibly taller, his eyes were the now-familiar Kiker blue. Some quality about him though—too elusive for her to pinpoint—rendered him less appealing. As she compared the slight differences in their features and attire, she put it down to the timbre of the first man's voice.

The hidden girl apparently agreed. Her eyes, wide as cherries, began darting about.

As the newcomer assessed Phoebe's predicament, his lips slid into a crooked grin. "You sure you don't want to come out, Miss Farrell? You look like you've spotted a cottonmouth."

"No," she answered, forcing a smile. "It's just a little frog."

Hugh shifted his position to block Charles's view of her abandoned clothing. "Let's leave Miss Farrell alone. She's trying to cool off."

"Cool off? She's shaking like a leaf. Did you ask if she's seen anybody?" He flicked his friend a less-than-friendly glance.

"I saw Mr. Foster," Phoebe answered, "and of course my father and little brother. The land belongs to the church, so the deacons sometimes visit; so unless you want to be baptized, you're not likely to find them in the river."

Hugh arched a brow, sending the color coursing back up her neck. She hoped she had not sounded rude, yet she needed them to leave.

"Come on, Charles." Hugh tossed her a quick wink. "You're ruffling the little partridge's feathers. You heard her. She's only seen a 'little frog.'"

"Ah, don't pay me no mind, Miss. It's not often we meet a true northern lady, and one as pretty as a peach—from what we can see." He angled his head to see if he might gain a better view. "If you happen upon a big slave..." He spun his head toward the other man. "Hey, I just realized she might not know one if she sees one."

Hugh shook his head apologetically.

"We're searching for a large man," Charles continued. "Dark and dangerous as the night. If you see him hanging around, send Foster to The Lilacs straight away."

"Which lilacs?" Her voice was quavering. "I don't think we have any."

Hugh's eyes flashed with humor as he swept up her clothing and laid it within easy reach. "It's the name of my home. Foster knows it well."

Bowing to her briefly, he signaled to Charles he intended to head north; and once she watched them crest the rise and disappear, Phoebe slipped out from behind the grass.

"They're gone."

29

The girl smiled, though only with her eyes. "You stay 'way from 'im, Miss Phoebe. 'Specially that one as was taunting you. Apples don't fall too far from the tree."

Climbing onto the bank, Phoebe unpinned her coil. Both had teased. While she wrung the water from her braid, she noticed the girl's arms were covered with goosebumps. "The sun feels wonderful. Why don't you come out? No one else's in sight."

The girl shook her head so barely Phoebe would not have noticed had she not been looking directly at her.

"Where are your clothes?"

When the young woman glanced down, Phoebe noticed for the first time she was wearing them.

"What possessed you to jump, clothes and all, into the river? You'll catch your death of cold." When she saw the look on her new acquaintance's face, Phoebe pressed her fingers to her mouth. "I've been taking care of Augie too long. I sound just like my Mama." She held up her dry dress. "Take it. I can run up to the house and sneak in the back."

"Can't, Miss."

"Of course you can. I have several others and some nicer ones besides."

"They'd say I stoled it."

"Who'd say that? I'm *giving* it to you. Besides, no one would recognize it. No one knows me, and they are certainly unfamiliar with any of my garments."

Though Phoebe smiled, the girl shook her head. "He know. I seed him pick it up and lay it down."

"Alright. Still, you are welcome on church grounds anytime, and not just to swim. Come visit me in the parsonage." Pointing up the hill, she stepped into her frock, pulling it up over her shoulders. "What about the boots? I have another pair. One pair looks much like another."

The girl's black eyes filled with both wariness and longing.

"I'm going to leave them here, and you can do as you like, although it would be a shame if some animal came along and chewed them to pieces. Much better if you would use them." Not knowing what else to do, Phoebe began to climb the rise, but a sudden thought whirled her around. "What's your name?"

"Got no name, Miss, leastwise none you can pronounce."

Phoebe knew her disappointment showed plainly, for instead of swimming out into the deeper water as the girl seemed about to do, she broke into a beautiful smile. "Birdie. My friends call me Birdie."

Dimpling deeply, Phoebe ran up the hill far happier than she had felt in weeks.

Chapter 5

PHOEBE LOOKED AT her reflection in the mirror. The ringlets she had gathered over her ears were already beginning to uncurl. By the time she arrived at the Wilsons', they would probably be drooping. Why had she accepted the invitation? It had sounded like a welcome chance to meet new people; now she wished Lisa would forget to call for her. She already had friends she could visit at will—they lived within the pages of her favorite books. Hearing two strikes from the mantel clock, she ran down the stairs, almost losing one of Mama's roomy hand-me-down slippers.

"Papa, does my gown appear too wrinkled?"

"Everyone knows you have just arrived. Isn't it the point of this tea?"

"Yes, but I don't want to give the impression I don't care for things properly."

"Anyone who draws that will be saying more about their heart than your appearance."

Phoebe suspected her father was right, nonetheless, she finger-ironed the front pleats. Although Mama and she had lined the folds with tissue, one of them had crimped badly. "I guess it will just have to do."

"It will more than do, Kitten. Of your better gowns, this is my favorite. It brings out the green in your eyes."

While Papa answered a brief knock, she flicked him an appreciative smile. Lisa had dressed impeccably in shades that enhanced the warm tones of her hair and skin. Phoebe felt pale and plain by comparison, a drab dove beside a vivid pheasant; however, her new friend's expression shooed away her fears. One day, she hoped to become just such a woman—one whose natural and welcoming self-assurance made everyone else feel wanted.

"You'll need a bonnet. The sun is bright and my parents' curricle offers less protection than a carriage. Here, let me help you with those." She circled behind Phoebe to refasten two buttons she had miss-aligned on the side of her neck. "Have you found your gloves?"

"Yes, and I made a pie for your mother."

"A pie? You didn't have to do that. What kind?"

"Rhubarb."

"I'll tuck away a slice for Father. It's his favorite. He is up at The Lilacs this afternoon talking with Mr. Kiker about growing rye in the far field."

"I hope he will like it. Augie says I don't use enough sugar."

"I'm sure it will be delicious, and anyway, my family prefers tart to sweet, except for Jordan. He has a decided sweet-tooth."

As they stepped outside, Phoebe saw an open two-wheeled chaise with only an awning overhead to protect them from the sun. "You can drive this?"

Lisa laughed. "I'd better be able to, or we'll find ourselves walking. Hold tight to your pie; I wouldn't want my father disappointed."

Driving up The Pike, she pointed out several homes belonging to Reverend Farrell's congregants, an excellent vegetable stand, and several commercial establishments of interest: a small apothecary, a general store, a blacksmith, a cooper and harness shop, and a well-known steam pottery. Many were familiar from their trip south from the station. Still, she was glad for a chance to fix their order in her memory.

When Lisa pointed out her own home, Phoebe felt heartsick: its white siding and green roof were charming, and the garden was full of irises and hollyhocks, but the trip by curricle had taken a good half hour. By foot, it might take her twice the time. She had hoped they lived close enough to pop over for frequent visits.

As they continued north, she remarked on the beauty of a two-story white house she glimpsed between oaks planted on both sides of a long lane.

Lisa turned to drive through its gate. "My parents have lived here as long as I can remember. My grandfather built the main part, and my father added the addition."

Four huge, round pillars extended from the house's porch to its roof, supporting an inviting second-story veranda. "It's just as Samuel portrayed it while telling us of his visit."

Before Lisa responded, her mother hurried through the door and down the steps. Her dark eyes flashed warmly. "Phoebe, I'm so happy you were able to come. Welcome to our home."

"Good afternoon, Mrs. Wilson. Thank you for inviting me. I baked your family a pie."

"Aren't you kind!" Mrs. Wilson lifted the towel and broke out into an appreciative laugh. "Rhubarb—John's favorite! I am looking forward to eating it. What am I doing keeping you out in the sun? Come in. Everyone has arrived except Lavinia and Clara, and of course, the Simmons girls could not come."

Looping both Lisa and Phoebe's arms within her own, she gathered her skirts and began to climb the stairs, however, all three turned back when they heard a carriage.

"Lavinia, I'm so glad you could make it. I was afraid you might still be feeling ill."

"I'm much better, Allison, thank you."

"This is Phoebe Farrell, our new pastor's daughter. Phoebe, this is Lavinia Kiker."

"Why, it's a pleasure to meet you, Phoebe. This is my daughter, Clara. I am sure you will become great friends."

Clara shot her mother a look that declared otherwise, though she acknowledged their prior meeting and punctuated her sentences with smiles.

If Lisa's mother was the epitome of welcome, Clara's was the epitome of elegance. Her words flowed in rich, dulcet tones announcing she was the unrivaled dame, and unlike her daughter, she instantly took to Phoebe. Why, Phoebe was less certain, but as Mrs. Kiker whisked her up the stairs, she felt like a squab protected beneath a peahen's wings. When they entered the parlor, an equally absurd image suggested itself: a clowder of sociable felines parting to offer a lioness her rightful place.

Emily Nelson handed Phoebe a sampling of finger sandwiches and some petit fours, though she struggled a bit to maintain her gaze. "These are my favorites. I am glad your grandmother's illness did not keep you away also. I look forward to knowing you better."

Phoebe felt encouraged. Between the girl's bashful smile and lack of artifice, she felt sure they could become friends. "I would like that also."

"Phoebe." The two glanced up to find Mary Nelson, Emily's grandmother, standing behind them. In her sixties or seventies, Mrs. Nelson's presence rivaled Lavinia Kiker's; however, it was of an entirely different quality. The only term Phoebe could think of was grace, though not a grace confined to tone or movement. Certainly, Mrs. Nelson possessed both, but whereas Lavinia Kiker's elegance spoke well of herself, Mrs. Nelson's grace was directed to others.

"Do you think your family might be able to come to our home for dinner Tuesday evening—if you are not too busy?"

"I believe we can and would certainly enjoy it; however, I will need to ask my father."

"Why don't we give you a ride home when Gary comes to collect us in our wagon? The parsonage is on our way. Then, we can see what your father says. Here's Lisa now. I will ask her if she minds."

While Mrs. Nelson spoke with Lisa, Mrs. Wilson sat down beside Phoebe. "So, tell me all about Samuel. Is he well? I thought he was looking too thin during his last visit."

Phoebe had never given his weight a thought outside of a similar comment Mama once made. "There isn't much to tell, though my mother agrees with you. Papa said he seems like a late bloomer who has not filled out yet."

Mrs. Wilson laughed. "John said the same thing. Lisa said you were asking about his family's adventures out west."

"Yes, she said your son's godmother is Samuel's aunt—of sorts."

Emily slanted her head to one side. "I don't understand. If she is Joshua's aunt, she is either your sister or Mr. Wilson's."

"She is neither, at least not by blood. She is the sister I always wanted and has grown very close to Samuel's mother. We did everything together when we were young. Shortly after I married John, she and her father received an invitation to visit her step-uncle in the territory north of Illinois."

"Did they go?"

"Yes, but the uncle turned out to be a real stinker. She ended up fleeing for her life."

The girls gasped in unison. "What happened? Did she escape?"

"Well, I will let you find out all about it for yourself. She wrote a book about her adventures and another about her daughter's, however, if I answer too many of your questions, I will spoil them for you. Would you like to read them?"

When both girls responded readily, she caught her daughter's attention. "Lisa, would you mind retrieving my friend Alcy's books from the library?"

"Not at all."

"Where is she now?" asked Phoebe.

Mrs. Wilson's sparkle dimmed. "We aren't certain. We have not heard from her in quite some time. I was hoping Samuel knew something."

Phoebe shook her head. "If he did, he didn't tell me."

"Let's make a point of praying for her," suggested Mary Nelson as Lisa handed Phoebe and her granddaughter the book. "What are the titles?"

"A River Too Deep," answered Emily, "and Light Bird's Song. Which is first, Mrs. Wilson?"

"A River Too Deep."

Mary Nelson opened the first page and then flipped to the last. "It—and I'm sure the other—would provide an excellent reason for a sleep-over."

The two girls smiled at each other and chatted for a while until Clara Kiker swished over and plopped into an adjacent seat. The fabric of her gown with its wide domed skirt perfectly set off the brilliant blue of her eyes. "Did you hear? Old Bett confessed to killing Mr. Simmons."

Phoebe whispered to Emily. "Who is…"

"That's absurd," declared Mrs. Nelson. "Granny Bett couldn't swing a hoe without falling over."

"Let alone," added Allison Wilson, "with enough force to harm a grown man."

"Why," asked Lisa, "would she confess to such a thing?"

"Father and Hugh," answered Clara, "think she's protecting Kitch. You know the hoe belonged to him. I thought Mother was going to have an apoplectic fit."

"Clara!" The young woman had not noticed her mother coming up behind her. "You needn't remind Phoebe of her grandmother's sufferings, and her welcome tea is hardly the place to air The Lilac's dirty laundry. I will have no more discussion of it. Allison, I came over to ask if Dahlia would share her recipe for Sally Lunn bread. It is so delicate, more like a cake. Undoubtedly, the best I have ever eaten."

"I'm sure she would be delighted. Girls, will you please excuse me?"

As they nodded, Emily's grandmother smiled. "I'd better join your mothers and leave you three to become better acquainted."

When Mary Nelson rose to follow, Clara leaned closer to Phoebe. "I hear you have met Hugh and Charles."

Her tone made Phoebe hope her curls *had* wilted. They might hide the redness of her ears.

"Ah, I can see they did not exaggerate. They each told me you made *quite* an impression."

How was Phoebe to answer? "I…they took me by surprise. The parsonage caretaker assured me no one would be about."

"Psh. Give no thought to *that*. Between sisters and slaves, both of them have seen their share of…well, not quite decorously clothed females. What did you think of them?"

"Honestly, I hardly had time to form an opinion."

"Not even of Hugh?" Clara slid an impish gaze to Emily, who not only turned red but also seemed to shrink into her seat.

"I…again, I spoke with your brothers only briefly. I was not in…in a position to carry on polite conversation."

"My brothers? I have only one, and he seemed to think you fetching. He…" Clara stopped as her mother once more loomed over her.

"Whatever Miss Farrell thinks of Hugh, I am sure she would prefer to keep it to herself." The expression on her face differed widely from her daughter's. "Now, gather up your wrap, Clara, and anything else you brought with you. Miss Farrell, I immensely enjoyed meeting you, and Emily, it is always lovely to see you."

As Mrs. Kiker walked toward the door, Phoebe shrugged and looked at Emily. "She may be having another one of her headaches."

Emily did not answer, though the uncomfortable pause did not last long. Her grandmother was beckoning both girls to join her in thanking their hostesses for their hospitality.

Chapter 6

PHOEBE HEARD A loud banging coming from the foyer. Taking the oatmeal she was preparing off the stove, she hurried to open the heavy wooden door.

Foster snatched his hat from his head and held it to his torso. "Sorry to disturb you, Missy. These here men wanna speak to yer pa."

"Papa's in his study at the church—the small room in the back."

"I know it, Miss, but do ya... "

Before he could get out the rest of his sentence, another man, burly and unshaven, barged past him to shove a garden hoe toward her face. "You seen this?"

Phoebe rocked backward, closing the door a tad. "No. Should I have? Foster cares for our garden."

"It ain't ours, Missy. Ours's just where I left it yesterday, hangin'..."

"Foster, shut yer trap. I want this here young lady to answer my question."

"My family only moved in last week, Mr..."

"Spry. Avery Spry. If it ain't the church's, whose is it?"

"I have no idea. I've not used any of the garden tools."

As door hinges squeaked in the kitchen, they heard approaching footsteps. "Sis! You're never going to believe it. They found the murder weapon—here! I told you the other night Foster was up to..."

Augie stopped, spotting Phoebe half-hidden in the open entryway. Stealing up beside her, he found Foster with two unfamiliar men. The nearest appeared to have been sleeping in a barn and the other was clean-shaven and tidy.

"What night?" asked the disheveled stranger, leaning forward as Augie shrugged his shoulders. "Speak up, boy." Beside him, Foster was twisting his cap so anxiously, it was barely identifiable.

"Uh…I don't know. Maybe Friday?"

"It was Wednesday, Mr. Spry, but my brother is spouting nonsense. It was too dark to see anything. Besides, Mr. Foster was pushing something away from the house, not toward it." Glancing at the caretaker, she read plain gratitude.

"Oh. I gets the night ya mean, Missy. I was pushin' a load o' them hostas I'd thinned out from the bed over yonder under the big oak."

Augie crinkled up his face, tilting it to one side. "But…"

Phoebe elbowed him. "Hostas are one of my favorites. I told Augie it was nothing, though you know how vivid little boys' imaginations are."

"Foster, why in blazes you be dividing 'em so early? An' you still haven't mentioned where you was takin' 'em."

"Down the lane a bit. Planted 'em next to the road."

"Gentlemen, if you don't need anything else, I will continue cooking breakfast."

As she tried to shut the door, the man who had remained silent swiftly placed his hand against it. "One minute, Miss Farrell. Apart from Mr. Foster—and your family, of course—who has visited either the parsonage or church since you moved in?"

Phoebe paused to think. "Many people. May I ask why you wish to know?"

"My name is Matthew Bentley. By the request of Asa Kiker, Governor McDowell sent me to investigate the recent murder at The Lilacs. Mr. Spry, who heads the local Slave Patrol, is showing me what he has learned."

"Oh!" Taking a step backward, Phoebe opened the door wider but none of the three stepped in. "Colonel Nelson, the head deacon, drove us here, then he and the other board members met with Father at the church. Foster was already on the premises. A friend, Lisa White, stopped by to say hello, and the Ladies' Welcoming Committee readied the parsonage in the hours before we arrived. I do not know which women belong to it, though Mrs. White would. Friday morning, Father performed the funeral for the…the late Mr. Simmons, and he preached his first sermon on Sunday in the sanctuary at ten o'clock. He or Colonel Nelson might be able to provide you a list of attendees. The list would be nearly identical."

"That won't be necessary. I'm sorry to have bothered you. Good day."

As the two strangers parted with Foster and walked toward the church, Phoebe stood in the doorway observing the contrasts between them. One was all brawn and the other more…gentlemanly. He was not as refined as Hugh was. "Oh!" She put her hand to her mouth. "I forgot!"

She stepped out the door to catch them, yet something held her back. What, she could not pinpoint. Perhaps she simply did not want to make a spectacle of herself before the governor's deputy, but she also was inclined to keep her introduction to the young Mr. Kiker private. It *had* been thoroughly embarrassing. Besides, surely Mr. Kiker's sons were not suspects. If they had been involved, their father would not have petitioned the governor for help.

Sons… Clara said she had only one brother, though how could that be possible? The two men were remarkably alike. Oh—and she had told them nothing of Birdie. Still, she was a mere girl and too frightened to… What of Birdie's warning about Hugh, or was it Charles? Moreover, why had Hugh—according to his sister—disliked the victim?

As she tried to remember exactly what Clara had said, she recalled the conversation she had overheard while in the Simmons' pantry. What hold did the dead man have over Asa Kiker, and why did it compel him to offer Charles his father's job? It made no sense to her, but then neither did much of that conversation.

"Why were they asking *you* questions?"

Phoebe jumped at Augie's voice. She had been so deep in thought, she had not noticed he had followed her outside.

"They wanted to know who owned the hoe."

"Why ask you? How would you know?"

"I can answer that'n." Foster raised up, holding a couple of weeds he had pulled near the front door. "They found it in the shed out back."

"The parsonage shed?" asked Phoebe. "What was it doing in there?"

"And how did they know where to find it?" added Augie.

"Both good questions. I went to get my waterin' can and saw that big one standin' inside, holdin' the hoe in his hand."

"How can we say *he* didn't put it there?"

"Well..." Foster scratched his head, tilting his cap forward. "That'd at least explain how they found it. Don't add up otherwise. I'm the only one as touches them tools. Why would I go all the way up to Kiker's place an' bash one o' our church member's husbands in the head? Pardon me, Missy. Not fit talk for a young lady. Still, it's a fair piece, and I don't own no horse."

Augie's eyes widened. "They think you killed him?"

"Now little fella, don't go takin' no fool notions. Never took no hoe to a varmint let alone Mr. Simmons, but I 'spect they's a wonderin'. Can't think it was you or Miss Phoebe, an' your pa wouldna' jumped the train in the wee hours to take a swipe at a stranger."

"That'd be a sight, eh Phebes?" Augie chuckled, though his sister only wrinkled up her brow.

"I thought a slave confessed?"

Foster looked down at the weeds and scratched his head again. "Told me Kiker don't give the notion no credit. All them up there got plenty o' reasons to do Simmons in. Kiker's slaves, I mean, but Kitch... He's big 'nuff he could have knocked Simmons out o' the county any time 'e wanted. Then again, if 'e did, Simmons would've whipped him somethin' awful."

Glancing up, he found both children staring open-mouthed. "Here I go again. Never you two mind. I shouldna' been tellin' you 'bout such evil goin's on."

"I'd heard it was a woman," said Phoebe, "named Bett."

"Old Bett? Nah, they's just tryin' to account for Kitch claimin' it was 'im. She's his granny—or his ma's granny. Hard to tell. They's let her go an' him too. I thank you, Missy, for comin' to my rescue a bit ago. Spry was set on grillin' me like a catfish."

When Phoebe shot her brother a frown, Augie hung his head and moved his toe back and forth across the threshold. "I'm sorry, Mr. Foster. I thought they were still searching the shed. When I overheard what they were saying, I just *had* to tell somebody."

"Never you mind, young'un. You got a keen eye. Y'll make a fine hunter once we git you a rifle."

"A rifle! When?"

"Well, that's somethin' y'll have to ask yer pa. Maybe he'll getcha one for yer next birthday."

Augie beamed at the thought for a second then furrowed his brow. "What *were* you doing that night?"

"Augie—stop it. He already said, and you heard just the same as I did."

Foster nodded in appreciation. Still, her brother was about to protest until they spotted Father climbing the path. Augie sprinted off to meet him, but she trotted back to the kitchen to see how much of breakfast she could salvage.

ONCE THEIR FATHER had given thanks and scooped a clump of cold oatmeal into his mouth, Augie began peppering him with questions. The reverend put up his hand and swallowed hard, taking a swig of coffee as he flicked a glance from one child to the other. "Mr. Bentley—the man the governor sent to investigate—suspects someone placed a hoe in our shed. I'm usually sequestered in my office. Have you seen anyone around?"

Phoebe concentrated hard on her oatmeal, trying to discern which was most important: answering her father or protecting Birdie. She could almost still feel the fear captured in the girl's eyes and did not see the point in telling Papa about her. When she slipped down to the river yesterday, Birdie had been nowhere in sight, and she had no way to guess where the girl might live.

"I saw two men on Saturday afternoon."

"Where and who?"

"Down the slope, this side of the river. One introduced himself as Hugh Kiker, though I am confused about the second. They resembled each other so closely, I took them for brothers. However, Miss Kiker told me yesterday she has only one."

Reverend Farrell shrugged. "Perhaps a cousin. Did he tell you his name?"

"Charles."

"Oh. He was likely Charles Simmons, the dead man's eldest. Although I suppose Charles is a common enough name. Hugh and he do favor each other."

"Hugh and Charles Simmons? I met Mr. Simmons at his father's funeral. He looked nothing like Hugh Kiker."

"Ah, now I understand your confusion. Charles was not present at the funeral. In fact, he had Mahala rather worried. You met William, her second eldest, younger than Charles by a year or two."

"William? So the maids were…"

Reverend Farrell leaned forward. "Were what?"

"Come on, Phebes," chimed in Augie. "Spit it out."

"Um…just something I overheard." Phoebe looked pointedly at her father. "It does not bear repeating."

Papa's expression changed so rapidly, she expected him to prod her further. Instead, he simply laid his spoon aside.

"Well?" Her brother prompted. "Are you going to tell us?"

"Your sister is quite correct, son. Overheard conversations do not bear repeating. Now get your chores done. The Nelsons have kindly invited us for an early dinner. Phoebe, Gary tells me you and Emily have struck up a friendship."

His daughter dipped up a spoonful of oatmeal and let it drop again.

"I take it you are not as fond of her as she is of you?"

"Oh no—I like her very much."

"What then?"

"We were getting along wonderfully at the Wilsons, then everything changed, and I don't know why. She barely spoke a word to me the whole way home."

"Well, I wouldn't think too much about it. Girls your age are given to rather puzzling changes, eh, son?"

"You can say that again. The other day, Phebes told me not to take her pie, then—when I told her I didn't want it anyway—she acted all bothered."

Phoebe flung her eyes to the ceiling as her father rose from the table and headed for the door.

"Oh—I almost forgot. Asa and Lavinia Kiker have asked us to a soiree of sorts in their home next Saturday evening. I hope the two of you do not mind, but I've already accepted."

"How formal will it be, Papa?"

"I really couldn't say; I never thought to ask. Your mother normally handles our social life."

Pressing her lips together, Phoebe picked up their empty bowls and took them to the pump. There was no point in pressing him further. Her admiration for Mama was certainly growing. She loved Papa deeply, however, half of the time his body seemed the only part of him truly present. Back in Princeton, she found it funny. Augie and she would ask him wild questions to prove he was not listening: "Papa, may we go swimming in the fountain?" or "May Augie and I jump out the upstairs window?" When he would answer affirmatively, their peals of laughter finally brought him back to earth. Now, she thoroughly understood why Mama frequently muttered: "What am I to do with him? He would lose his head if it were not attached." She would wait and ask Emily's grandmother about the required attire.

Chapter 7

AFTER YET ANOTHER afternoon of unpacking, Phoebe collapsed on the parlor's settee and gulped down an entire glass of lemonade. She was thankful for the Nelson's invitation for dinner, as she needed to tackle the creases in Mama's gowns if everything was to be perfect for the day she arrived. When she would, Phoebe could not guess. The stationmaster had received and dispatched a brief telegraphed message this morning saying Grandmother had been partially paralyzed and was unable to speak.

Once she had hauled the steam-kettle back up the stairs to her parent's bedroom, she began holding the spout close to a particularly stubborn fold until something blocked the sun from the northeast window. No doubt it was a hawk, plenty existed in the surrounding woods, or a vulture or eagle. The shadow had seemed massive. Darting to the window, she craned her neck in every direction; and while searching the thick branches of a nearby maple, she heard the same scuffling overhead she had on the night Foster wheeled his handcart toward the road.

She picked through her conclusions that evening and caught a mistake in her logic: squirrels were not active after dark. Perhaps it had been an opossum, as Foster may have hinted. Recalling the attic dormers were only decorative, she plucked the candle from Papa's holder and shoved it and some matches into her pocket. At the end of the hall farthest from the landing, stood a slender door she carefully opened. Just beyond, two triangular steps doubled back to a narrow staircase running over the one descending to the foyer. At its top, she spied nothing but darkness.

The silence of the empty house amplified the match's scrape and the wick's fizzle, and the flame flickered and twirled toward some unseen source of air. As she was climbing tread upon tread, the seventh step creaked so loudly she halted, and, hearing an answering scurry, she whirled around so quickly the candle blew out. Running down to the hallway, she slammed the door, leaning back against it while catching her breath. Something *was* up there: an opossum or...or...

"Phebes!" Augie came bounding up the foyer staircase and rounded the landing. "They caught the murderer! Foster saw him hanging around here a couple of days before that hoe—hey, what's wrong with you?"

"Nothing. I just heard some noises in the attic. Who was it?"

"The victim's son! A witness who was at the plantation that day said he was arguing with his father."

"Which son? He has three."

Augie shrugged. "He couldn't have been Jeremiah; he's only nine. Must be...what are the older brothers' names?"

"Charles and William."

"Yeah—one of them. Somebody else said he was spotted standing over the body with the hoe in his hand."

Phoebe shuddered. William was all civility. She could not picture him murdering anyone, nor Charles, despite his taunting. Whichever it was had intended to cover his tracks or throw suspicion elsewhere—but on whom?

"I'M SHOCKED!" Mrs. Nelson was setting the meal on the table. "I was with Mahala the morning she delivered Charles. I cleaned and wrapped him myself."

Colonel Nelson dropped his eyes to his plate. "I'm as surprised as you, Mary, but a witness has come forward. He—or she—swears he saw Charles standing over the body with the hoe in his hand. And speaking of the hoe, Foster spotted him near the shed on Saturday, not long before it turned up."

Once Reverend Farrell had said the blessing, he sat tugging at one side of his mustache. "The time I've spent with him is not sufficient to form any opinions. What do you think? Does he seem the sort to kill his own father?"

The Nelsons flicked each other meaningful glances. "I don't know," answered Gary. "This is my first brush with murder, so I can't say what sort that would be. Charles has appeared troubled at times, even resentful. Simmons was a hard man, and a good deal of friction existed between them."

"Any idea why?"

"For a long time, a rumor has circulated claiming Simmons was not Charles' fath…"

"Gary!" Mary cut in. "Not in front of the children. 'Little pitchers have big ears.'"

"They would have to be deaf not to hear them, though I guess you are right. Since no one truly knows—except Mahala of course—I shouldn't have brought it up. To answer your question, Ernest, I've learned the hard way to hope for the best from a man without letting the worst take me by surprise."

"I quite agree. I've seen angry people do things I would never have imagined, still, the hoe didn't belong to Simmons. Governor MacDowell's man—what was his name, Phoebe?"

"Matthew Bentley."

"Yes, Bentley. He said it belonged to the Kiker's carriage driver."

"Kitch. It was his alright, but how could Kitch have come all the way down to the parsonage to hide it?"

Augie perked up. "Wasn't the dead man found behind his cabin?"

"Yes, but…" Emily was crumpling her brow. "Clara—Miss Kiker—told us Granny Bett already confessed."

Mary shook her head. "The poor old woman. When Avery Spry hauled Kitch away, she fell to her knees and grabbed him by the boots. It took both Lavinia and Mitilde to lift her back onto her feet."

"I'm afraid you have me at a disadvantage," replied the pastor. "Lavinia's grandmother confessed?"

"Not Lavinia's," Gary answered, "but most every slave at The Lilacs."

"I still don't understand. If she already confessed, why arrest Charles?"

"Not even Spry believed her, and Bentley let her go."

"That may have been Lavinia's doing," offered Mary. "Asa told Gary she was beside herself. He insisted she drink a glass of whiskey just to calm her down."

"She must care a great deal for the woman. You say she is a slave?"

Gary nodded. "The Kikers' oldest, passed down from one generation to the next."

"Had it not been for Granny Bett," added Mary, "Lavinia would have died giving birth to Clara. Dr. Ridley was visiting relatives in Richmond and would never have made it."

"Still…" Reverend Farrell sat back in his chair. "If she confessed to killing Simmons, they cannot simply look the other way. And what of Charles?"

"I don't know how strong the evidence against him is," responded Gary, "but Granny Bett could not have done it. She has to be over a hundred, and her hands shake so severely, she can barely steady a spoon."

"Colonel Nelson," asked Phoebe. "Why do they fix Saturday as the time the weapon was hidden?"

"Well…I guess because that's the day Foster saw Charles. Sort of circular reasoning, if you ask me."

"You have a point, Gary," agreed his wife. "And so does she. How do they know it was not placed in the shed on Friday, while we were all occupied with the funeral?"

"I can answer that," replied the reverend. "Foster sharpened all the tools before he left that evening, and it was not among them then."

"What about Sunday?" asked Augie.

Colonel Nelson raised an eyebrow. "I reckon it could have been during church. Half the village came to hear your father speak."

"And Charles," added Emily, "was noticeably absent."

Phoebe pushed her peas around her plate. "Is Foster certain it was Charles he saw? Hugh Kiker was with him Saturday, and they look very much alike." Despite the heat she felt rising beneath her collar, she lifted her eyes. "Don't you remember, Father, I told you at breakfast this morning?"

"You told me they were down by the river but not anywhere near the church's shed."

Colonel Nelson arched his eyebrows. "What were the two of them doing?"

"Tracking an enslaved man." Phoebe hoped he would ask nothing of the circumstances.

49

"They can't have been searching for Kitch; none of the slaves left the plantation. Maybe Manuel Jackson, though I don't suppose it could have been. He purchased his freedom several years ago."

"Lavinia said Hugh was home with her all Saturday," added Mary. "And he was in plain view of everyone at Sunday's service. I remember admiring how attentive he was toward his mother."

Pastor Farrell frowned. "What about during the tea the Wilsons held for Phoebe?"

"No, after I dropped Mary and Emily off, I rode up to see Asa and him. It made little sense for me to come all the way home just to turn around and pick them up again."

As Mrs. Nelson and Emily rose to clear the plates, Reverend Farrell sat back in his chair. "Mary, you must forgive me. We've been so thoroughly occupied, I've completely forgotten to mention how much I've enjoyed this meal. It was delicious. When Amelia returns from her parents', we would enjoy having the three of you come to dinner."

"I'm glad you enjoyed it, Pastor. We look forward to meeting her."

While Emily finished clearing the table, Reverend Farrell turned to his daughter. "Why didn't you mention seeing Hugh and Charles to those men who questioned us?"

"I...I didn't think of them until the men were halfway down the path. Besides, I thought they were both Mr. Kiker's sons. If he had suspected one of them, he surely would not have sought help from the governor."

Mary sliced and served a freshly baked apple pie before taking her seat. "Phoebe, I found what you said earlier very interesting. What do you think, Gary? Those two boys do greatly resemble each other."

"Well...Foster might have taken one for the other, but what about the person who saw Charles standing over his father with the weapon?"

Augie sat up straight. "Somebody saw the murder?"

"Not the act, the aftermath."

"Colonel Nelson means they saw what happened shortly afterward," explained the reverend, noticing his son's puzzled expression. Setting down his fork, he began toying with his mustache. "I wonder who identified him and from what distance? Could he—or

50

she—have mistaken Hugh for Charles? Certainly, no one would be surprised to find Hugh on his own family's property."

Emily cleared her throat. "Mrs. Kiker wouldn't lie. I mean, Phoebe, I know you would not say Hugh was at the parsonage Saturday if he was not, however, Grandmother said..." As she tried to reconcile both stories, she grew pink.

"You raise an excellent question, Emily," replied the reverend. "I have full confidence in what my daughter recounted and can think of only one reason Mrs. Kiker might lie: she fears for her son."

"But Reverend Farrell, I've known Hugh all my life. He would never hurt..."

Colonel Nelson placed his hand on her arm. "Mr. Bentley is considering every possibility. Murder is a capital offense. You wouldn't want them to hang Charles if he didn't do it, would you?"

All color drained from Emily's face.

The colonel folded his napkin. "I've got to admit, he might have a far better reason to..."

"To what?" asked Augie, when the colonel trailed off.

Phoebe swatted his leg under the table. "Hugh seemed both thoughtful and gentlemanly to me."

"We've always thought him so," replied Gary. "But the location of the incident raises Hugh's motives. He did not approve of Simmons' harsh methods. Not many did—including Asa."

"Why," asked the reverend, "did they keep him on?"

Phoebe leaned forward, wondering if Colonel Nelson might shed light on the conversation she had overheard from the pantry. Instead, he began squirming as if his chair had grown uncomfortable.

"I cannot answer without revisiting the rather base speculations we agreed we wouldn't discuss."

"Then you mustn't. As your pastor, of course, I hope you will always follow the dictates of conscience, however, this question of slavery troubles my whole family. Amelia and I prayed mightily before accepting this position and would not have done so were we not sure of God's leading. The need is obvious, but I felt befuddled about the board's reasons for my call. I know little more about the area or congregation than what I read in your letters."

Colonel Nelson considered his words before answering. "As someone who genuinely desires your friendship, Ernest, I must warn

51

you straight away to tread lightly. With the growing tensions in Congress, folks are expecting a northern preacher like you to look down your nose on them. If you try to convert our people to abolitionists, more than a few will be upset. Some might grow madder than a wet hen. "

"I intend to teach only what is inherent in the Scriptures."

"Good. Then we should not have any trouble. Most people in these parts have been raised in the church and think God put slavery into place as part of His order; and frankly, men like Kiker see it as essential to much of our economy."

Reverend Farrell groaned inwardly. He had hoped to delay discussing the topic, yet before he could decide whether to debate or sidestep it now, Deacon Nelson reached for his Bible.

"They will quote Mt. 10:24—the second clause. 'A slave is not above his master.' And if you argue, they will tell you, 'Jesus met many a slave and master, but He never demanded they set their slaves free.'"

As Reverend Farrell weighed his answer, he glanced from Augie to Phoebe. "And what about you, Gary? What do you believe?"

"I believe I am to love my neighbor as myself."

"Who is your neighbor?"

Colonel Nelson arched a brow. "I suspect you are purposefully taking the lawyer's part—the one Jesus told about the Good Samaritan. As I understand it, my neighbor is anyone I meet, whether Ed Simmons, his housemaid, Ruby, or Asa Kiker. Each has needs, though they differ from one to another."

Reverend Farrell could not help but smile. "I confess, I am relieved. For a minute, I wondered if you wanted me here."

"Want you? Why, I cast the deciding vote!"

Chapter 8

AS PHOEBE WAS placing the bowls on the high shelf, her brother brushed into her. "Watch what you are doing, Augie. You nearly made me drop the dishes. Oh—and what have you done with my quilt?"

"What quilt?"

"The blue and green log cabin quilt from the chest by my bed. I took it to the parlor so I could wrap up while reading, but now the weather's warmed up again, I wanted to take it down to the river."

Augie shrugged his shoulders. "Haven't seen it. The weather around here is crazy. Hot then cold and now it's warmed up again."

While he slipped out to fill a water jug, Phoebe assembled a picnic lunch, and when she thought of Birdie, she decided to pack double. "What are you doing today?" She did not want to risk him finding out about the girl.

"Maybe hanging out with Foster, even if his eye still gives me the creeps. He knows about all sorts of things."

"Like what?"

"Building and fixing stuff mostly, but..." His eyes began to sparkle. "I'll tell you something if you promise not to tell."

"Alright, I promise."

"I think he's up to something. He told the governor's agent he was planting hostas by the road, remember? He doesn't know I had sneaked into the shed and peeked at his hand cart the next morning—Friday before we went to the funeral. It was perfectly clean, not a smidge of dirt anywhere. And Sunday, while you were sipping tea at Mrs. Wilson's, he pulled a little raft from a bunch of thick bushes and ferried over the river. I would have followed him, except I didn't have a way to get across."

"Where did he go?"

"Once he hit the other side, he disappeared up a trail."

53

"I don't know, Augie. He may simply clean things after using them. I hate to think he lied—and he can do as he pleases on Sundays. Still, if he's doing something he ought not…"

"Aw, he's alright. Just like he told those men, he doesn't even hurt the mice he traps. He takes them out in a field and sets them free."

"How do you know?"

"Haven't you been listening? I've been following him."

"You better be cautious. What if he caught you? You're a pest, but I don't want you getting hurt, at least not while I'm taking care of you."

"Aw, don't worry. I plan to gracy ate myself to him."

"Ingratiate—and how do you plan to do that?"

Augie shrugged. "I don't know. I'll help him do chores and such."

"Well, mind you don't go getting into mischief—and stay on the church property."

"Oh, alright." Not until he scampered off did it occur to her he might not know where the property ended.

BASKET AND BOOK in hand, Phoebe trotted down the hill to the river and flopped down on the grass near a weeping willow. Birdie was nowhere in sight, leaving Phoebe to wonder if she would ever see her again. Lying back against the cool grass, she debated whether to eat first or read, however, the sun was so deliciously warm it began lulling her to sleep. She watched a cloud wafting above the new leaves until every fiber of her sprang awake. "Birdie, why are you up *there?*"

"He gone?"

"Who?"

"That little boy. He always down here catchin' things. He better watch out—gonna catch hisself a cottonmouth one day if he ain't careful."

"Augie? He won't hurt you. He's my brother."

"Where he at?"

"Off following Foster, the church's caretaker."

"Again? He done tracked the man all week."

"Come on, down. I packed too much lunch and don't want it to go to waste."

Birdie narrowed her eyes. "How come you pack so much?"

Phoebe's dimples started twitching. "I was hoping I might find you. I see you made use of those old boots."

"Like you said, ain't no use of letting no raccoon drag them off." Scrambling down to a lower branch, she dropped to the grass.

"Here." Pulling a dishtowel from over the basket, Phoebe drew out two sandwiches and two large slices of pie, chuckling when Birdie snatched one of each. "Now hold on. We haven't said grace, and if you eat too fast, you'll give yourself a stomach ache."

Looking sheepish, Birdie stilled her hands.

"Thank You for this food, Lord, and thank You for my new friend."

As Phoebe opened her eyes, Birdie bit into her pie. "Um-hm. You make this? It's almost as good as my aunt Mitilde's."

Phoebe paused mid-bite, immediately recalling where she had heard the name. "Mitilde?"

"Uh…" Birdie cast her a quick sidelong glance. "She don't live 'round here, Miss Phoebe."

"Just Phoebe. Don't you remember? We're friends."

"I never called no white woman by her first name before."

"What else would you call a friend? Do you want me to call you Miss Birdie?"

The girl put a hand up to her mouth to cover her giggle. "No, no—that's okay. I'll call you Phoebe if you want me to, but don't tell no one."

"I promise. Now you've got to promise me something."

The girl fell silent.

"Promise you'll stay while I fetch us another couple of pieces of pie."

When Birdie broke into a wide grin, Phoebe hopped to her feet and bolted back up the rise. She dashed passed the larder and up to her room, pulling a serviceable frock from the wardrobe. Birdie had refused the last one, but the condition of her garment, without a river to hide it, appeared even worse than Phoebe had expected. Hurrying back to the kitchen, Phoebe rummaged for spoil-resistant foodstuffs and lit on a round of cheese the Nelsons had sent home with them. She cut a huge wedge.

"Yuh goin' fer a swim, Missy? I see yer takin' an extra frock."

Foster's question stopped her in her tracks until she reminded herself she had nothing to fear. As long as she was playing housekeeper, everything in their kitchen fell under her jurisdiction. "Just a picnic. I'm using this old frock to wrap my food in. I'll be back in time to make dinner."

Trotting down the hill, the corners of her mouth sank. Birdie was nowhere to be seen, but as Phoebe peered into the willow's canopy, she laughed. The girl was already clambering down.

"You know, Birdie, you have just as much right to be here as anyone."

"What you mean?"

"You don't have to hide. This is church property. It belongs to God. Then again, I guess everything does."

Birdie was too busy eating to answer. She had already stuck a chunk of cheese in her mouth then stopped, growing sheepish again.

"Don't worry. Our last prayer covers this food, too, so eat all you would like and take the rest with you."

Birdie smiled. "Hey, looky." She tipped her head toward a brown bird with a red breast. "A robin. Spring's sure to stay. What you got?"

"A book a friend loaned me." She held it up so Birdie could see the front cover.

"You read?"

"Sure. Would you like me to read it to you?" When Birdie's eyes lit, she cracked the novel open to chapter one and flopped back onto the grass. "'Escaping Henry was so effortless I could hardly believe I had succeeded.'"

"Who Henry and who saying that—a slave?"

"I don't know. I've only read the first line." She was surprised Birdie looked so vulnerable. Her shoulders were hunched and her head drooped down. "Do you know any slaves?"

"Some. You know any?"

Phoebe laid the book aside. "Not really. Slavery is illegal in Princeton, where we just moved from, but I may have met your aunt at Mr. Simmons' funeral. Did you know him?"

Birdie nodded.

"Why is your aunt a slave when you are free?" As the girl's eyes darted around again, Phoebe groaned. "I'm sorry, Birdie. Papa cautioned me about asking uncomfortable questions—only, sometimes I don't know they'll be uncomfortable before I ask them. The truth is, I did the same thing with your aunt."

"How's that?"

"After Mr. Simmons' funeral, I offered to carry a platter of fried chicken for her—or maybe it was Ruby. A new acquaintance, Clara Kiker, told me both of their names, but she didn't point out who was called which."

"Don't worry 'bout that none. Likely, they didn't want them Simmonses thinking they's shirking, that's all."

"Oh. I hadn't thought of that. If you see either, please tell her I'm sorry and meant well. Do you live with your mother and father?"

"No. They's dead."

"Who do you live with?"

"I lives in...uh...in a *friend's* house. I got me a man—a free man. We gonna jump the broom."

"Why?"

Birdie smiled at Phoebe's bewildered expression. "It's what you folks call gettin' hitched."

"When?"

"Soon as he gets back from...from a place he's...stayin'... an' he comes to collect me."

"Oh." Phoebe's dimples disappeared. "I am happy for you, though I confess I wish you didn't have to go. I mean, we haven't known each other long, yet I already feel I can be myself with you more than anyone else I've met so far."

"Why's that? You don't like folks here?"

Phoebe shrugged. "I've met several I like, however, one is a busy wife and mother who lives too far away to visit often. The other is closer to my age and seemed to like me enough, but I'm afraid I've offended her somehow. While we were talking with some of my other new acquaintances, she just went all quiet. Then, while my family ate dinner in her grandparents' home, she nearly implied I was lying."

"Was you?"

"No!"

"Some folks don't say what's eatin' at 'em less you ask."

"I will—if she gives me a chance. Then there is this whole slavery issue. I just can't see how it's right to own human beings. The Bible

57

talks about slaves, however, Papa told me yesterday the circumstances were different. Ancient cultures captured enemies instead of slaughtering them and often gave them a good deal of freedom. Like the Romans. They highly respected the Greeks and employed vast numbers as teachers, but God strictly forbade snatching and selling unsuspecting persons."

Birdie lay down in the grass by Phoebe and sighed. "I don't know any o' them Romans you is talkin' about or them Greeks, though I gets being lonely an' all. I's lonely too. Still, you best keep all them thoughts 'bout slavers to youself. Last preacher got into a heap o' trouble. Ran him out o' town and..."

Phoebe gasped. "What happened to them?"

"Took shelter with them funny-talkin' folks as lives south o' us— call themselves somethin' crazy soundin' like Minnow..." She rubbed the corner of her mouth, trying hard to remember the name. "Minnow Nights."

"Minnow Nights? Oh—Mennonites?"

"Ain't that what I said?"

"Where are they now?"

"Don't know." Birdie shrugged. "Never heard no more. Maybe they's still there."

Shuddering, Phoebe picked up her novel. She was unwilling to spoil their visit by paying attention to the nerve Birdie had struck. When she read a page describing the protagonist's step-uncle, the girl sat up and pulled her legs up under her chin.

"Shall I stop?"

"No," the girl answered, although she seemed to shrink further within herself the farther Phoebe read. Then, for some unseen reason, she began shaking her head. "He need to stop!"

"What?" Phoebe also sat up and snapped the novel shut.

"That man. He tryin' to take liberties." As Birdie flicked a glance to the bottom of the page, Phoebe skipped to the last paragraph.

"You read ahead. You didn't tell me you could read."

"Uh...I reads a bit. My uh...my *aunt* teached me."

"Mitilde?"

Birdie shook her head a little too strongly. "No, uh... 'nother aunt—ain't my real kin an' ain't no one you knows, but promise me you won't tell no one."

"I won't say anything. I haven't even told anyone you exist. Why does it matter?"

"Against the law in these parts. They'd put my...aunt...in jail."

"That's awful. No wonder you seem scared. I didn't mean to upset you."

Birdie began casting her eyes about again as if a lawman—or the novel's step-uncle—might pop up from behind the bushes. "I gotta be goin' now anyway."

"Oh. Well, here." Phoebe unfurled the frock "This is mine to give, and don't worry—you are the first person in Virginia to see it. It will fit you admirably. Please take it and the remaining cheese—as a favor to me."

Birdie ran her hand over the light blue cotton. "Sure is beautiful, but I got nothin' to give you in return."

"You've already given me what I want most: your friendship. It is worth far more than old clothing."

Birdie slid her a sidelong grin. "If you's sure. I'll wear it on my weddin' day."

WHETHER FROM THE newness of Phoebe's surroundings or the lonely silence within the parsonage's thick stone walls, a thud sent a shiver up her back. She shrugged it off. Augie or Papa had likely come in, shutting a door behind them. If she hurried, she might finish steaming the last of Mama's gowns before the sun altogether set.

She glanced from the window to her parents' Argand lamp, dreading the additional heat of an oil flame. The afternoon had been pleasant, despite the steam making her feel sticky. Less desirable still was the risk of scalding Mama's only taffeta in poor lighting. While trimming the wick, a distinct footfall froze her in place. The bedroom door was wide open; had either Augie or Papa passed it, she would have seen them.

Yesterday, she had felt too embarrassed to confess her fear to Augie; now she wished he would come bounding up the steps again. As her imagination presented threatening possibilities, she discarded one after another. She did not believe in spirits—at least not the unholy kind—and though Mr. Bentley may have apprehended the wrong man, Simmons' true murderer could not have gained entry. Most likely, it had only *sounded* like a footfall. Unfamiliar houses came with unfamiliar noises, and six days were not enough to acquaint her with all of them.

Grasping the lamp, she headed for the narrow upper staircase, opened the door, and climbed the stairs. This time, she was prepared for the seventh step's squeak, but she held her breath as she heard a repeat of yesterday's scrambling. A door closed snugly as if it had swelled in the day's warmth and needed a firmer tug to pull it into place. As she stepped around the half-wall dividing the stairway from whatever lay beyond it, she lifted the lamp aloft.

The attic proved much like any other: full of items the Ladies' Hospitality League thought her family was not using. A wooden rocking horse stood in one corner and a child's bed—too large yet for her baby sister, Lucy—graced another. An old lectern stood close by, perhaps stored after the church replaced it with the one she had seen in the sanctuary. A shame, she thought, briefly studying its carvings. Though old-fashioned, it was far prettier.

Gaining courage, she slipped between their trunks and winter items to raise and lower the lamp along each wall. Not one was marred by a tell-tale seam betraying a hidden door. Tomorrow, she would enlist Augie's help, pushing everything to one side and then the other to search for rodent holes. For now, she dusted off her skirt and descended the way she came, feeling much better for having faced her fears.

Chapter 9

ONCE HER FATHER closed the kitchen door, Phoebe leaned over her pancakes. "Augie, do you ever hear noises in this house? I mean sounds you cannot account for naturally?"

He leaned in closer, nearly half-way across the table. "You hear them too?"

"Yes. Last evening, I was sure I heard footsteps in the attic and a door pulled shut."

Flopping against his chair, he rocked on its back legs. "I asked Foster about them. He said the kids before us heard them too!"

"Did he say *what* they heard?"

"Ghosts!"

Phoebe rolled her eyes. "There is no such thing."

"How do *you* know?" He dropped the chair back onto all fours. "The Bible even says there is. A ghost visited King Saul."

"You'd better ask Papa about that. I suspect God let him see an apparition of some sort or gave him a one-of-a-kind warning. Would you help me?"

"How?"

"Go with me into the attic. I want to see if we can find evidence of opossums or squirrel nests up there."

"Right Phoebe—an opossum who closes doors?"

Phoebe shrugged. "What else could it be?"

"Maybe the murderer!" Augie beamed. "I bet he's hiding up there."

Both started as a door swung open.

"Kitten." Papa stepped inside. "Would you be free to visit the Simmonses with me? I'm sure her children and she are distressed over Charles' arrest and may find a woman's presence helpful. Her daughters are around your age."

Phoebe smiled. He had called her a woman. "Yes, I'd be glad to go. What about Augie?"

"Would you like to come too, son, and play with Josiah?"

"Jeremiah. Sure. I'd love to go."

AS THE WAGON rolled up to the Simmons' residence, a tall, dark-haired man came out of the barn.

"Charles!" The reverend called. "I'm glad to see you're already home."

"So am I, and I'd like to thank you—or rather your daughter—for getting me out of jail."

"Phoebe? She hasn't left church property since Tuesday."

Charles tossed her a wink. "The governor's agent dropped by Colonel Nelson's home this morning, following up on information I gave him about a bootlegger. The colonel told him what Phoebe said about Hugh."

Augie started squirming. "Did they arrest him?"

"Who, son?" asked his father. "Mr. Kiker?"

"The bootlegger. Before he sneaked the hoe into our shed, I bet he was hiding it in his still."

"You could be right, little man, but I doubt they've found him yet." Charles bobbed his head toward the house. "Mother doesn't know, so I'd appreciate you keeping him a secret."

"What about your friend?" fretted Phoebe.

"No, you alibied us both. Seeing you dipping in the river was a piece of luck."

Phoebe reddened as her father spun his head her way.

"You left out that part."

"Don't trouble yourself none, Pastor." Charles grinned. "The water was clear up to her neck."

Reverend Farrell appeared far from reassured. "Is he from around here? The bootlegger, I mean. What reason would he have for hurting your father?"

"Pa and he were…business partners. Together, they …"

"Why it's Pastor Farrell and his children." Mahala Simmons and her older daughters, Virginia and Megan, streamed out the door to greet them. "I can see you know our good news. I knew it was

62

nonsense, accusing Charles. Hello Phoebe, Augie. Come in. Ruby has just made us a fresh batch of sweet tea."

When Phoebe recognized the housemaid, she tried to catch her eye, but Ruby offered only the slightest nod before receding into the background. Phoebe could not tell whether or not Birdie had conveyed her apology.

Sidling up to Augie, Jeremiah whispered. "Wanna see my lamb? He's two weeks old today."

"Sure! Can we, Papa?"

"You *may*," Reverend Farrell answered, and the two ran outside so eagerly the door had banged shut before little Sarah, who chased after them, had reached it. When she glanced back toward her family and guests, her mother motioned for her to come back.

Crowding Phoebe on both sides, Virginia and Megan asked for any tidbits of gossip she could supply about the Wilsons' tea and looked disappointed when she was not particularly forthcoming.

Virginia clasped hold of Phoebe's hand. "Surely you can tell us something more. I feel I shall go mad if we have to stay in this house for another week—and to miss the Kikers' dance! They are not likely to hold another until the harvest."

Megan leaned in on her other side. "Mother did not think it appropriate to accept such a happy invitation while the household is in mourning."

Phoebe agreed. Had her father been murdered, she would have found feigning any degree of gaiety very taxing; but, hoping to assuage the sisters' loneliness, she described all she could remember about the food, attire, and conversation. When William came in from outside and sat by his mother, talk turned to Charles' detainment, their father's murder, and the most likely suspects.

"I still suspect Kitch," answered his mother.

Charles shook his head. "More likely Manny to my way of thinking. That's why Hugh and I were tracking him in the first place. He's been saving to buy a girl from Kiker nigh on three years."

When William noticed Papa intently studying the braided rug, he cleared his throat. "I'm sorry if our conversation is making you uncomfortable, Pastor, you being a northerner and all."

"What *are* your views, sir?" asked Charles.

Reverend Farrell shifted in his chair. "I was aware of the differences in thought between most southerners and northerners when I took this position."

"I'm glad," said Mrs. Simmons, "for the good living the Kikers afforded my husband and now Charles, however, I cannot abide the buying and selling of human beings."

"I do not mean offense, Mahala, but am I mistaken in assuming your housemaid is a slave?"

"She is, indeed, Pastor, though I had no say whatever in the decision to keep her. She was a gift to me from Lavinia, and while I was inclined to return her, I was up to my elbows in dirty diapers, and Edward insisted she stay."

"And now?"

She began to fidget. "Well...I am no longer worn ragged by a troop of children, and Edward clearly has no more to say. Now, I find I cannot let her go. I have become accustomed to her help, as has my whole family. Besides, what would we do—put her out to fend for herself? She has served us well for years; I refuse to let her starve."

"See, Pastor," continued Charles, "The trouble is Ruby's kin are living in this valley, most of them up at The Lilacs. All she knows is cooking and cleaning, and who would pay her wages? Anyone rich enough to afford a maid is rich enough to buy one. The initial outlay might be costly, but it's a bargain in the end."

William looked Reverend Farrell squarely in the eye. "You have not shared your views, Pastor."

"Well, while I did not accept this position to convince anyone of my political views, God created all of us from one set of ancestors. We were all—your housemaid, included—made in His glorious image. God meant us to rule over beasts not become them."

"With all due respect, Pastor, what about Ham, Noah's son? As a preacher, you are bound to be acquainted with the curse on his descendants."

"I am. Do you have a Bible handy?"

"Yes, of course. Go fetch the one on my table, Sarah." Her mother nodded toward her bedroom.

When the child brought it to Reverend Farrell, he read: "'Cursed be Canaan; a servant of servants shall he be unto his brethren.' William, who is this Canaan?"[ii]

"Noah's grandson, the son of Ham."

"So why was he cursed and not the other sons of Ham?"

William frowned. "I can't say."

"Neither can I. It's rather puzzling, isn't it? And what about the content of the curse? Sarah, you are the youngest among us today, but I'd guess if I asked you, you could tell me what the curse amounted to."

Sarah looked at her mother.

"Go ahead, child. Tell the Pastor what you heard him read."

"It says he will be a servant."

"You are a good listener and have answered correctly. So *if* we could conclude the descendants of Canaan *must* serve, who are they, and which kind of service is required?"

When William did not answer immediately, Charles spoke up. "Isn't it obvious?"

"Not to me. Can you prove Ruby descended from Canaan?"

"That would be impossible."

"Indeed, and wouldn't you say you serve the Kikers?"

"You know I do."

"Well, I've heard you and Hugh are like brothers and have been since you were knee-high to a grasshopper. Is yours the kind of friendship a slave enjoys with his master?"

"No," Charles mumbled, glancing away.

"So which of these kinds of 'servant' did Noah intend Canaan to be?"

William rubbed his lip. "It doesn't say."

"Ah. So here we have an important lesson on interpreting the Scriptures. The Bible states most things as clearly as the crystal vases on your hutch. Other passages offer such little and murky information we can't use them honestly to justify a position."

"But what do you think, Pastor?"

"What I think is insignificant. The question concerns what God thinks, and for that, we need to look at what He has clearly expressed."

"How?" asked Sarah.

"Well, for one, He said, 'Treat other people as you wish to be treated'[iii] or something very like it. I never can get the quote quite right. It's in Luke's gospel, chapter six or seven, if you want to read it for yourself."

Charles' blue eyes simmered. "But surely you cannot apply the same standard to everyone. Take Asa Kiker. I don't expect him to treat me exactly as he treats himself. He's my employer."

"But he can treat you exactly as he would like to be treated by his boss if he had one, and I hope he does."

"Asa has been nothing but kind to us, Charles," replied Mahala. "I don't know what you are going on about."

"Just an example, Ma, to help me understand what Pastor Farrell is saying."

"If any of you wish to know God's opinion, you have only to search the New Testament for passages about masters and servants. If you compare those instructions with how the enslaved are treated in this valley, you can arrive at your own conclusions."

Both Mrs. Simmons and Sarah looked satisfied, even pleased. The girls on either side of Phoebe had long appeared bored. William offered Reverend Farrell a polite if inscrutable nod, and Charles seemed almost too silent. As the pastor and his family rose to their feet, he held out his hand to each.

"My children and I thank you kindly for the excellent tea and stimulating conversation. I am eager to know each of you better and my door is always open. Girls, will you please show Phoebe where she can collect her brother?

Charles tossed her a brief wink. "I'll do that."

As he walked her toward the barn, he stopped at the gate, however, he held it shut. "I owe you a great debt, Miss Phoebe."

"I only mentioned what I saw."

"Whoever spotted us—or one of us—must have done so from a distance. When Bentley posed your question to them, they could not swear which of us it was. Bentley had no choice but to let me go."

Phoebe dropped her eyes. While she did not wish to suspect him, she could not help noticing he omitted a claim to innocence. Besides, he was standing so close she was able to detect all the minute variations of hue in his curling sideburns. He did not bother to hide his scrutiny of her. He had examined each of her features, and his gaze now rested on her lips.

"I was accurate, nothing more, nothing..." Catching herself in a half-truth, she trailed off and surveyed the barn looming just beyond his dark hair. She had *not* told them everything, even though why she so keenly wished to conceal Birdie's presence was a question she did not care to ask herself.

"Go on. You were saying..."

"My father will be wondering what is taking me so long. Can I find the lambing pen within the barn?"

"Yes, you cannot miss it." He unlatched the gate, yet though he held it open, he moved insufficiently to let her pass. "They used to burn women who had fairy rings."

"I'm sorry?" Phoebe glanced into laughing eyes.

"The circles ringing your irises. They are distinct and much darker in color than the mossy green toward the center. People used to think they marked a woman as a *witch*."

He pronounced the last with such relish, Phoebe took a step backward. "I assure you, I am nothing of the sort."

"No, you are more in the mold of Colonel Nelson's sweet little granddaughter."

What he was about, she could not decide, nor if he intended to compliment or insult. "Thank you, Mr. Simmons. I like Emily very much."

His lips lost their curve as he allowed her to squeeze past, but as she reached the barn's half-door, he called out. "Did you happen to see anyone else, Miss Phoebe, while you were...bathing?"

Ignoring the question, she ducked into the barn only to be knocked aside by Augie and Jeremiah.

"Charles, that's him!" Jeremiah pointed to a head bobbing through an early sprouting field. "He swiped something from Bessie's stall."

As the thief's cap disappeared beyond the crest of a small rise, Charles clambered over the far fence and sped after him.

"Who is he?" asked Phoebe as she ran with the boys. Climbing onto the lower rails, all three gained a clearer view of his progress.

"What is going on?" shouted Pastor Farrell. He, Mahala Simmons, and her other four children poured into the paddock.

67

"Momma, it was the man Charles and William chased off last week."

"We were watching him!" cried Augie. "He was digging in the hay."

Mahala began wringing her hands. "Land sakes, why didn't you tell someone, son?"

"He'd have seen us. We were hiding in the loft."

"Did you see what he stole?" asked the reverend.

Both boys bobbed their heads, Jeremiah so eagerly his whole body shook. "A box."

"And you recognized him, Jeremiah?"

"Yep. Pa met him out here when Ma was gone to prayer meeting."

The boy's mother nudged his shoulder. "Well, tell us his name."

"Don't know it." Jeremiah shrugged. "I was watching from the window when I was sick with the chickenpox."

Everyone turned as Charles pounded back into the paddock. "I…" He leaned atop the fence, his chest heaving in and out. "I couldn't catch him, but he was one of the men Hugh and I found hanging around Kiker's distillery. Reverend, do you have time to go fetch that lawman? I'm saddling the horse to follow his tracks."

"I will surely try. William, I take it you will stay home with your mother and sisters in case he returns? Mahala, may Jeremiah come with us? We've been here less than a week, and I have yet to venture beyond the post office. Afterward, if it's alright with you, I thought he might enjoy spending the afternoon with Augie."

Both boys lit up, though Augie cast an apologetic glimpse at his sister. They would need to postpone exploring the attic.

"Of course. Now mind the Pastor, and be sure to let him know beforehand he is coming up to a turn. He won't know our local landmarks yet. The girls and I will give Phoebe a ride home."

Reverend Farrell glanced at his daughter to make certain she liked the idea, but although he could tell something had not pleased her, she nodded. "Thank you, Mahala. I don't know how long I'll be. I'll either see you at the parsonage or when I bring Jeremiah home.

"Excellent. I dare say the girls and I will enjoy a drive."

Chapter 10

THE WIDOW SIMMONS drove her buggy up the church's lane and pulled it to a halt in front of the parsonage. Allowing her eyes a moment to roam the stone exterior and surrounding trees, she exhaled deeply. "Those walls hold dear memories for me."

"Memories of what, Ma?" Megan Simmons and her little sister, Sarah, spoke nearly in unison.

"Nothing really, I suppose. Just many happy hours in that room, up there by the chimney, with one of the former pastor's daughters. I think I spent more of my youth in this house than in my own parents' home, Father being...sick...so often."

Phoebe dimpled. "It's my room. You are welcome to come in and see if it has changed."

"I would like it very much if you are sure."

Virginia almost knocked Sarah over scrambling down from the buggy. "Me too! I feel like we've been locked in jail for the past week."

"It's great to see something besides our parlor walls," agreed Megan, patiently waiting her turn to climb out.

Phoebe mentally searched her pantry. "Would you like some tea or lemonade? I'm afraid I haven't fixed supper yet."

"Of *course* you haven't, deary," answered Mrs. Simmons. "You've been thoroughly occupied this morning with your kind visit and all this hoopla over our thief. Funny, but he seemed familiar to me." She paused, digging through her memory, and then brightened. "Foster— the parsonage caretaker—and yet..."

"Somebody call me?" Foster, as seemed his habit, popped up, this time from the kitchen herb garden. "Hello, Mrs. Simmons." He doffed his hat. "How're ya gettin' along?"

"We are managing, thank you. I was just telling Miss Farrell a man we saw at our farm reminded me of you."

69

"Been here all mornin'."

"I saw he wasn't you, still something about him…"

"Got heaps o' cousins, but you best be stayin' away from most o' them, you bein' a widder an' all. Some o' them'll cheat ya blind."

"I appreciate the warning and will relay it to Charles and William. Phoebe, some lemonade will be fine. First, though, I'd enjoy seeing the parsonage. The last pastor's wife did not take to people calling unannounced."

"Stop clinging." Virginia made a face at Sarah. "You'll wrinkle my gown. We called on her once, just after they moved in. She pretended she was not home. She had laundry hanging on the line—plain as day—and we could see the church's wagon pulled just behind the house."

Sarah frowned. "When was that?"

"Ages ago, while Mother was still carrying Jeremiah. You were still toddling about—clinging to her skirt instead of mine."

"That was the only time we called," added Megan. "She was nice enough during Sunday service, but," she leaned toward Phoebe, "we know where we ought not to intrude."

"Now, Meg, some women are just less suited than others to be pastor's wives, and anyway, we don't want to give Phoebe the wrong impression. All three of you were young, and childhood memories are notoriously faulty."

"I was at least eleven," protested Virginia, "and Megan was close to nine."

"And why would Phoebe care?" asked Sarah. "She never met them."

"First of all, Virginia, I'd rather you not contradict me. Second, Sarah, you don't know if Miss Farrell knows them or not, and third, my concern is for *us* not *them*. We don't want to give the impression we are a family of gossips."

"Yes, Mother."

"If you will just follow me, Mrs. Simmons, I will take all of you anywhere in the parsonage you wish to go."

Stepping inside, Mahala looked around, a wistful smile softening her face. "How delightful. It hasn't changed at all. The walls were not this blueish green—they were a sort of mauve if I recall—but the banister and paneling appear just as they did. Grieving Edward

70

prevented us from helping clean and arrange everything for your family or we would already have seen it. I helped pick out this carpet before the last pastor came. It's held up well."

Phoebe tried to think of what her mother would reply. "We are grateful to have it, Mrs. Simmons. I like the way it picks up the color of the walls, and I'm doubly glad it quietens Augie's leaps from the steps."

"Boys find any way of filling the most mundane doings with fun."

"I'm glad to hear it." Phoebe's crinkled brow wrestled with her smile. "I was afraid he's been growing incurably wild. He does things that would have never entered my mind."

"If you are like my girls, you are more interested in reading about adventures than manufacturing them."

Virginia and Megan looked as if they might dispute the description, though Phoebe could easily believe it of Sarah based on her responses to Papa.

"If you will follow me, I'll take you to my room, unless you would like to see something else first."

"Just your room, if you are certain you don't mind."

"Not at all." Climbing the stairs, she pushed her door open, relieved she had made her bed before breakfast; however, when she turned, she saw clear disappointment register on Mrs. Simmons' face.

"Don't take my frown as censure, dear. I was just surprised not to find my old friend's canopy bed. It was lovely, and so were the hours we spent lying on it talking over our hopes and dreams. Undoubtedly, you thought it too old fashioned."

"Not at all. The furniture had been arranged as it is when we arrived. I may have seen the bed you recall—or part of it—in the attic. I didn't notice the canopy. It may be stored elsewhere. Would you like us to go and see?"

Mrs. Simmons' face lit up, making her answer obvious. Lighting the candlestick in her dresser, Phoebe lead her and her three daughters into the hall and up the narrow staircase.

Mahala cocked her head. "How odd. This room seems smaller than I remember and so dark. The dormer used to let in a glorious amount of light."

Phoebe thought of telling her they had always been merely decorative, but she decided to keep silent. Though Mrs. Simmons must be even older than Mama, she did not wish to imply her memory was declining.

"It *has* been a very long time, three decades, and as I told the girls, childhood perceptions and recollections are often faulty. Perhaps…Oh, there it is, only what happened to…" She wended through some other items to examine the bed more closely. "Oh. I see now why they allotted it to storage. Look. This post has been split so badly it would not support the top."

Phoebe weaved past a crib and an overstuffed chair that would have made a wonderful place to escape with a book had the attic been well-lit. "What a shame." She felt the splintered post, sliding her fingers along the break more than half-way down to the headboard. "My current bed is more than serviceable, but this must have been quite lovely."

"Perhaps it can be repaired."

Tilting her head, Phoebe examined it further, though she knew her father's scant salary would not afford such costly workmanship. Why congregations thought men who loved Jesus could live on less than others was beyond her ability to comprehend.

"Oh, here they are!" Mrs. Simmons ran her fingertips over the headboard's backside in a slow, gentle caress.

When the girls crowded closer, angling to discover what she deemed so special, they found two sets of intertwined hearts carved where no one would be likely to discover them. One contained an RL and AV, the other an MV and AK.

An idea seemed to occur simultaneously to all three Simmons sisters. "Those are your initials, Ma."

"But Pa's were ES."

"Then who is AK?"

"Wait—the AV could be for Uncle Adam."

Mrs. Simmons smiled. "Indeed they are. My friend Rose adored my brother."

"Uncle Adam didn't care for her?"

"Things do not always turn out as you hope they will. Well, children, we have taken up far too much of Miss Farrell's time."

"But what about our lemonade?"

Mrs. Simmons scooted away and hurried to the slender steps. "I'm sure Phoebe can treat us to some another day."

"I'd be delighted—anytime you can return."

Like a line of ducklings, the girls followed their mother down to the first floor, though while Megan was crossing the lower landing, she looked back at Phoebe apologetically. "We'll come as soon as Ma lets us. She says it's not yet proper to be out and about."

"Alright, or maybe…" As Phoebe was about to suggest she visit them, the rattling of a wagon drew everyone's attention to the foyer window. They could just make out her father's salt and pepper hair bobbling above the rhododendrons as they opened the door and spotted Avery Spry riding a few paces behind.

Once the slave catcher dismounted, he drew his felt hat from his head and nodded. "Mahala. Girls. Have you seen Charles?"

"Not since he rode off after the thief, *Mr.* Spry."

Mrs. Simmons seemed piqued. Whether because of the man's familiarity or her haste to be away, Phoebe could not tell. Augie and Jeremiah had already leaped from the church wagon and were running down to the river to catch frogs.

"Mr. Spry," called Reverend Farrell. "I'll go down with you to talk to the boys as soon as I help Mrs. Simmons and her daughters into their buggy." Ensuring each of them was safely seated, he lingered while the widow gathered up the reigns. "We stopped by your farm before coming here. Charles had not yet returned. William stayed to wait for him."

"If anyone can track that man, my Charles can."

"Still, you seem troubled. Are you worried?"

"I am perfectly fine. Our visit stirred ancient memories, that's all."

"It's only been a week since Edward's funeral. If your grieving is like I've witnessed in many other widows, it will come in waves and be triggered unexpectedly: a place, a story, even a smell."

"Thank you, Pastor. I will bear that in mind."

"We'll bring Jeremiah home before supper."

"Very good." Clicking her tongue at the horses, Mrs. Simmons nodded to Phoebe before jostling the reins.

Once she had guided the buggy down to the lane, the reverend headed around the side of the house. "Did you find the boys, Mr. Spry?"

"Over here. Can either o' yuh tell me what the man looked like? How tall? What color o' hair?"

73

"Brown," Jeremiah answered. "But Augie saw his eyes better than I did."

"Nuh-uh. His head was down all the time."

"Any impression? Dark? Light?"

"Sort of in between, like Phoebe's or Jeremiah's, or a greenish-blue."

"Well, which?"

"I'm not sure. He only glanced our way once, when my elbow hit the latch and it fell loose. Even then, he never really looked up."

"What about his weight and height?"

Jeremiah squinted hard, trying to bring his recollections into sharper focus. "About like Pastor Farrell, not tall, not short, and sort of thin but not too thin."

"Nuh-uh."

Reverend Farrell frowned. "Augie, do you think you could find a politer way of offering your observations?"

"Yes, sir. Sorry, Jeremiah. I thought he was a bit shorter than Papa and thinner, more like Foster. In fact, he almost could have been Foster."

"What way?"

"Kind of boney-looking though also strong. He lifted that box like it was full of feathers."

"Old? Young?"

Jeremiah scrunched up his face. "Hard to say. His skin was pretty wrinkled, but his hair wasn't as gray as my Pa's."

Mr. Spry glimpsed up at the reverend over his shoulder before turning to the boys again. "So maybe between forty and sixty?"

Both nodded their heads.

"How 'bout 'is clothes? Workin' man's or a gent's?"

"Dirty looking and all wrinkled," answered Augie. "Sort of like yours."

Shifting uncomfortably, Mr. Spry cleared his throat. "He may have been working sun up to sunset and sleeping where he can. Now, take a minute, boys, and think hard. Was there *anything, anything at all,* unusual about him—what he wore, the way he combed his hair, a scar or mark on his face, anything?"

"He wore a brown cap. Not like the one Mr. Kiker wears. It was sort of flat or smashed down."

Jeremiah's head popped up. "And no brim. His hair was pulled back, sort of old-fashioned like..."

"Like President Washington."

"Long like an injun's?"

Jeremiah crinkled his brow. "About the length of my pointing finger."

"Anything else?"

The boys looked at each other, back at Mr. Spry, and shook their heads.

"Where'd you see 'im, an' what was he doin'?"

"Digging in our cow Bessie's stall."

"We heard the clank when his spade hit the box. That's when we looked down from the hayloft."

"What sort o' box?"

"Metal, I guess—about this big." Jeremiah used his outstretched hands to measure one foot by one foot of air.

"Why do you s'pose your pa buried it there?"

Jeremiah winced. "My pa?"

"Had to be. Who else?"

"Well, now, hold on Mr. Spry." Reverend Farrell put up his hand. "The man may have buried it without Mr. Simmons knowing."

The slave catcher's glimpse announced what he thought of the suggestion. "Plenty 'o places to bury sumthin.' Why pick another man's barn, 'specially knowin' he'd be in it several times a day?"

"I see your point, though shouldn't we try to separate facts from conjecture?"

"Just let us as has the experience do our jobs." Spry spotted Phoebe walking toward them and rubbed the stubble on his chin. "If you don't think it was yer pa, what about one o' yer brothers? I ain't accusin' no one, but Charles or William could've hidden it just as easy."

Tears sprang into Jeremiah's eyes.

"Now don't yuh go to frettin' none, son. We're just lookin' at the...the buried treasure...from every angle."

Augie's head flew up. "Treasure?"

Phoebe nudged her brother's shoulder, however, one glance showed his friend had recovered.

"Really? If we find it, can we keep it?"

"All depends on its owner, young fella." Spry ruffled Jeremiah's hair. "Might o' belonged to your pa or might belong to someone else."

"Someone else?" asked Phoebe. "Who?"

"Any number o' folks, Miss Farrell, but maybe now's not the best time to speculate." He tossed a telling look at Jeremiah. "We'll find 'im in good time."

Chapter 11

ONCE PHOEBE COMPLETED her chores, she hoped to spend the afternoon with Birdie. The female portion of the Simmons family had absorbed yesterday's free time, and even after Avery Spry had ridden away, she had still needed to consider Augie and Jeremiah. They might be lurking anywhere, and she had not been willing to take the risk.

Gathering leftovers for a more-than-ample lunch, she spied Mrs. Wilson's book beneath her Bible and grabbed them both.

"Lord," she prayed as she trotted down the long hill. "Birdie appears hungry and her garments are threadbare. She worries me. Please show me how to meet her needs, even spiritual needs only you know about. I want to reflect Your heart toward her."

Reaching the river's edge, she looked up and down the bank. "Birdie? Are you here?" Her heart sank as she glanced behind the clumps of grasses and up the tree. The girl was nowhere in sight. Putting aside her lunch for later, she lay back on the grass beneath the tree, drew out her Bible, and began reading John's gospel.

When she was little, she used to love to listen to the Bible's stories. Of late, she took joy in the unity of the parts in between. They were like an intricate pattern embroidered on a quilt, unfolding a whole and coherent picture through every tiny stitch. The part[iv] she was now reading was a prime example, reaching back to the creation[v] and forward to the wonder of Philippians.[vi] *Who but God could imagine such a thing, holding in mind the end from the beginning?*

"Boo!"

Phoebe sprang upright, a smile spreading wide between her dimples. "Where did you come from? I couldn't find you."

"I heard you callin.' What you got, another one of them storybooks?"

"In a way, however, I know this one is true."

"What's it about?"

"God, and how He left His home to come to rescue us."

"Don't I wish? I needs rescuing."

"What's wrong?"

"Nothin'." As Birdie seemed to curl up deep inside herself, Phoebe wished she had not asked. "I's just tired of waitin' for my man to come an' claim me. Startin' to wonder if he's comin' at all."

"Oh, Birdie, I'm sorry. Maybe something has held him up."

"Somethin' or somebody. I's scared he's hurt…or…or he decided I ain't worth the trouble."

"Of course you are. God made you to reflect how wonderful He is, to show what He is like."

Birdie pulled back, peering at Phoebe like she had lost her mind. "You been drinkin'? Ain't no way I look like God."

Phoebe chuckled. "I honestly don't know what God looks like, though by creating people in His image, He made it easier for us to understand what He is like."

"I gotta think on that one."

"Here. Let me read you this." Phoebe flipped to one of her mother's favorites. "'Can a woman forget her sucking child? They may forget, yet I will not forget thee.'[vii] Mama's always fussing over my baby sister, helping me picture how God feels about me."

"Don't know, Phoebe. I know'd me an awful bad man. If God's like that, I ain't wantin' no part of Him."

Phoebe dropped her eyes, unable to decide if she should probe further. Birdie might draw deeper inside herself. "Some people corrupt His image so badly you can't see Him at all."

"What's that mean—corrupt?"

"Um…like tarnish. You know, the stuff that turns silver dull."

"Why folks go and do that—make themselves…what's that word?"

"Corrupt." Phoebe shrugged. "I guess we think God's trying to keep us from something good—as Eve did in The Garden. See this?" She held up the fingertips of her right hand for Birdie to see. "Ugly, aren't they. Mama told me not to touch an iron she had set on the fire. I didn't listen."

"Ooo, you is lucky they's not worse."

"She was quick to snatch me away."

78

"I ain't got no Mama. She died when she was birthin' me."

"Oh, Birdie. I'm so sorry."

"I never know'd her, so I guess I don't miss her none, and I got my two aunts—Mitilde and Ruby. The ones I told you 'bout. They's been like mothers to me."

"So they've given you a taste of God's love. Speaking of tasting, are you hungry? I brought plenty for us both."

After finishing off a couple of sandwiches, Birdie peered at Phoebe over a slice of last night's cake. "If God loves me like my aunts do, how come He made my skin so black?"

Phoebe shook her head. "I'm not sure, but I think it's appealing. When I first saw Lucy, all I could think of was a naked field mouse."

Birdie laughed as Phoebe crinkled her nose.

"Papa once told me skin is darker the closer a person lives to the sun and lighter if they live farther away. Maybe your darker tone is a gift."

"A gift?" Birdie tucked in her chin and looked askance as if she thought Phoebe was fibbing.

"You ought to have seen Augie when he stayed outside too long last summer. His skin turned so red and hot, he'd wail if anyone touched it. Until the burnt parts peeled away, he was miserable. You don't like the color?"

"I don't like the way folks treat me."

"Oh. I wouldn't either. Do you mean the man you were talking about?"

Birdie nodded.

"Papa says, 'Changed hearts change habits.' That's why he agreed to come here. He's praying God will change the people in his congregation on the inside so they will reflect God better on the outside."

"How that happen?"

"Through God's Word. He uses it to make us clean."

Birdie grinned. "Aunt Mitilde polishes Ms. Kiker's tea service until it shines, though sometimes she frowns at her reflection. Says she spots a fresh wrinkle every time."

Phoebe lay back on the grass. "I feel the same way."

"You ain't gotta wrinkle on you."

"Oh." Phoebe's cheeks twitched. "I meant in my heart."

"You got a good heart, Miss Phoebe. I knows it. I feels it."

"Then God's answering my prayers. I've been asking Him to polish off all my tarnish so I can reflect Him clearly."

"You..." Birdie sat up. She had heard a man calling. "I gots to go." She jumped up so quickly she upset her cup of water.

"Wait. It's my father. I want to introduce you."

"Sorry, Miss Phoebe. I'm sure he's nice 'n' all, but I stayed longer than I shoulda."

By the time Pastor Farrell crested the hilltop, Birdie was already running along the river, and when he ambled down the hill to speak with his daughter, the other girl was nowhere in sight. "There you are. For the life of me, I cannot remember if the Kiker's party is this evening or tomorrow."

"Tomorrow."

"Where did Augie go?"

"Augie? I thought the two of you went to town."

"We arrived home a bit ago. Isn't that his cup?"

"Uh...he might be searching for leaves. He said he wanted to find new ones for his collection. Do you want me to look for him?"

"No. I'm sure he's around somewhere. I was sure I saw him scampering into the tree-line and wondered what he was up to."

Phoebe hid her face inside her novel.

"Do you mind if I join you? This is a lovely place. I can understand why you chose it for reading. After our first week here, have you formed any opinions?"

"I still miss my old friends, though I'm making some new ones." She looked in the direction Birdie had just run. "Papa, if someone you are getting to know behaves in unexpected ways—ways, for example, which might raise concerns—what do you do?"

Reverend Farrell stroked his short, well-trimmed beard. He was fairly certain he knew who she was thinking about. He had noticed the glances Emily had cast her during Tuesday evening's dinner. "It depends. Have they hurt you?"

"Not a bit."

"Give them time. Better yet, if the two of you are friendly enough to be frank, ask what's wrong."

"I have, or I've tried to, but she clams up."

80

"Well, maybe she doesn't yet realize what a wonderful friend you can be. Just give her time. Any other thoughts?"

Phoebe creased her forehead, peering around as if she were afraid of being overheard. "Mr. Simmons' murder has put such a pall over everything. It's hard for me to say what I feel, and many conversations I've been part of are nearly indecipherable. They talk about things I'm not sure I understand, and some matters they discuss are too delicate for me to feel comfortable probing."

"Like what?"

"Miss Kiker's cryptic comments about Charles Simmons and her brother. Lisa was saying they are very close. Miss Kiker portrayed them as jealous rivals."

"Clara may simply have voiced her own opinion or, if what she said is accurate, it's not too hard to understand. Since you are female and Augie male, you do not compete for the same prizes. Augie doesn't care, for example, how he appears or how well he can cross-stitch, and you care nothing for tadpoles. A younger sister might compete to be a better cook or excel in an area you do not, and since people would inevitably compare you, one of you might be hurt. Of course, it is the same with brothers."

"But they aren't brothers—or at least, they are not acknowledged as such."

"So you, too, have heard the gossip. I wouldn't put any faith in it. Since Charles' father worked so closely with Hugh's, I suspect they grew up in and out of each other's pockets. What do you think about our new home?" He glanced up the hill at the parsonage's chimneys.

"Other than the odd noises, it's quite comfortable. I love the rolling hills and living so close to the river."

"I guess a house is like a pastor." He chuckled. "As it ages, it's beset by its own peculiar groans and creaks. You don't miss Princeton...your old friends...all the debates you used to enjoy with my theology students—one in particular?" As he slid her a sidelong look, color flared up her neck.

She looked away, though she had not missed his teasing twinkle. "I miss all of them."

"You really held your own. I was proud of you. And Princeton itself?"

"Not as much as I feared, though I do miss everything's close proximity. To see anyone here requires a ride."

"I guess Augie and you are far enough apart in age and interests, you don't afford each other much company. Would you like to learn to drive the church's wagon?"

"Could I?"

"I don't see why not. Then you could go visit Emily at will or even Lisa."

"Thank you, Papa." She leaned her head against his arm. "You're the best."

"Oh, I could say the same of you. Not my little girl anymore. Quite the efficient young woman and household manager. Your mother will be pleased."

"Thank you, Papa. I could never hope for a better father."

.

Chapter 12

PHOEBE HAD BEEN wishing for her mother ever since she set foot in the parsonage. As she appraised her reflection, she felt the need for her desperately. She had been to soirees before, even attended one ball, however, Mama had been present to guide her in both manners and attire. When her brother came up to see if she was ready, she dropped her eyes to his feet.

"Augie, put on your better shoes."

"Why? I'm not dancing. Soon as Jeremiah arrives, we'll head outside."

"He won't be there, remember? His family is still in mourning."

"Aw, you're right. I forgot." While Phoebe descended the stairs, he dashed off to change out of his well-worn boots, but when he returned, he clomped slowly down all twelve steps.

"Son, are your shoes pinching? I thought your mother just bought you them."

Augie thrust his hands into his pockets and plopped heavily onto the entryway bench. "Papa, do I have to go?"

"Yes, I'm afraid you do."

"But the Kikers don't have any boys my age."

"Some of their friends may." Turning to Phoebe, he held her at arms' length, affection and admiration so softening his face, he looked just a boy himself. "Blue becomes you, Kitten. You remind me of my sister, Jane. She often wore gowns of just that shade."

Closing the gap between them, Phoebe leaned up to kiss his cheek. "Thank you, Papa. So, I look alright?"

"Never prettier. I don't know what to expect from this shindig, but the young men are sure to form a line." As she tucked her chin in shyly, he became as tongue-tied as she seemed. "Well...I've brought the wagon up, so we'd best be on our way."

THE FARRELLS TRAVELLED north, passing the Simmons' farm along a seemingly interminable split-rail fence. By the time they reached the gate, Phoebe's ribcage felt as jarred as her confidence. The Pike's plentiful ruts attested to its continuous use, and holes the size of pots reminded passengers of the recent ups and downs in the weather.

As far as the eye could see, rolling hills and pastures stretched toward the Alleghenies; though where the plantation's western border lay, the Farrells could not guess. The lane curved around the stone walls of a modest outbuilding, so lowering their expectations, the first sight of The Lilacs took their breath away. It was as grand as one of Princeton's halls. They were all relieved to see John Wilson lifting his wife, Allison, from a carriage.

Once her father pulled around a huge bed of blossoming lilacs, Phoebe perused the highly formal façade. Wide white steps led to a porch raised so high off the ground, it towered above the sprawling lawn. As she followed its pillars upward, she was surprised they were both narrower and shorter than the Wilsons', however, the reason became evident. The Kikers' columns reached only one story; the Wilsons' supported a balcony and second-story roof. Indeed, these reminded her of sentries standing guard on a high castle wall scanning the drive for hostile invaders.

When the Whites pulled alongside the Wilsons, Phoebe nearly bounded off her wooden seat. Both Lisa and Allison were as lovely as she had previously found them, the daughter in golden cream and mother in rich currant; and their husbands rivaled Phoebe's father for looking distinguished in their finery.

"We're so glad you could make it, Phoebe," crooned Allison, though when they turned to include Lisa, they found her occupied. Jordan was sneaking a sweet, brief kiss. As he placed Lisa's hand in the crook of his elbow and queued up in front of the expansive stairs, Lisa tossed a quick smile over her shoulder.

The reverend followed Jordan's example, offering his arm to his daughter, and Augie embarrassed them both by racing past the other guests and into The Lilacs' foyer. While the butler greeted her father, Phoebe breathed a sigh of relief. At least her brother had not knocked the old gentleman over.

Surveying the large parlor, Phoebe admired the well-crafted woodwork. The paint was slightly bluer in color than the parsonage's parlor, but the detail was astounding. Turning her attention to the guests, she found most were strangers, though several appeared attached in one way or another to persons she had previously met. Chief among them was Tandy Bentley, who looked up at her husband, Matthew, with all the adoration of a recent bride.

When the crowd swept them toward the receiving line, Phoebe keenly felt the difference in station between her family and the Kikers. Lavinia had woven a spray of ivory lilacs into her hair, matching the ribbons to the sapphire silk of her gown. It shimmered in the hanging lamps, picking up the deep blue of both her eyes and her husband's. After welcoming Phoebe, she introduced her to Asa who then guided her toward their son, Hugh.

She had thought him handsome when they met at the river; dressed in a silken waistcoat and tails, he was positively dashing. While he held her hand in his, her cheeks threatened to turn the color of Mrs. Wilson's gown. So fixed was his attention, he made her feel she was the most entrancing woman in the room. Shrugging off the notion—she was certain he focused on every young woman with equal intensity—she gently tugged away her hand and stepped toward his sister, Clara.

"Your gown is exquisite, Miss Kiker. I've always loved indigo. You and your parents have the deepest blue eyes I have ever seen."

"It's kind of you to say so, Phoebe. I've always thought it a shame Hugh didn't inherit them as well, though I suspect you find his brown eyes pleasing. The color of your throat matches the sweet roses pinned to your gown."

Phoebe had no idea what to reply. Grateful her father absorbed Hugh's attention, she smiled politely and hurried to the safety of Samuel's relatives-in-law. They were listening to a Haydn quartet when Allison Wilson, taking her by the arm, pulled her into a quiet alcove.

"We received a letter from Samuel today asking if he might come for a visit."

"Samuel, coming here?"

"Yes, and we can all guess why he is so suddenly eager to see us." Her eyes sparkled as she waited for Phoebe to catch her hint.

"He seemed genuinely attached to your whole family, even apart from his sister's connection."

"As we are of him, though I suspect he has another reason—but here come the Nelsons."

As the colonel shook hands with her husband, Allison and Phoebe greeted his wife and granddaughter.

"Oh, Allison, aren't all the peonies just beautiful?" Mary Nelson leaned over to inhale the fragrance. "Gary and I are not having much luck with ours. Perhaps the tree cover where we planted them is too thick."

While they encompassed Lisa in their discussion, Emily smiled shyly at Phoebe, but before they could begin a conversation, Hugh Kiker joined them.

"Miss Farrell. Emily. Are you enjoying the string quartet?"

"I am, indeed." Phoebe nodded. "I didn't think we'd find such accomplished musicians this side of the Blue Ridge."

"We aren't entirely in the backwoods. The nation's capital is within a few days' carriage ride. And you, Emily?"

"Very much so."

"And are you still enjoying that nice little trotter?"

"Oh, yes." She made an effort to meet and hold his gaze. "I exercise her each morning, and she has a nice, even gait."

"An excellent piece of horse-flesh. I was happy to secure her for you."

As they talked longer on the subject, Phoebe observed them uninterrupted and felt quite certain of her earlier conclusion. Emily was obviously delighted with his attention, albeit greatly discomfited. Hugh's feelings were harder to discern. He certainly exhibited more ease with Emily than he did with her, though this was only natural. The two families were of long-standing acquaintance.

"Would you honor me with this dance?" The quartet had begun playing a piece by the elder Strauss. "Miss Farrell?"

"Oh. I'm sorry, Mr. Kiker. My mind was elsewhere."

Leaning toward Emily, he whispered. "Apparently, Miss Farrell finds us impressively boring. We haven't been speaking five minutes and already she seeks entertainment within. Or do you think she fears, as a backwoodsman, I may step on her toes?"

Phoebe's cheeks turned crimson. "I think nothing of the sort."

"Then will you allow me to vindicate our valley's claim to culture?"

Emily's expression showed her clear disappointment, however, Phoebe saw no alternative but to accept. Once he had conducted her into the line of dancers and joined in the steps, she realized how ridiculous her surprise over the quartet must have appeared. By comparison, even Samuel, for all his Boston upbringing, seemed inept. What Hugh thought of her execution of the steps she was afraid to imagine.

"Are you enjoying your new home?"

"It is lovely, though I fear we have a large opossum or some such living under the eaves of our roof."

"What makes you suspect that?"

"Noises heard at odd times."

"Of what kind?"

"Augie is half-convinced we have ghosts."

Hugh's eyes lit with humor. "Miss Farrell, your conversation while dancing is distinctly unconventional."

"Truly," Phoebe teased. "You *are* more cultured than I am."

"What? A pastor's daughter who grew up at an old and honored university?"

"Now you are making fun of me."

"Not at all. I find you refreshing."

"Surely, the other young women attending this party are just as backward in their ways as I am."

"Backwards? Is that another word for backwoods?"

"You will not let me live that down?"

"No." He slid her a teasing smile. "I intend to torture you with the memory of those words until my dying day."

"Are you expecting an early demise?"

His features filled with mock horror. "First she thinks me a bumpkin, and now she introduces my death!"

Phoebe could not help but laugh. It was very easy to see why Emily felt so smitten. "I would not, truly."

With the final meeting of hands, the dance was over and they parted ways; yet when a glance over her shoulder showed he was watching her retreat, she became so unnerved, she stumbled into Emily. "I'm sorry. I was not looking where I was going."

"No harm was done. There is a large bed of lilacs in the center of the lawn, some quite tall and old. Would your father mind if you came out with me to look at them more closely?"

"I don't see why he should; he is well-occupied, and I would relish the cooler air."

Sweeping through the front door and onto the high porch, they descended the steps to a large island of both bushes and trees. "I suppose these are the lilacs that lend the home its name."

Before Emily could answer, they turned to the patter of shoes on steps and saw Hugh carrying three cups of punch. Handing one to each of them, he leaned toward Emily.

"Miss Nelson, the ribbon you've woven into your hair is my favorite color."

Watching the exchange, Phoebe smiled. His interest in Emily showed clearly in his eyes, still, he made whomever he addressed feel like the only person in the room. How deep his feelings were, she simply lacked knowledge of him to say. Though she had not caught what her friend had replied, she saw he was listening attentively.

"What are the three of you doing, huddled out here?" Hugh's sister swished down the steps to loop her arm through Phoebe's.

"It has become intolerably warm inside," he replied. "By the way, while we were dancing, Phoebe informed me she's been hearing noises in the attic."

"You don't say?" Cocking her head, she considered Phoebe a moment before remembering her errand. "Hugh, before I forget, Mother asked if you would kindly engage one of our young guests in a reel."

"Gladly." Hugh bowed briefly and extended his hand to Emily, who startled before breaking into a smile. Within moments, Phoebe and his sister spotted them through a window performing the dance's vigorous steps.

Clara sighed. "It's horrid to have so few single men for partners. Charles can be glum and William has two left feet, but I cannot wait for them to get out of mourning."

"You may need to wait a good while. The loss of their father cannot be easy."

"Edward Simmons? Believe me, none of them are unduly grief-stricken. Their mother more likely feels relieved. He was a, hmm—what's a polite way of put...."

A crash from inside had them gathering their skirts, dashing up the stairs, and hurrying through the entry. A silver punch bowl was skittering across the wooden floor, its contents rapidly spreading toward the rich-hued Oriental rug.

The overturned table on which it had set lay next to Augie, a swath of red staining his dress-shirt. "I didn't mean to. The dog was thirsty, and when I was setting down some punch for him to drink, I backed into it."

As the boy knelt to blot it up with napkins, Papa looked every bit as mortified as Phoebe felt. "I am very sorry, Lavinia. If anything is damaged, please send me the bill of repair."

"It's just a spill. Mitilde will have it cleaned in no time."

Mitilde cast Augie a sharp glare as she dropped to her knees. "You go on now. You is ruining Missus Kiker's best table linens."

"I'm sorry, ma'am. I was trying to help."

"I knowed you was. Best get yourself out to the kitchen to clean your shirt or the stain'll set. Go on. Kitch'll help you."

"Yes, ma'am." Augie arose as inconspicuously as he could manage, avoiding the plentiful eyes watching his progress. In the kitchen, he found the tallest, blackest man he had ever seen. "Sir, are you Kitch?"

The man's brows darted up, though he smiled. "Yes, young sir, I is."

"Miss Mitilde told me to come in here so you could help me get the stain out of my shirt."

"Um-hm." He looked as if he thought Augie had meant to cause the damage. "You just take it off and climb onto that stool. I'll see to cleaning it up."

Once Augie pulled the long hem out of his best britches, he handed it over to Kitch, who left him sitting by the door. At first, every housemaid who entered stared at him as if he had green hair. As they passed him going in and out, in and out, he soon became just another part of the kitchen.

A younger girl pushed open the door for Mitilde. "You seen the mess that boy made?"

Mitilde jerked her head toward Augie to remind her he was present.

"He knows it." The girl scowled. "I better get these napkins a soakin'."

Watching Augie hang his head, Mitilde slid him a warm grin. "You wantin' sumpthin' to eat? You's all skin and bones. Got me a heap o' puddin' left over from last night."

"Yes, ma'am." Augie's eyes started to sparkle.

"Kitch'll be back with your shirt in no time." She handed him a large bowl of chocolate pudding.

"Thanks." As Augie scooped spoonful after spoonful into his mouth, he studied the people passing through the kitchen. Mitilde was clearly in charge. The younger woman seemed tentative and less friendly, as if having a stranger watching made her uncomfortable. When Kitch ducked under the doorframe, he seemed to fill every space. Not only was he tall and amply built, but he also had hands the size of Mitilde's head. Still, unlike Augie, he moved through even the tightest spaces without bumping into a single item.

"Here ya go, young massa. It's still a bit damp, but I took the iron to it."

"Thank you, sir." Augie slipped it on. "You got out every spot. Wait 'till I show Phoebe."

Kitch broke into a broad smile. "You got a name?"

"August, though everyone calls me Augie. Oh, and please thank Miss Mitilde for the pudding. It was much better than the fancy stuff we ate in the dining room."

As Kitch chuckled, Augie jumped off the stool and ran back through the doorway, nearly colliding into Asa Kiker.

"Slow down, young man." Mr. Kiker caught him by the shoulders. "You'll upset something else. Augie, isn't it?"

Augie looked up into Asa's startlingly blue eyes. They reminded him of the light shining through a small pitcher his grandmother kept on a shelf set in the window. "Yes, sir. I'm awfully sorry."

"I know you are. We could tell by the color of your ears."

Augie's ears reddened all over again.

"Would you like to see some puppies?"

"Could I?" Although the boy stood in place, his whole body seemed to ripple with excitement—until he spotted his father approaching.

"Ah, there you are August. I think we'd better head back home before you knock over the cake."

"Yes, Papa."

Asa watched the boy's face fall. "Ernest, do you think you could bring Augie by sometime this week? My favorite spaniel just had a litter. If it would be alright with you—and if you think your wife wouldn't mind—I'd like to offer him one of the pups no one has already spoken for."

"Could we, Papa, could we?" Augie looked like he might explode from happiness.

"Well, I think we'd better consult Phoebe. She's playing mother, Asa, while Amelia is away, and I don't want to add to her load."

"I'll take good care of it, Papa, I promise."

"Well don't convince me; convince Phoebe—but wait until we get into the wagon."

Asa's blue eyes twinkled. "Come on over on Tuesday, if it suits. The pups aren't ready to leave their mother yet, so if your daughter says no—and I wouldn't blame her, boys are apt to promise more in the way of chores than they deliver—we can keep the one he chooses until a more convenient time."

"A puppy?" Phoebe had just joined them. "Mr. Kiker is giving Augie a puppy?"

"Yes, Phoebe, a very kind offer, indeed. Thank you, Asa."

The boy grinned. "Maybe I should knock over more punch bowls. I got to meet Kitch, eat pudding, and now get a puppy."

Asa's smile widened. "Better not, son. I don't want your father to get mad at me—or my wife. Now you listen to your sister." He turned his startling eyes on Phoebe.

"We had a lovely time, Mr. Kiker. Thank you and Mrs. Kiker for including Augie and me in the invitation. I hope your silver bowl is not dented."

"It was our pleasure, Miss Farrell, and don't worry. Hugh was every bit as rambunctious when he was a boy. Have a safe trip home."

Chapter 13

"GOOD AFTERNOON, MR. KIKER." When Phoebe had answered the knock on the parsonage door, she had found her most frequent dance partner from the previous evening. "Father is still at the church, in his study."

"It's you I've come to see, Miss Farrell, and your brother. I thought, if he is willing to play chaperone, we might discover what is causing the noises in your attic. You don't seem like a girl who is given to flights of fancy, and I would like to ensure you are safe."

Phoebe's dimples deepened at the well-aimed compliment, and the playful glint in Hugh's dark eyes sparked a reaction she would not have expected. A bevy of butterflies seemed to take flight through her stomach.

"Forgive me if I am too bold," he continued when she did not immediately answer, "but your father strikes me as someone who resides mostly in his mind—not the sort to rummage around in attics."

"No apology necessary. Your assessments are accurate, and you are kind, however, I'm afraid it's not possible right now. Augie ran off on one of his adventures directly after our Sunday meal, and it's Foster's day off."

"That's too bad. I was hoping after our hunt to take Augie back home with me to choose a pup." He glanced over his shoulder toward the church, around at the maples flanking the house, and then craned his neck toward puffy white clouds floating in the brilliant blue sky. "If I remember correctly, a comfortable bench sits on the ridge crest, looking down the slope to the river. Do you have time to spare for a thirsty man who has ridden a good ways to see you, or must I go home disappointed? We will be in the open. Surely no one can fault us if they see we are simply sitting side by side."

Phoebe hoped Colonel Nelson would not happen by. She did not want to cause Emily pain. Still, Hugh had ridden all the way from The Lilacs, and she did not wish to appear rude. "Do you prefer sweet tea or lemonade?"

"Lemonade."

"I'll meet you there."

As Phoebe passed through the entryway, she paused at the mirror to check her reflection. It was passable. Cranking up a jug she had lowered to the cellar's cooler depths, she poured two glasses and exited through the kitchen to the bench. Hugh was already seated on one end atop an old cushion Augie had dragged down from the attic to soften the hard wood.

"The river is so peaceful, and from here, you can see anyone who travels up it. Since you have moved here from a more populous northern town, I imagine you find our way of life very slow."

"Again, I must disappoint you. Since my mother is not with us, I've spent most of my time cleaning, preparing meals, or unpacking and arranging our belongings."

Hugh searched her face. "Surely, you allow yourself some free time. I saw you myself floating in the river."

As Phoebe's face grew hot, she looked away. She was certain she was standing upright when they met. If he had spotted her from this ridge, she had no way of knowing how much he had seen. "I steal a moment here and there, though I spend most of them reading."

"Oh? And what have you been reading recently?"

"My Bible and a novel—or perhaps I should say journal—Mrs. Wilson loaned me."

"Quite a lonely pastime. Your father and brother are not around often—have you made some local acquaintance? I can think of several young ladies who appeared to enjoy your company as much as I did last evening."

"I have yet to invite anyone over. I will be freer when my mother returns."

"And there is no one else?"

Phoebe glanced down. She was unsure what he wanted and afraid he might have spotted her picnicking with Birdie. "Papa is always working, and Augie never sits still for anything but food."

Hugh chuckled. "He is a healthy young boy. Does he never tell you about his adventures?"

"On occasion. He brought home a couple of frogs, insisting I allow him to keep them in the house." The face she pulled announced her feelings. "Then there are his spy games."

Hugh sat up straighter.

"He's been reading about the spies Washington employed during The Revolution and likes to pretend he is one of them."

"On whom does he spy?"

"Just Foster. Who else could he? Papa forbade him to leave church property."

"What about your strange noises? Does Augie also hear them?"

As she imagined how absurd her fears must have sounded, she busied herself tracing the small flowers printed in the fabric of her smock. "Yes, and he promised to explore the attic with me, though he only offers far-fetched notions."

"Such as?"

"To ghosts, he has added murderers."

With twinkling eyes, he stood up and held out a hand; and when she offered him her own, he secured it in the crook of his arm. "Can you point out the section you were in when you heard them?" Leading her toward the house, he let her guide him to a northern window.

"There." Phoebe pointed. "That is my parent's room. I was in it when a large shadow passed by."

After studying the eaves, they strolled around the front, to the northern side, and half-way back to the front again. Hugh trailed his eyes up a vine creeping around a high and sizable maple limb when they heard a voice from above.

"Hi, Mr. Kiker!"

Phoebe's mouth fell open. "August Timothy Farrell, how did you get up on there? Come down this instant!"

"There's nothing to it." Grasping the dormer's overhang, he balanced on the sill, gripping a handful of leafy branches, and swung into the maple's thick canopy.

"Augie, I don't know what to do with you. If Papa had seen you on that roof, he'd..."

Before she could finish her scolding, he had dropped onto the soft grass by their feet. "Want to see the toad I caught?" Augie grabbed a makeshift cage he had set against the trunk and held it up for Hugh's examination.

"He's a beaut."

Augie grinned.

"Did you happen to peek into the dormer window?" Hugh directed his attention to the bubbled glass.

"No. Why?"

"Just curious to know what you might find."

"Don't waste yer time. Ain't nuthin' to see."

Turning, they saw Foster gaining on them from behind, carrying an armful of peonies.

"Miss Phoebe, I been pruning my garden this afternoon an' thought you might enjoy these more'n me."

"They're lovely—such a dark pink. I'll go put them in a vase. Would you like some lemonade?"

"Sure. An' Augie, I brought this for you." Foster pulled out a slim pouch holding a large number of sticks of similar length.

"Gee, thanks! What are they?"

"Jackstraws. Injuns use'em to train their young to grasp one item without unsettlin' the whole bunch."

Hugh thrust his hands in his pockets, watching the handyman dump the sticks onto the grass to show Augie how the game was played. Gazing at the window, he frowned, forcing up his lips only when Phoebe returned.

"Thank you, Miss Farrell. I enjoyed our afternoon, though we have gone from too few chaperones to too many. I doubt we can tear Augie away from the jackstraws to explore the attic."

Foster glanced up from his game. "Pardon me for interruptin', Mr. Hugh, but I wouldn't be goin' into the attic if I was you. It needs some new planks fer walkin.'"

"Miss Farrell was exploring it last week."

Foster darted an eye toward Phoebe. "She's a mite lighter 'an you, sir, and all the same, children, I'd rather you stay out 'o there."

Phoebe chafed at being called a child in front of Hugh, however, the retort on her lips died when she spotted Papa closing the church

95

door. Hugh followed her eyes as Reverend Farrell began his climb up to join them.

"Look Papa!" cried Augie. "Foster made a set of jackstraws."

"You are very kind to my children, Foster. Mr. Kiker, it is nice to see you on such a pleasant afternoon."

"I came to take Augie up to The Lilacs so he could choose the dog he prefers. It'll be about eleven more weeks until they can leave their mother, but Father wanted him to have his choice."

Augie sprang to his feet. "Can I?"

"May I, Augie."

"Sure, if it's all right with Mr. Kiker."

"No. I meant the question to ask is 'May I?' if you are seeking permission. You obviously *can*."

"Yippee!"

Phoebe wondered if *all* little brothers had putty for brains.

"I said you can, not you may. What about your game?"

"Foster, can we leave it for tomorrow? Mr. Kiker is giving me a puppy."

"That'd be fine," answered the caretaker, though Phoebe could not tell if his eyes were fixed on Augie or Papa. "I'll just put these back in the pouch."

"Thanks!" Augie smiled from ear to ear while Hugh glanced from Phoebe to their father.

"What about it, Pastor Farrell? Would you and Phoebe care to join Augie and me?"

"What about your mother? She may be tired from last evening's festivities. I would not wish her to suffer from another one of her headaches."

"I suspect she'd appreciate the company. She hasn't been herself lately."

Reverend Farrell looked at him quizzically.

"And you, Phoebe? Would you like to come?"

Phoebe dimpled, but before she could answer, her brother ran toward the house.

"I'm going to put my toad away."

"Not in the house, son." Reverend Farrell shook his head. "Your sister has enough to take care of between the two of us."

Hugh winked at Phoebe when Augie ran back to the bench and set the make-shift cage beneath it. "I'm ready!"

ONCE THEY ARRIVED at The Lilacs, Hugh dismounted, handed off the reigns to a coffee-skinned young man, and lifted Phoebe from the wagon. Augie had already jumped down and was scanning the far lawns for the place the puppies might be hiding.

"They're in there." Hugh indicated some outbuildings behind his home. "The calving barn—right next to the main one. I'll meet you in a minute. I want to let Father and Mother know we are here."

As the Farrells walked the short distance to the barns, they heard the door of the plantation house fling shut. Lavinia Kiker streamed down the steps, bunching up her skirt to keep it from dragging across the grass. Asa loped behind her, his hands thrust into his pockets. Hugh outstripped both, and Clara brought up the rear.

Seeing Miss Kiker's pinched expression, Phoebe wondered if they had interrupted a pastime she found more pleasing. Of all her new acquaintances, Clara presented the greatest challenge, extending herself in all ways polite and welcoming while somehow conveying the opposite.

Augie bounced up and down while Hugh unbolted the latch. "I can hear them. I hope my pup will like me."

Asa Kiker ruffled the boy's hair. "If you treat a creature well, he cannot help but take to you. These pups are smart ones, and yours will soon learn which way his bread is buttered."

"Is that what I should feed him—bread?"

Asa's eyes crinkled at the edges. "Just an expression, son. You've got the gist of it. A pup knows who feeds him and feels beholden. By mid-summer, they'll be ready to leave their momma. If you come over every chance you get, the two of you can become well-acquainted."

Smiling warmly, Lavinia took hold of Phoebe's hand. "Ernest, I'm so glad your family could come to see the spaniels, however, we'd appreciate it even more if you stayed for supper. Mitilde is preparing smoked goose breast, and we have plenty to spare."

"Thank you, Lavinia. We would be pleased, wouldn't we children?"

Phoebe smiled at Mrs. Kiker, though Augie was too busy with the puppies to pay the invitation any mind. Once he had plopped onto the straw, several warm furry bundles had begun scrambling over his legs and others were pouncing on his moving hands. A little one with brown curly hair and white markings pressed her paws against his chest and stretched up to lick his chin.

"Is this one spoken for, Mr. Kiker? I think he likes me."

Hugh softly chuckled as Augie leaned back on his elbows, and the little dog tried to nuzzle inside his shirt collar. "He's a she and the runt of the litter. Anyone claimed her yet, Father?"

"No, but it's clear she's made her choice. She's yours, Augie, if you want her."

"Really?" The boy was grinning from ear to ear while fending the pup off from licking his teeth.

"If you give her proper attention, she'll grow into a fine hunter."

Clara leaned over the stall to find Augie buried under squirming fluff. "What are you going to call her?"

"Sparkles."

She cast her father a disparaging glance.

"Let him call her whatever he wishes, Clara. As long as he trains her well, her name won't make a lick of difference. Augie, after supper we'll come back out, and Hugh and I can start. Best to begin young."

"Oh boy—thanks, Mr. Kiker!"

Clara sidled up to slip her fingers into Phoebe's free hand. "Did you discover what's making those noises? Hugh said he was going to help you explore."

Her brother turned his head. "Maybe tomorrow. I arrived when Miss Farrell was quite alone, and once her brother and father arrived, we decided to come here."

"Now, Hugh," said his mother, "and you too, Clara, I don't want you filling Phoebe's head with nonsense about a parsonage ghost."

"Ghost?" Phoebe flicked a glance from Lavinia to her son and daughter.

Clara explained. "The last pastor had a daughter also, closer in age to your brother. I sat with her on occasion when her parents were both answering parishioners' calls. She heard odd sounds at night, while everyone else was asleep—even an occasional moaning—as if the home were…"

Phoebe's eyes grew round as saucers. "Haunted?" She had discarded the idea as ridiculous. Hearing someone else's suspicions made the possibility seem real. "I…I do not believe in ghosts."

Lavinia waved a dismissive hand. "Do not give it another thought. She was a very imaginative child."

"She hasn't been the only one, Mother. I've been hearing of the parsonage's ghost most of my life. I was told one pastor's child or another kept a diary detailing the occurrences."

Sandwiched between them, Phoebe found her position nearly as uncomfortable as the topic. "I have heard footfalls and seen…shadows for which I haven't any logical explanation."

"Never you mind. Clara just loves to tease. The wind is rubbing that old maple against the roof, that's all."

When the back door opened, Mitilde stepped onto the porch. "Massa Kiker, Missus Kiker, supper is ready. You wants me to wait to put it on the table?"

"No, Mitilde. We'll be there in a minute. Is everybody hungry?"

"Starved!" Augie jumped up from the puppies and brushed the straw from his slacks.

"Well, dinner is served."

Chapter 14

AS LAVINIA SWISHED into the dining room, she pulled out the chair to the right of the table's head. "Phoebe, as your mother isn't here this evening, I'd like you to take the seat to Asa's right. Reverend, you will sit to mine, and your son can sit across from Clara, next to Hugh."

Augie tossed Hugh a series of looks from bashful to thrilled. Hugh kindly reciprocated each, though Clara wore a barely concealed pique. As Phoebe wondered why, a coffee-colored footman offered her an array of choices from his platter.

Reverend Farrell studied twin paintings on the wall opposite his seat. "Lavinia, these portraits of you and Asa are exceptional. The artist caught your essence so well, I almost feel they might take part in the conversation."

"They were among Polk's last portraits. Of course, I was much younger. He painted them when Asa and I were first married. Tell me, are you settling in well?"

"As well as can be expected. Phoebe has been wonderful, running the parsonage as if she'd been at it for years, but I naturally miss Amelia."

"When will she join you?"

"I wish I could say. We've received only a brief telegram appraising us of her mother's condition. The mail naturally takes longer."

"As soon as she arrives, I trust you will bring her by." Lavinia offered him her most gracious smile. "We will not be holding any dances until harvest time. However, I would enjoy giving a tea in her honor, similar to the one the Wilsons hosted for Phoebe."

"Amelia would enjoy that. You are commendably welcoming."

Asa reached for a decanter and a couple of tulip-shaped glasses. "Whiskey, Ernest? We make it from our rye in the plantation distillery."

"No, thank you."

"Don't drink?"

"No, I've never acquired the habit."

"Probably best." Asa stared at the amber liquid as he swirled it around his glass. "Mahala Simmons tells me the subject of slavery has already come between the two of you."

"Well, yes, since one of her sons asked about it. However, when the board invited me to become your pastor, they told me quite clearly I was not to make abolition the topic of my tenure."

"And you agreed?"

"I'd much prefer the gospel be front and center."

During the exchange, Phoebe noticed Mrs. Kiker had begun squirming in her seat. The footman, who was serving his mistress the next course, perked up. Clara appeared indifferent, and the two Mr. Kikers exchanged relieved glances.

"I'm glad to hear it. Hugh and I were just discussing the gamble we took by inviting a pastor from the north to take the church. A few of our local slave owners were decidedly against you."

"I expected as much. Even when topics are not so volatile, I would imagine few preachers receive a unanimous vote."

Hugh cleared his throat. "What irks the slave states most is the tendency of the abolitionists to impose their sensibilities on us. Our government, as I understand from The Academy, is supposed to be a confederation of states, not a central government imposing its will. Wasn't the War for Independence primarily fought to ensure the right of self-determination?"

Asa nodded. "And to disavow taxation without true representation. As long as the free states do not muzzle the slave states' voices, the union should remain sound. I've heard similar concerns from men returning from out west. One area differs from another, just as individuals do, not to mention the influence of religion. It varies from person to person, depending on a man's motherland, and some decisions should be left up to an individual's conscience. Don't you agree, Reverend?"

"I do, so long as the subjects at hand have several viable alternatives in accord with the Scriptures. These potatoes are delicious, Lavinia. What are they?"

"We've always called them yams. I believe people in northern parts call them sweet potatoes."

Phoebe, supposing her father hoped to change the subject, turned to ask Clara a question at the same time Hugh began speaking.

"What might those decisions be, Pastor? The ones with several viable alternatives."

Pastor Farrell rested his fork. "Well, Paul lays out a few, one regarded eating of meat. In his day, almost all—if not absolutely all—of the meat available for purchase had been dedicated to one or another idol. Jesus did not address this issue while He walked on earth because it wasn't a question within Israel. The people of Corinth—or was it Rome—had begun to wonder if they could eat only vegetables."

"Ugh! Even for breakfast?" Augie had been paying more attention than his sister thought. "What did they decide?"

"Paul concluded each person should do what they thought right."

Asa sat back a little from the table in a more relaxed posture. "So you agree: we—north and south—need to follow the dictates of our own consciences?"

"Well, if you would allow me to be truthful rather than politic, this is where the issue becomes a bit thorny. In addition to an individual's conviction, Paul laid out a pervasive rule we should always keep in mind: the rule of love.[viii]"

"Love, Ernest?" Lavinia leaned into the empty space where her plate had just been.

"Putting the other person before yourself. He went on to say the man who feels it's perfectly fine to eat meat—after all, those idols were nothing more than clever fabrications—should refrain if the friend he is with considers it wrong.[ix] Whether our actions help those around us becomes a better question, not whether or not we are free to indulge. Next, we have a repeated refrain from the book of Judges: 'In those days there was no king in Israel. Every man did that which was right in his own eyes.'[x]"

Lavinia tilted her head. "Surely, Pastor, that is the ideal. Aren't we to listen to our consciences?"

"Not everyone's consciences are the same. Some speak loudly and clearly. Others have been ignored so often, they no longer speak. If you desire to see what comes of everyone doing 'right in their own eyes' read the chapters after 17."

Augie's perked up. "I'm going to read it soon as we get home."

"Oh, no you're not, young man—not until you are *much* older."

Asa began tugging on his mustache. "So, what would you have the slave states do?"

"Well, for the reason you've already cited, the government can only legislate so much. The real problem lays in our hearts."

"Are you dodging my question?"

"No, just trying to answer as accurately and succinctly as I know how. I doubt you asked us to dinner so I could preach a sermon."

"I for one," began Lavinia, "wish to hear what you have to say."

"As do I," replied her husband. "Though I cannot promise to agree with it. Lavinia and Hugh are the true believers in our family."

"Asa, darling, you go to church every Sunday. I know. I sit right beside you."

"Yes, but Clara and I are not so…heavenly minded, are we daughter?" Raising his glass, he tipped it in her direction.

"Ugh, all those rules," she replied.

"What *is* your answer, Pastor? I am willing to listen."

"Well, to your daughter's point, the real issue has nothing to do with rules, and I am sorry, Clara, you were led to believe it does. It's all about a change of heart—being born from above, born into His kingdom—and anyone born of God takes joy in pleasing Him. He is a kind and loving father and king. Therein lies the trouble. Most people would rather rule their own kingdom, circling us right back to those men in the book of Judges."

Asa cleared his throat. "You have given us much to think about, however, I see Mitilde is about to bring in dessert, and Augie and I need to go back into the shed to further acquaint him with his pup. Don't we, son?"

As Augie bobbed his head, Phoebe glanced around the table. Asa poked at his cake, as if he found the flavor offensive, and Hugh hardly touched his. Clara ate hers with relish, and Lavinia was still—the kind of still that bespoke a mind avidly at work.

Once Asa rose to his feet, he nodded toward the rear door. "Ready, Augie?"

"Yes, sir!"

"If you grin any wider, I'm afraid your teeth will touch your ears."

Augie caught up with Mr. Kiker while the other diners pushed their chairs back from the table. While Phoebe watched her father and Hugh amble after the other two males in their party, she began to wonder what they were discussing. Their faces were serious to the point of growing somber, and they had lowered their voices. Returning the smile Clara offered as she bid her good night from across the room, she was considering whether she should follow her family when she felt her hostess capture her hand.

Lavinia, in what Phoebe had come to consider characteristic fashion, laid it within the crook of her arm and guided her across the hall into a small, well-appointed room. The painted woodwork was a pleasing shade of bluish-green, quite like the walls of the parsonage, and the door she shut behind them had been finished to look like grained mahogany.

"Please, sit." Lavinia indicated a diminutive chair adjacent to a writing desk.

"This room is lovely." Ivory and fuschia blooms sprung from teal vines woven into the fabric of her chair and the tall draperies, and cabriole legs on all the room's pieces added femininity absent in the straight lines of the bookcases.

"I'm delighted to get a chance to speak with you alone. I am in need of a new secretary companion and believe you would suit me perfectly. The position has been vacant for several months, so you will have much to do. However, a young woman with your upbringing, education, and temperament will be able to put everything in order in no time."

"I...I don't know what to say, Mrs. Kiker. I would be pleased to help you in any way, however, I will need to ask my father. And what about my brother? While Mother remains in Baltimore, he is my responsibility."

"Oh, that is no problem at all. The Lilacs boasts many acres. He will be free to roam and find as much mischief as his heart desires. I remember what my son was like at his age. Speaking of Hugh, I am sure he will find plenty for... I know your family calls your brother Augie, but what is his given name?"

"August."

"August. Delightful. Hugh often prayed for a little brother. As I was saying, I'm sure he will find plenty for the lad to do. Perhaps he can even earn a bit of income of his own, and both Hugh and Asa can help him train the pup he has chosen. There is also the matter of my daughter."

Phoebe was unsure what Lavinia meant.

"She spends too much time alone, Miss Farrell, and I suspect you could be a...brightening influence. Since Charles Simmons has replaced his father, it places their..."

A gentle knock pulled their attention to the door. "Missus Kiker, the young lady's father is fixin' to go."

"Alright, Mitilde. You outdid yourself with supper tonight. The smoked goose breast was just delicious, and so was the cider cake. Thank you, and please let Job know how pleased we all were with his service."

"Yes'm. I'll tell 'im."

As the cook backed away, Lavinia rose from her desk. "I will keep you no longer. Suffice it to say, I think you are just what I—and Clara—need. Many a girl blooms in the company of another and, though you are a few years younger than she, you are proving yourself just the sort of young woman with whom I'd like her to associate."

When Lavinia ushered Phoebe through the front door, they found Reverend Farrell and Augie waiting in the wagon.

"May I give you my answer later this week?"

"Most certainly." Sweeping slowly down the steps, Lavinia extended her hand to help Phoebe climb into the seat. "A daughter must consider the wishes of her father and mother, is that not so, Ernest? I will await your reply."

With a smile and a wave, Lavinia gathered her skirts and ascended the steps leaving Phoebe to wonder what she had been about to say when Mitilde knocked. Indeed, the short conference had given her many things to think about.

"CHILDREN, I WAS very proud of your behavior this evening." Reverend Farrell beamed as he glanced from his son to his daughter. "Augie, your manners were what any father would hope for an eight-year-old, and Phoebe, I was not aware of how poised you've become."

"Thank you, Papa."

As they rounded the curve, her father stretched sideways, almost leaning out of his seat. "Who is that?"

Phoebe stared at the fleeing figure. "He reminds me of the man Charles chased from the Simmons' paddock."

As Augie also leaned out of the wagon, Phoebe grabbed his suspenders. "It was him. I'm sure of it. Lamb's tail and all."

"It's called a queue."

"Huh?"

"A queue, not a lamb's tail."

"Son, your eyes are better than mine. Can you tell me which way he went past the bushes?"

"Yep, he went right—into the trees."

"I don't like this. There's a lamp lit in the office. I'm going to pull up and see if the manager's inside. Stay here. Climb in the back and lie down, just in case I find trouble."

As he climbed out, the children repositioned themselves as they were told, though Phoebe had to yank Augie's shirt more than once to make him lay flat. They were listening to crickets chirping all around them and the occasional lowing of a cow from a nearby pasture when the office door flung open with such force it whacked the stone wall. Before they had a chance to peek over the wagon, a shadow was hopping onto the seat.

"Stay down!" Reverend Farrell barked as he turned the wagon around.

"What happened, Papa? Ow!" Augie's head bumped the wagon side as he tried to see where they were heading. "Why are we going back?"

"Down!"

In minutes, they reached the house's circular drive.

"Quickly. Get upstairs." Jumping off, the pastor helped his children hop out, and when they reached the porch, he began banging on the door.

The man Lavinia had called Job pulled it open. "Reverend Farrell, may I…"

"Call Asa and Hugh—hurry. Children, go inside."

Phoebe did not know what was wrong. She had never seen her father behave in such a manner. He shoved them into the foyer without waiting to be invited and then brushed past the dumbfounded manservant as soon as he heard Asa's voice.

"Asa, come quickly. Where's Hugh? We'll need him also."

"Good heavens, man, what's all the commotion?"

"Asa," called Lavinia. "Is everything all right?"

"Where did Hugh go?" asked her husband.

"I have no idea. The last I saw him, he went to the barn with you and the boy." She seemed embarrassed that she had not used Augie's name once she saw him in the entry hall.

Asa sharply drew his brows down. "We'll have to go without him. Did you overturn your…?"

As their voices trailed off, both Farrell children were left in the hall. Phoebe smiled sweetly, watching Augie sweeping his toe back and forth along the striped Venetian carpet.

"What is it? What has happened to upset your father so?"

Phoebe lifted her shoulders apologetically, telling her all she knew, and Augie only perked up when they began talking about the Simmons' thief. In a short while, they heard hard footsteps hurrying up the stairs onto the porch, and Hugh flung the door open.

"Mother, stay inside and bolt the door. I'm riding for Bentley—or Spry—whichever I can find first."

Lavinia began wringing her hands, the first clue to any onlooker, she could not keep her thoughts as composed as her face. "Matthew hasn't come back in several days. I thought he was pursuing the thief Charles was after, however, the children said they saw the man here—tonight. Try the tavern. He may be there taking a meal. What has happened?"

"I have to fly. Father and the new pastor…" He faltered, taking note of the younger Farrells. "Pastor Farrell will explain everything." Grabbing his hat, he spun on his heels and raced for the stables. They could hear him galloping away as they bolted the door.

A quarter-hour went by as the three sat awkwardly, their minds striving without success to fill in the blanks. When Clara swept down the staircase, she came to an abrupt halt. "What on earth are you all doing, just sitting around as if your fates hung in the balance?"

Before her mother could attempt an answer, her father and Reverend Farrell pounded the door. "It's us."

Lavinia threw back the rod. "Asa, you look as white as a sheet."

"Father, what's the matter?"

As Pastor Farrell came inside, the three adults exchanged glances. "They will hear about it anyway," he answered. "They may as well hear it from us. Lavinia, may I have a glass of water?"

"Of course." She left the room, calling over her shoulder, "I'll ask Mitilde to bring some lemonade."

Once everyone else was seated around the dining room table, Lavinia took her place. "What is all this about, Ernest?"

"As the children no doubt have told you, I went into Asa's office assuming I'd find Charles Simmons." He ran his hand over his face as if wishing to wipe a memory away. "Instead, I saw the thief from the Simmons' farm—yet I still can make no sense of it. We had just seen him sprinting into the tree line. He was laying across the desk, over a book, as if he had fallen asleep. Asa identified it as the ledger from The Lilac's Whiskey Distillery. His body was positioned strangely, and when I went to shake him by the shoulder, he slumped to the floor."

As every drop of color drained from her father's face, Phoebe went to stand beside him, worried he might faint.

"My whittling knife—the one I lent you yesterday, Augie—was lodged in his ribs."

Augie's eyes grew as large as cherries. "But..."

Asa pinned him with a firm though gentle look. "When did you last have it, son?"

"Th...this evening. I...I loaned it...to Hugh."

Lavinia moaned, dropping her face into her hands. "This is awful, just awful."

"Hugh said he'd cut a leather strap to use as a collar for Sparkles, to show everyone he was taken." The boy seemed like he was making a plea, whether for Hugh or himself remained unspoken. "Papa, I forgot to ask for it back."

"Never mind, son. I can easily buy another, but it...it will be difficult to explain to Matthew Bentley how it found its way there."

108

Chapter 15

JUST PAST NINE, the sound of scattering gravel alerted the families inside the manor of Hugh and Mr. Bentley's arrival. Bentley doffed his hat, acknowledging everyone briefly, before asking Reverend Farrell and both Mr. Kikers to accompany him to the scene of the crime. How they proceeded, Phoebe could only imagine. From the scene her father had described, she had a reasonable idea of what they would find, however, the time she spent waiting with Lavinia, Clara, and Augie seemed to stretch for weeks. At last, they heard several sets of firm footsteps ascending to the porch.

Lavinia raised her head as Asa strode through the door. "Well?"

He motioned toward Hugh, who had come in just behind him. "Bentley is set on taking him, though first, he insists on talking with Augie." He skewered the boy with eyes full of hope and worry.

On their heels, Matthew Bentley and the pastor slipped in. "Do you have a room I can use to talk with Ernest's son—alone?"

Asa opened the door of a small room off the foyer. "Here, in my study."

"It's alright." Hugh flashed Augie a smile. "Just tell him everything you remember."

Once Mr. Bentley pulled the door shut, Lavinia and Clara peppered the remaining men with questions.

"One at a time." Asa took Lavinia's hand. "Beyond what Ernest told us earlier, we don't have anything else to tell."

"Except for the name of the victim," added Reverend Farrell. "Hugh recognized him as one of Edward Simmons' cohorts."

Lavinia peered at her son. "Whoever can he mean?"

"Silas Rugger," answered Hugh. "We caught his brother and him rolling a barrel out of the distillery. Now I understand why Augie and Jeremiah thought he looked like Foster. They're cousins—same scrappy build and coloring. Always made me think of tough plucked chickens—all sinew and no meat."

"But Hugh," asked Clara, "what has any of this to do with you?"

"Rugger was killed with a knife Augie loaned me while we were in the barn."

"If the weapon is Augie's, it implicates him, not you."

Pastor Farrell cleared his throat. "The knife is not Augie's. It's mine, and Bentley cannot fathom me killing a man I've never met. He also knows I couldn't have committed the first murder."

Lavinia sat up straighter. "Ed Simmons' murder? Matthew thinks they are connected?"

"Maybe yes, maybe no," answered her husband. "And to further answer your questions, Clara, Hugh neglected to give the knife back. Besides, Augie is eight. He lacks the strength to...to commit such an act. And—like his father—he lacks a motive. Bentley thinks your brother has both." He blew out a frustrated breath.

"Asa, you still haven't told us why."

"I did not wish to worry you, darling, but for several months before his death, Hugh and I had suspected Ed Simmons was stealing from the distillery."

"Stealing? How? You keep a careful watch over the inventory. It would have shown on the books."

"That's why Rugger was in the office. Since Simmons died, he's stepped in to alter our figures. Not much: a few barrels here or there, and then looping a three so it would look like a two or turning a one into a seven or a seven into a nine."

"And that's why Matthew supposes the two may be connected?"

"Yes, and it offers both Hugh and I a motive."

"Oh, how dreadful."

Hugh raked a hand through his hair. "It gets worse. I was here when both murders took place."

Lavinia was about to protest when Reverend Farrell spoke up. "That seems awfully weak. Why not simply have them jailed? Asa, you know everyone in this community. Who has a stronger motive?"

Mr. Kiker peered out the window toward the slave quarters. "I can think of many. Many killings, according to Bentley, are spontaneous—acts of rage or jealousy, but some are well-planned. In cases of the latter, he said he always asks the same question: who has the most to gain?"

"Then why arrest Hugh?" asked Lavinia. "He had nothing to gain from Simmons' death and certainly not from this Silas…"

"Rugger. Not directly, but since we suspected Simmons was stealing from us and caught Rugger outright, we *gain* by stopping the distillery's losses."

Phoebe, whose presence they had all but forgotten, scooted to the edge of her seat. "Surely not all gains are financial?"

Reverend Farrell narrowed his eyes. "Good point. Perhaps revenge or relief. I've known cruel or oppressive men whose wives and children resent being beaten—and battery is not always a matter of fists. Words can wound deeply. Or a man with ample means who holds his wealth so closely he forces his dependents to live in poverty. His family might gain relief from either."

While her father looked from one Kiker to another, Phoebe watched Lavinia trap her lower lip between her teeth.

"You appear to be describing Edward Simmons," suggested Asa. "Do you suspect something you have not told us?"

"No, though you know all the Simmonses far better than we do."

Clara stood so abruptly, Hugh had to catch her chair. "The idea is absurd. I've known the Simmonses my whole life. Mahala is one of Mother's closest friends. Besides, if Mr. Simmons were wealthy, why would he be robbing us?"

"Settle down, pet," said her father. "Ernest isn't accusing anyone. He is offering us an example."

While Clara regained her seat, Phoebe puckered her brow. "We were all with you, Mr. Kiker, the entire evening. You could not possibly have done it."

As Hugh glanced at her warmly, her father shook his head. "Sadly, that is not quite true."

Lavinia sucked in her breath, and Clara glared.

"Now don't blame the pastor, either of you," cautioned Asa. "He is stating what we all must face and what he will be sworn to admit in court if it comes to that. Hugh was with us in the barn and during dinner, but…" He cast his son a probing stare. "Where did you go when you walked off? I paid no attention. I was concentrating on acquainting Augie with his pup."

112

As Hugh picked at his thumbnail, the color deepened beneath his shirt collar. "To craft Augie's puppy a collar."

When the study door opened, Augie emerged with tear-stained cheeks. The moment the lawman let go of his shoulder, he ran to his father to bury his face, flicking Hugh a look of deeply felt shame.

"Asa, Lavinia," began a grim-lipped Mr. Bentley. "I have no choice but to detain Hugh. I will understand if you prefer me to move my belongings from your guestroom and seek lodgings above the tavern."

"You will do no such thing," replied Lavinia, pulling on her most imperious air. "Our son had nothing to do with either of these murders, however, we are aware you must do your duty without prejudice. Of course, if *you* would feel more comfortable..."

Clara curled her upper lip. "We wouldn't want you to fear you'll be murdered in your bed." As her father shot her a reprimanding scowl, she shrugged and smiled sweetly. "What? It would be the quickest way to free Hugh, and we wouldn't wish our guest to be uncomfortable."

"Clara, while I appreciate your desire to protect me, it is not necessary. Matthew, I agree with Mother and hope you will continue here. No doubt I will be freed like Charles was and cannot hang for a crime—or even two of them—I did not commit."

Everyone started as they heard voices from the other side of the kitchen door. "Granny, stop. You can't go in the dinin' room. They has company."

"Then gimme that pot o' tea. I'll take it to them. I got somethin' to say as cain't wait."

A dark-skinned woman burst through the door, older than any Phoebe had ever seen. Brandishing a trembling teapot, she wobbled backward to regain her balance before shuffling unsteadily toward the table.

"I'll take that, Granny." Lavinia reached for her burden. "You're spilling it all over the rug."

"I's sorry, Missus. I *gots* to speak wit' dat man." She pointed her bony finger at Matthew Bentley. "He mus' be deaf as a plank. I telled 'im I done killt that sorry piece o'..."

"Now Bett, I will not have you insulting a guest in our home." Setting down the pot, she guided the shriveled old woman back to the kitchen. "I expect you to apologize to him in the morning."

"But Missus Lavinia, I ain't..."

As the door closed behind them, Asa turned to the governor's agent. "Please pardon her outburst, Matthew, and my wife's indulgence. She's been in our family for generations."

"Is she Granny Bett?" asked Reverend Farrell. "She seems to feel free to speak her thoughts. Pardon my ignorance, but I have little experience with slavery. Isn't she afraid you might sell her?"

"Bett? Never. Raised my father before me and my children after. If not for her, both Lavinia and Clara would be lying in our family cemetery. Besides," he chuckled, "if I tried, she'd take me out to the woodshed. When she's not down with rheumatism, she thinks she still runs the place."

The reverend's eyes sparkled as he pictured the old woman pulling their host by the ear, though Asa once more grew somber. Staring at his empty teacup, he turned it over and over, as if it held some hidden answer.

"Oh, Matthew," sighed Lavinia as she resumed her seat. "I'm not any happier than she is about your suspicions, however, I am deeply embarrassed. Asa, I just don't know what to do with her anymore. She's clearly slipping."

Seeing Pastor Farrell's questioning glance, Asa tapped a finger against his right temple.

"Hand me your cup, Ernest." Lavinia smiled thinly. "I will pour you some tea."

As she did so for the entire table, passing around sugar and cream for anyone who liked it, Reverend Farrell solemnly stroked his mustache. He studied her, then Hugh and Mr. Bentley. "Matthew, what of the man I saw running away? Surely Augie mentioned him. He saw him better than I did. Isn't it far more likely this man killed Silas..." He looked up at Asa as Lavinia had earlier, hoping he would once more supply the name.

"Silas Rugger."

"Yes. The man running appeared so similar to the victim, it struck me at first they were one and the same. Of course, I realize that is impossible."

"Yes." Mr. Kiker slapped the table. "Could he have been Silas Rugger's brother?"

Matthew shrugged. "I cannot say. I didn't know he had a brother."

"A miserable sort locals call Lyin' John. He was the other man we caught trying to steal our whiskey."

Mr. Bentley leaned back in his chair. "It might help if you tell me more about it. What did you do with the two of them?"

"Ed Simmons persuaded us to issue a distinctly stern warning and let them go. This was, of course, before we suspected his involvement or had learned it had happened more than once. It's what tipped us off."

"Sir," ventured Phoebe, "isn't running a sure signal of guilt?"

The agent paused, rubbing his knuckle back and forth across his lips. "I take your point, Miss Farrell, though he may have run for the same reasons your father hurried away from the scene—especially if he is, as we speculate, the dead man's brother. We must also consider the good possibility he ran for Spry, not wanting to alert the Kikers he was trespassing again on their property. If that's the case, we'll know shortly. I assure you, Asa, I will pursue this avenue until I discover its end."

"But, sir," persisted Phoebe as the agent rose to his feet. "Surely, his very presence removes your reason to arrest Hugh as it offers you a plausible alternative."

"I am not arresting him, only holding him for questioning. For one so young and feminine, you have the makings of a fine lawman; but you are neglecting an important fact. This...Lying John...was not in possession of your father's knife."

A HEAVY PALL lay over the Farrells as they rode home; and the new moon provided so little light, they were grateful for The Pike's deep ruts. If they veered right or left, the feel of the wagon announced the error with the sharpness of a quirt.

"Son, you were visibly upset when you came out of the study. Was Mr. Bentley harsh with you?"

"No." Augie reached up to pull his father's arm more tightly around him.

115

"What sort of questions did he ask?"

Augie only shrugged.

"Did he imply you had any part in the deed?"

"No." Augie sniffed. "But the Kiker's have been so kind to me, first when I knocked over the punch bowl at their party, and then by giving me Sparkles. I didn't mean to get Mr. Hugh in trouble."

By the way the boy shook, his father knew he was weeping and gave him a firm squeeze. "You didn't. Only Hugh could do that, and we can't yet say the extent of his involvement. Where did he go, when he left you?"

"He…he told me he was going to…to the office."

Chapter 16

REVEREND FARRELL RAN up the path from the church, flung open the parsonage door, and waved a letter at his children. After the night they had just spent, he was glad to bring good news. "Look what the postman brought!"

"From Mama?"

"Is she coming home?"

"Yes, on Wednesday's train!"

"Yipee!" cried Augie, bounding off his chair.

"How is Grandma Ada?"

"She's frustrated and probably scared, although she's progressing. At first, your mother writes, tears streamed down your grandmother's cheeks. Her facial muscles were unable to hold them back. She has now regained some control—just not as rapidly as she would like. She's beginning to form intelligible syllables."

"Oh, poor Grandma. Will she fully recover?"

"Hard to say. I know very little about medicine."

"And Mama—how is she?"

"She sounds exhausted, but at least Lucy has continued sleeping well through the night. She's a very contented baby."

Augie cocked his head. "How old is she now?"

Papa's lips tipped up at the edges while Phoebe rolled her eyes. "How old was she when they left, Augie?"

"Four months?"

"And how long have we been here?"

"Uhm..." He ticked off the days on his fingers. "Only a few weeks? Seems like ages."

"It does indeed. Phoebe, you have done an admirable job with the unpacking. Your mama will be quite pleased."

"I'll be glad to have her home."

"Me too!" said Augie. "No more of your cooking."

As she rolled her eyes, Papa began to exit the way he had entered; yet as he patted his pocket, he turned back. "Oh, I forgot to give you this, Kitten. The postmark says Princeton."

Taking the missive from his hand, she quickly tore at the flap.

"What's it say, Phebes?"

"It's private." Pushing her chair from the table, she waltzed through the parlor and ran up the stairs.

"Oooo….Phoebe has a beau. Phoebe has a…"

Pulling out the letter, she closed her door and flopped back against it.

April 27, 1843

Dear Phoebe,

Are you enjoying the Shenandoah Valley? Have you met my brother-in-law's family or made any other friends?

Though I was sad to see your family leave, in one way it has been good for me: it forced me to extend myself elsewhere and with immediate benefit. A classmate named Phillip invited me for dinner this evening. He grew up in town, and his two younger brothers remind me much of Augie—always fidgeting or into mischief. He also has a sister, Hannah, you may know. She looks a few years older than you and has my mother's auburn-colored hair and amber eyes.

I have so much more to write, but I hear the bugle call. I'll fill you in on everything later.

Please tell your whole family hello from me and give Allison—Mrs. Wilson—and Lisa my regards when you see them next.

Your friend,
Samuel

As Phoebe reached for her inkwell, she frowned. She knew an auburn-haired Hannah. She was a few years older and a great deal prettier.

Dear Samuel,

I was happy to receive your letter. Is the young woman you describe Hannah Shockley? If so, I do not know her well. However, our fathers taught together and are friendly if not friends. When they moved to Princeton, she was just enough older than I am to regard me as too young for friendship. You know how it is. A child of seven seems rather immature to someone who is ten. If we had not met until now, we would probably see each other as peers. Her brother Philip was always gentlemanly, even as a boy.

The valley is lovely and your brother-in-law's family is delightful; but before we debarked the train, we learned of a horribly unsettling event: a murder on a nearby plantation. The victim's family belongs to Papa's new congregation, so many of our earliest days were occupied with their grief.

Then—I promise I am not making this up—after dinner last evening on that very plantation, Papa discovered a second murder victim. It was awful, especially since they have detained a man I was just beginning to trust. Papa and Augie have become the chief witnesses.

As for friends, besides Lisa, I have made two others. The first is our head deacon's granddaughter. Everything about her is lovely, especially her heart. The other is like no one I have ever met. She has not yet introduced me to her family. Her mother passed away and, now that I think of it, she has not mentioned her father at all. Between you and me, I am deeply concerned for her. Not only is she always hungry and ill-clothed, but she also evades many of my questions. Furthermore, she often takes to hiding.

The rest will have to be a discussion for another day. I had not intended to write you a novel.

Phoebe lifted her hand, wondering how she should close the letter. She had received occasional attention from the students who discussed theology around her family's table. Some treated her as if she were a little sister or a comfortable piece of the furniture. Occasionally one would debate with her as if she were an opponent. From a small number, and all of them unappealing, she sensed a desire for more. Only with Samuel had she felt unsure. She knew he enjoyed her company. Whether his intentions lay beyond that, she had never been able to conclude. Since he had simply called himself her friend, she decided to do likewise, tucking the letter into a homemade envelope and running over to the church to place it with the outgoing post.

"Papa, it's me." She rapped lightly on the door before swinging it open. An individual she had just been writing about rose politely from the wide, black leather chair beside her father's desk.

"Miss Farrell." Hugh briefly inclined his head.

"Oh—I'm sorry. I didn't mean to disturb you."

"That's quite alright. Your father was just answering some questions he raised in my thoughts concerning our discussion last evening."

"When did Mr. Bentley release you? Did you walk? I didn't see your horse?"

"Just this past hour. As you were so kind to point out last night, he didn't have enough to hold me. My mount's around the other side, tied to the hitching post out front."

"Oh. I am glad you are free. Papa, I'll just leave this for you to mail." She could not help but notice Hugh's eyes dropping to the address as she was laying her letter on the desk.

"Thank you, Pastor, for taking the time to talk with me. If you still feel you can trust me after last evening, I'd like to walk your daughter back up to the parsonage."

"I'm sure she'd be delighted. Bentley's suspicions could have fallen on me just as easily as they did you. While I do not know Silas Rugger, it was my knife. I enjoyed our conversation." He looked up at his daughter. "Phoebe, I'll see you around suppertime. I'd bet you will be glad to hand over the responsibility of making our meals."

Phoebe nodded, glancing at Hugh as he lightly pressed his hand against the small of her back and ushered her out the door.

"What did your father mean—about your cooking? Do you cook well?"

"Depends on whom you ask. We received great news today." She could not suppress her happiness. "My mother will return to us on Wednesday."

"That *is* great news. My parents are eager to meet her. As you have seen, our parcels of land place all of us at a distance from each other, so our circle of friends is small. If your mother is like you, she will be a welcome addition, and as an educated woman will have much in common with my own."

"You are too kind." She tried and failed to look him in the eye. "Mama will be happy to finally meet everyone."

Hugh cleared his throat. "Her arrival smooths the way for another matter my family and I were discussing just before your family joined us."

She stopped and offered him her full attention.

"As Mother mentioned to you, she has recently lost her secretary-companion and has had difficulty finding another. I overheard you telling her you were busy with your current responsibilities."

Phoebe wondered how. He had left the table with the other men. Had he come back into the house without them?

"Since your mother is arriving and your time will be freer, she would very much like you to consider the position."

Hoping to hide her mixed feelings, Phoebe ducked her head down. While she would be glad to supplement her father's barely-adequate salary, she could not relish spending her days on the spot of two unsolved murders. Furthermore, she was not sure either of her parents would allow it. She longed for more time with her mother. "May I wait until after my mother arrives to give my answer? I do not yet know if she can spare me."

"Exactly the sort of answer to commend you for the post. You are a sight prettier than Miss Halifax and much more enjoyable company."

Phoebe wished she had thought to put on her bonnet. The brim might hide the warmth flooding her cheeks. "You mustn't say such things, Mr. Kiker. My head will grow so large, my neck will no longer support it."

"You never met Miss Halifax. Her jawline was floppier than a hound's, though she didn't slobber half so badly." Watching

Phoebe's dimples fade, he slowed to examine her more closely. "Are you so unaware of your appeal, Miss Farrell?"

"I suppose the parsonage has as many mirrors as any home, and if she is as you paint her, any woman might be an improvement."

He flashed her a charming grin. "Hardly my point—or rather you are proving it. Mind you, Miss Halifax *did* remind me of Beowulf's monster."

As he mimicked the beast, Phoebe pealed with laughter.

"You think I'm teasing. She was every bit as menacing. Had the story not been written a thousand years ago, Charles and I would have been convinced she was the author's model."

"The two of you studied literature together?"

"Yes. He joined my tutor and I every day while his father was working with mine. Ed Simmons was The Lilacs' foreman. Once old Brandhorst had taught us all he knew—or perhaps had run out of patience—my father sent us to Washington College, a day south of us in Lexington."

"So you really are like brothers."

Hugh's eyebrows jumped toward his dark waves. "Who's been saying so?"

"Your sister." Phoebe was relieved to see the tension soften from his face. "She said you have always been close."

He cleared his throat. "When we were younger, we were together so often people referred to us as the twins."

Although another reason flitted through Phoebe's mind, she thought it impolitic to mention it. Besides, something in his eyes belied his calm tone.

Once they had reached the parsonage, Hugh leaned a hand against the kitchen door. "Before I go, I wonder if you will answer a question for me?"

She looked up at him.

"Did you happen to see another stranger by the river the day Charles and I met you?"

"The slave you were chasing?"

Hugh shot her so sharp a look, her neck grew warm.

"Charles mentioned the two of you were searching for a man. Did you ever find him?"

"No." Hugh glimpsed the gently lapping water, shimmering in the strong afternoon sun. "I meant someone else—a girl who has gone missing."

"A girl?" Phoebe tried to force the surprise from her face. "A little child?"

"About your age. She was a great favorite of my mother's."

"A slave?"

He nodded, though he looked away. "We are afraid she might be...in trouble."

"What sort of trouble?"

"I suspect she witnessed Edward Simmons' murder."

Phoebe gasped. She had known Birdie was hiding something—but this.

"I was hoping to find someone who can exonerate...me...of at least one of the murders. I am also frankly afraid of what the...true culprit might do to keep her from testifying."

"I...I..." She wanted badly to help him, for Birdie's sake if not for his own. Still, his inquiry might be a ruse. How could she guarantee *he* was not the true culprit? Could a man be perfectly charming during dessert and then casually slip out to commit murder? Her father obviously did not believe so or he would not have permitted her to be alone with him?

"You what?"

She wished he would stop peering at her so intently. "I hope the girl's alright. What do you call her?"

"Birdie."

"Birdie. It is a name I will not easily forget, and if I discover any information to clear you from suspicion, I will immediately tell you."

"I'm grateful, Miss Farrell."

As he removed his hand from the door, she pulled it open. "Would you like anything to drink before you go? I cannot invite you in. Augie is playing somewhere in the park, and you know where my father is."

"No, thank you. I only stopped because the church was on the way. My parents will be eager to know Bentley has released me. Good day." With a slight bow, he walked back the way they had come, skirting the church's other side to reclaim his mount.

123

Slipping inside, Phoebe lay back against the closed door, racing through her recollections for bits that might condemn or acquit him. He *was* every bit as amiable as Emily thought him, yet she had often felt, as she did just minutes ago, he was prodding her for information. It was natural enough to ask questions of a new acquaintance, however, his were not of a sort to deepen a friendship.

"Hey, Phebes."

"Augie, I thought you were outside."

"I was, but when I saw Foster shimmying down the tree, I remembered we never explored the attic."

"Which tree?"

"The big one. He showed me a baby squirrel he had tucked inside his shirt."

"I want to see." She ran out the front and spotted the caretaker half-way up the tallest tree, placing the tiny creatures into a pile of bunched-up twigs and leaves wedged into the crotch of a sturdy limb. "Oh, they're so cute! May I hold one?"

"Best not. Their ma will smell you on 'em and might leave'm be. They're too young to live on their own." When Phoebe crumpled her brow, he held up a hand. "Gloves."

"I see. Why are you putting them there?"

"Fixin' to saw off that branch tomorrow." He jutted his chin toward the one encroaching on the northern dormer. "Growin' too close. Summers comin' on soon. A good storm could whip it against the window an' bash' it to pieces."

She saw what he meant and also noticed some traces of the old nest. "Will their mother be able to find them?"

"Don't worry none about that. Might be right puzzled for a time, but she'll hear' em callin' 'er."

"May we peek?"

"Sure. C'mon."

Her brother scrambled up with the ease of a little monkey they had once watched in a traveling menagerie. Phoebe had more difficulty. Her skirts proved too difficult to hold free while hoisting herself up without immodestly displaying her legs.

"Ah, Phebes," called Augie. "You've got to see them! They're all… Quit worrying about your skirt. I've seen your legs a hundred times, and Foster doesn't care."

Phoebe's cheeks began twitching when she noticed Foster's expression. "Perhaps you should let Foster speak for himself."

"It's ok, Miss Phoebe. I'll shut my eyes and keep 'em shut."

He did—so tightly he began to wobble; however, when she thought of Hugh or Charles springing up from nowhere, she decided to stay rooted to the ground.

"You can open them, Foster." Dropping her skirts into place, she climbed the branch with her gaze: first up to Augie, then to the gray fluff nestled in their caretaker's outstretched palm, and lastly to something moving past his shoulder. The hair stood up on her nape.

Augie stopped what he was doing. "What are you gawking at, Phebes?"

"Nothing." Nothing she wished to admit. She glanced back at the two in time to see Foster press his lips into a thin line and swallow.

Chapter 17

PHOEBE'S LEGS FELT a bit weak, though she was more determined than ever to search the attic. In less than an instant, the face—or what looked like a face—had disappeared. Surely, it was just a chance reflection. Scanning the opposite treetop, she searched for an animal: a raccoon or cat, perhaps a hawk. Owls and opossums were too pale.

"Augie, I will meet you inside."

She was determined to see if she could find...what? A well-disguised door? A secret panel? As she gathered fistfuls of her skirt to ascend to the kitchen, a chill ran up her spine. She stopped at once. If she did find a door, was she ready to meet whatever—or whomever—she had seen framed in the bubbled pane?

"Miss Farrell, where're you headed in such a hurry?"

Turning, she found Charles a wagon's length away. "Good afternoon, Mr. Simmons. I...I was just going...inside. I have yet to plan what I will make for supper." She dropped her eyes to the herbs sprouting in the kitchen garden, hoping to hide her frustration. During each of her day-lit attempts to steal into the attic, someone interrupted.

"Mr. Simmons!" Augie waved at him from the tree. "Come see the squirrels Foster's been showing me."

Charles looked from him to Phoebe and back again. "Maybe another time, Scamp. I'm here to talk with your sister—if she can spare the time."

"Certainly." She plastered on as genuine a smile as she could manage. "What can I do for you?"

Charles slid her a lopsided grin. "You get right to the point, don't you?"

"I did not mean to be rude, sir. From what you told Augie, I thought you were seeking something in particular."

"I am." He moved a little closer. "And I found it."

Phoebe did not know what to make of his answer, but seventeen years as a pastor's daughter fashioned her instant response. "Would you like some lemonade?"

"I would if it comes with the pleasure of your company."

"Although I cannot guarantee my company will be a pleasure, I will be right back with your lemonade. The parsonage has a nice bench, just atop the ridge, where we can..."

Augie darted up the garden steps. "You ready, Phebes?"

"To get some lemonade? Yes."

"I'm not even thirsty. Are you ready to explore the attic?"

"Mr. Simmons, please ignore my brother's poor manners. I will be right back."

"Explore the attic?" Charles had squatted down to Augie's level. "Sounds like great fun."

Phoebe threw her eyes up toward the sky, though she was glad neither noticed. Augie was engaging Charles, imitating the odd noises they had heard. Maybe she should be grateful for a man's presence, especially if something threatening appeared beyond the panel.

"Mr. Simmons and I are going upstairs, Phebes. We'll meet you there."

Since Augie had left her no choice, she climbed to the attic, tray in hand, every few seconds puffing a stray strand of hair out of her face. Charles was wiping his brow with his sleeve when she rounded the top landing.

"Why, thank you, Miss Farrell. While we need the lamp to see, the rising heat has made it hotter 'an blazes."

Augie and he had shifted all the cast-offs into the middle of the space to afford a clearer view of the walls. Starting beside the stairs, all three began tapping: Charles toward the ceiling, Phoebe about mid-wall, and Augie toward the floor. Knock after knock proved unfruitful. The answering sounds were all solid and brief.

The air Charles disturbed while he moved behind her felt close and overly intimate. She was about to slip aside when Augie burst out, "Did you hear that?"

Charles froze where he was standing, his warm breath in her hair. "Do it again."

As Augie did so, Charles dropped to his knees. This time, he did not wait. He rapped on the wood and peered up at Phoebe with eyes all alight. "Now, you knock on that other wall."

She did so and lifted her eyebrows.

"You hear the difference?"

"Yes." Kneeling beside her brother and him, she also knocked, listening intently.

"Spread out. Augie, you go to the far corner. Miss Farrell, if you take the other, I'll take the middle. No, Augie, wait. Let's knock in succession so we can hear any differences."

They followed his plan, but other than the original section, each sounded identical. Traveling with his fingers along the molding where the wall joined the ceiling, Charles let out an irritated sigh.

Why was *he* annoyed, Phoebe asked herself. If she ever wished to sleep again, she *needed* to explain that face.

Stepping back, Charles rubbed the channel in his mustache between his upper lip and nose. Hugh, she recognized, did the same thing while deep in thought.

"Miss Phoebe, does the placement of this molding strike you as odd?"

She shook her head. Although she admired the way moldings made a room appear, she had never considered their function.

"Why would someone bother trimming out an attic?"

"Hey, that's right," added Augie, though Phoebe wondered if he was just being agreeable. He had taken a shine to Charles, perhaps due to his friendship with Jeremiah or merely the attentive help the man was offering.

"Installing it in an attic does seem excessive," she answered. "But what about the difference in sounds we noted?"

"The wall is solid. Likely, when they were filling it with horsehair, they missed a hollow between the studs." He looked up and down the molding. "The way it faces, I assume it runs across the front of the house."

"Perhaps they installed it to hide the dormers."

"Yep, but why?"

"Deacon Nelson," spouted Augie, "said they're just pretend. The first pastor added them because his wife liked a fancier roofline." He looked pleased he could supply the answer.

"Maybe so. Seems like a waste of money. The glass in those windows is real enough. Even from the ground, you can see the bubbles blown into it, and they'd make a good source of light." He ran his hand atop the molding again, where it met the roof, as if seeking a loose section. Augie did the same with the floorboard, but neither found anything amiss.

"Well now…"

Nearly jumping from their skins, the explorers whipped around to find Foster on the landing. He had crept up the stairs with his characteristic silence.

"Didn't mean to scare yuh none. Most log'cal explanation was t' keep the pastor's kids from climbin' onto the roof. Don't see how it matters, 'less y'all are wantin' to pry the wall apart. If you do, I'll fetch my prybar, though I doubt the church board'll cotton to the idea."

Augie began springing up and down on the balls of his feet. "Can we, Phebes?"

While her eyes mirrored her brother's excitement, Phoebe shook her head. "Think of the mess. It's not the way Papa will wish to greet Mama."

"Fact, yer Ma's the reason I'm in the house. Yer Pa said the hinge on 'er wardrobe needed fixin'. An' when I came in, I heard a bunch o' tappin'."

"Your Ma's arriving soon?" asked Charles. "I'd better clear out and let you make dinner."

"Not for a couple of days," replied Augie. "Why don't you stay? Papa won't mind."

"I'd be pleased, Scamp, if the lady of the house agrees."

"Well, Phoebe?" asked Augie.

Charles's presence was the last thing she desired. His liberal compliments set her ill at ease. "Of course, Mr. Simmons, as long as you do not mind very ordinary fare."

Charles winked. "Any lack in its fineness will be made up by the loveliness of the cook."

REVEREND FARRELL TOOK his place at the head of the table. "Charles, to what do we owe this honor?"

"I stopped by in hopes of speaking with you, but I was waylaid by your charming daughter and son. They tell me your wife will arrive on Wednesday."

"I thought," interjected Augie, "you stopped to see Phoebe. That's what you said."

"Yes." The boy's father ignored the comment. "And I can hardly wait. While Phoebe has proven herself adept at running our household, I miss Amelia terribly. I can only imagine, Charles, how difficult these past weeks have been for *your* mother."

"Some days are easier than others, but, naturally, we keenly...feel Pa's absence."

Plunging through her memory, Phoebe tried to locate those exact words. She *knew* she had heard them, and a comment Mr. Bentley made last evening bubbled to the surface: 'Once a witness repeatedly reports what he has seen, he begins to remember his story rather than the actual events. That is why it's so important to examine them quickly.'

"Silas Rugger?" asked Charles.

As the question pulled Phoebe back to the conversation, she surmised her father had identified the latest victim. Oddly, she had the distinct impression Charles already knew, and when her father began filling in the details, the face she remembered in the window gave her a sudden chill.

"You're cold?" asked Augie. "I've got sweat running into my shorts."

As the pastor slid his son a censorious look, Charles threw back his head and laughed. "I agree, Scamp. It's hot enough to melt a candle, though this morning was downright cold."

Reverend Farrell put down his glass. "Yes, I've been meaning to ask if late springs in this valley are always unpredictable? This morning I considered dressing in my long..." He flicked his eyes to his daughter. "...my heavier clothing. Just now, as I came up the walk, I began peeling off my top layers."

"You just never know. Despite the heat, The Lilacs didn't begin spring planting until last week. Seen too many snows in April. Heading on into summer, the weather should straighten out. It'll be right humid come July."

130

As Phoebe thought of her dip in the river, she determined to change the subject. Charles was such a tease, she did not trust him to keep her confidence. "Papa, have you heard yet whether Mr. Bentley has apprehended the man we saw running away?"

"Who was that?" asked Charles.

"Mr. Kiker called him Lazy John."

"Lyin' John, Phebes. You're so dumb."

"Augie, don't insult your sister. I haven't heard anything as of yet."

"If it was Lyin' John," answered Charles, "Bentley may never find him. He's as comfortable as a bobcat in the mountains. Likely, he headed west over the Alleghenies."

Pastor Farrell frowned. "This will be some way to welcome your mother, children. She'll be afraid to leave the house."

Chapter 18

THE SUN WAS high overhead when Phoebe finished sweeping. Hanging up her apron, she was trotting down the slope toward the river until she stumbled over Augie's pouch of jackstraws. Her basket flung from her hand, rolling topsy-turvy until it smashed against the trunk of Birdie's favorite willow.

"Ugh! That brother of mine."

She brushed off her skirt, freshly streaked from her tumble, only to jump aside as an unfamiliar hound streaked past. Heading straight for her basket, he tugged at the tea towel, spilling out the contents, and thrust his nose into the middle of her elderberry pie. As Phoebe lunged for the sandwiches, he raised his muzzle. It was dyed a dark purple.

"Bowser! Git back 'ere this instant!"

Bounding up the hill with a longing backward glance, Bowser eagerly circled Avery Spry, the man who had banged on the parsonage door last Thursday. He was running toward the river, his rifle in one hand and a tattered scrap in the other. As Phoebe raised up, he took in her predicament, set both against the tree, and grabbed the dog by the collar.

"Afternoon, Missy."

"Good afternoon, Mr. Spry." Returning to the foodstuffs, Phoebe rescued as much as she could while Bowser wiped the filling his lolling tongue had missed onto the slave catcher's britches.

"Git!" Shoving the hound's muzzle away, he brushed debris from a sandwich near his boot and eyed the extra loaf she was tucking into the basket. "Let me help you with that. You got an awful lot o' food fer one little gal. You fixin' to meet a friend?"

Phoebe found his question impertinent and too direct for a ready obfuscation. As she searched for a polite reply, she spotted Augie sneaking up behind him.

"My brother plays down here during warm afternoons, and it's my favorite place for a picnic."

She could not tell what Augie was up to. He had snatched Spry's rag to wipe out the pie tin and then tossed it back down beside the rifle. Backing away, he signaled for her to keep his presence secret, and she decided to play along.

"Are you hungry, Mr. Spry? You are welcome to take the sandwich you are holding. I have plenty. Or you may join me if you like. I'm afraid we'll have to forgo dessert." Augie was encouraging the dog to lick the crumbs from the tin. "And if you are still hungry after your sandwich, I brought an extra loaf. I baked it fresh just this morning."

"Thank you, Miss. If you don't mind, I'll just take the sandwich with me. You seen a young slave woman 'round the park—'bout yer age?"

Before she could answer, Bowser began barking at Augie, who offered Spry a disarming grin. "I like your dog." He was holding the tin up high, waving it back and forth. "Come on, boy, come and get it. Jump!"

As the hound leaped, he knocked Augie over, and both boy and dog began wrestling on the ground.

"Ick! You sure give wet kisses." Augie wiped his face with the back of his hand. "I bet he's a fine hunter."

Spry nodded. "Best in the county, but we better be goin'." He retrieved his rifle and the scrap, which on further inspection appeared to be a tattered blouse. "You sure y'all ain't seen nobody?"

Phoebe shook her head. "I've seen no one at all since I woke up, besides you, of course, and my brother and father. You might ask Papa. He's probably in his study at the church."

Spry squinted as he angled his head. "What about Foster?"

"No." Phoebe shrugged. "He's probably around the front of the house. He told us yesterday he intended to saw off a branch that had grown too close to one of the dormers. You can't miss him."

"Yep," said Augie. "I was just talking with him about the squirrels."

"Squirrels?"

"The ones he took down yesterday. He didn't want them getting hurt when the limb fell."

133

"Hmm." Mr. Spry held out the scrap to the hound. "Ok, Bowser. You remember that scent?"

The dog returned his eager expression, pressing his chest toward the ground as if ready to spring off.

"Go get her." As Spry loped toward the other side of the stone church, the dog tore off beside him.

"Don't worry, Phoebe." Augie grinned. "He'll never find her."

Phoebe's mouth fell open.

"Mr. Kiker taught me a thing or two about hunters Sunday evening. You saw that blouse he shoved in his dog's nose? Bowser'll be tracking alright." Augie chuckled. "Tracking elderberry pie!"

"You know? About Birdie?"

"'Course I know. You think Foster's the only one I've been following?"

"Where is she?"

Augie shrugged. "We seen him…"

"Saw him."

"We *saw* him coming from up in the tree, and she skedaddled down to where…" He stopped as if he had said too much already. "To a boat hidden in the rushes. She's long gone now."

"Oh, Augie, I could just kiss you!"

Augie screwed up his face. "Not you, too. I've had enough of sloppy kisses for one day."

"Then, I'd better stay here and have my picnic in case he comes back. Would you care to join me? I'm afraid Spry and his dog ate most of my lunch, but I'll gladly share what's left."

"Nah. I need to wash this pie plate up. It wouldn't be good for his dog to head right for it."

"Here, take the sandwich—and the loaf if you want it. I'd intended it for Birdie. I'm going to read a while."

"Thanks. I've worked up an appetite."

"Phoebe! Augie! What's all the excitement?" Their father called down from the rise. "Did I see Avery Spry?"

"Yes sir," answered Augie. "He's hunting." He slid Phoebe an amused glance. "Maybe he'll bag himself a berry large rabbit."

Reverend Farrell's eyebrows shot up. "Bag? You're picking up the local way of speaking, eh? Perhaps it's a good thing, though I don't like the idea of him shooting rabbits on church property, especially as

134

you children are so often out and about. If he comes back, please tell him I'd like to speak with him."

"Yes, Papa," answered Phoebe. "Are you going back to your office?"

"For a while. I'll see you two around supper."

Once he was out of earshot, Phoebe turned back to her brother. "What are you going to be doing? Do you wish to explore the attic again later?"

"Nah. Didn't you listen to Foster? There's nothing there. Papa would have our hides if we damaged that wall. Besides, I already have plans."

"Alright." Phoebe smiled. "But don't get too dirty. I won't have time to wash a bunch of clothes before Mama comes home."

As he galloped to the top of the hill, passing the garden shed and disappearing from view, she shook her head. She was not sure what surprised her more: her brother's awareness of Birdie, his ability to outwit Spry, or his refusal to join in an adventure. Sitting down beneath Birdie's willow, she brushed off the remaining sandwich and had bitten off far too large a portion when a shadow fell across the grass.

"Miss Farrell, may I have a word?"

Looking over her shoulder, she found Matthew Bentley, hat in hand, standing just behind her. She held up a finger to signal for him to wait a moment. "I'm sorry, sir." With her hand, she shielded the lower portion of her face lest he notice the contents she was choking down. "I was just finishing my lunch." Her growling stomach argued otherwise. One bite, however, large, could hardly be considered ample. "Papa was just here. He said he was returning to his study."

Glancing up the hill, she recalled Hugh implying he had observed her floating and wondered how much her current visitor had seen. By throwing Spry's hound off Birdie's trail, Augie might have committed a punishable offense.

"It's you I have come to see."

"Oh."

His eyes warmly twinkled. "You appear surprised. Do you think we could sit and talk on that bench?" He tipped his hat toward the rise. "While my bride is sure of my heart, you are of an age that might give passersby a wrong impression if they spied us picnicking."

135

Phoebe saw what he meant. "I enjoyed meeting Mrs. Bentley at the Kikers' soiree last Saturday. She is lovely."

"I cannot argue, and it brings up my reason for seeking you out."

"Is something wrong? Is she ill?"

"No, no." He shook his head vigorously. "Nothing of the sort."

"That's a relief. I am quite parched and was about to fetch something more to drink if you can wait a few moments."

"You have a jug next to your basket."

Phoebe dimpled. "It's empty." She was glad he had missed it flailing through the air with her basket. "May I offer you something? Lemonade? Sweet tea?"

"Tea will do nicely, thank you."

After she gathered up her belongings, they trudged silently up the hill, leaving her to wonder exactly what he desired. "I'll only be a moment." She ducked through the kitchen door as he was brushing dogwood petals from the worn bench cushion. Lifting his coattails, lest he soil them, he claimed his seat just as she arrived with two tumblers.

"Here you go, sir." She handed him the tallest. "I hope it has enough sugar."

Putting it to his lips, he smiled. "It is perfect."

Phoebe sat beside him, willing herself to remain still. She wished he would hurry up and tell her what he wanted. He was taking an extraordinary amount of time to approach the subject.

"Miss Farrell, I suspect you find yourself in a unique position to help me."

"With something for your wife?"

He flashed her an awkward grin. "No. However, your observations about her confirmed some opinions I've formed."

She was at a loss as to what he meant, but he had surely captured her attention. "I will do what I am able, though I do not know how much that will be."

"I need your eyes and, perhaps more importantly, your ears."

"You wish to enlist me as a spy?" She thought of Augie's stories about General Washington's secret troop.

"Not a spy, exactly. As a newcomer, you are sure to have been meeting a multitude of persons, particularly those from your father's congregation who held an association of one sort or another with

136

Edward Simmons. A few might know those two bootleggers as well. You have been forming fresh opinions, unprejudiced by family ties and allegiances. It would interest me to listen to them. I fear your father, if you will pardon me, might be less forth-coming. He will be concerned with protecting his flock. And—again, if you will excuse me—he strikes me as a man who is absorbed far more by his intellectual and theological pursuits, worthy as they may be, than by whatever is standing before him. You, on the other hand, have already demonstrated a great deal of perspicacity."

Phoebe folded and unfolded her hands. "I am afraid, I do not know the word."

"Clear-sightedness. You strike me as keenly observant and as someone who ruminates amply before speaking."

One of her dimples began to twitch. "You are as well. I confess I often feel overlooked, more scenery than a participant."

"A quality that enhances your usefulness to me, if I may be blunt."

"What would you have me do?"

"If you are amenable, I would like to list some persons and ask you to describe them. For you to be of help, however, you must be candid. While I am certain you are admirably delicate in social situations, this is not a time to hold back information."

"I will try. Honestly, I know little of anyone here. We arrived at the end of April."

"You likely know more than you realize. People tend to clam up when speaking with an official. You, on the other hand, not only have gained entry to places I cannot without raising someone's guard, your gentleness invites confessions. Investigating is much like putting together a puzzle. The most insignificant appearing piece may begin to reveal the whole."

"I will do my best. Who would you like to hear about?"

"Let's start with Hugh Kiker. He seems particularly attentive to you, and you have spent considerably more time with him than anyone else I have noticed." Seeing her color, he added, "Nothing inappropriate. You simply appear to enjoy each other's company."

"I...Mr. Kiker has been kind, not only to me but to my little brother. His father and he gave Augie a puppy, which is why we were all in the barn before dinner."

"And other times? He engaged you for several dances during the Kiker's soiree, and I've gained the impression the two of you had met previously—by the river with Charles Simmons, wasn't it?"

His question did nothing to calm her color. Worse yet, she feared he could tell if she carefully picked through her answer.

"Yes. It was a particularly hot day. I was cooling off in the river when the two of them happened by. They were searching for a lost slave."

"Who gave you that impression?"

"Charles Simmons told me outright or implied it by his questions. He asked if I'd seen a large dark-skinned man and told me to send information to The Lilacs if I did."

"And what did Hugh say?"

"Nothing." She blushed deeply. "He introduced himself and shielded me from Mr. Simmons' teasing."

"Did you see either approach the garden shed?"

"No. I was concentrating on...getting cool."

Mr. Bentley pressed no further, having a good idea of why she appeared embarrassed. "What was your initial impression of Hugh?"

"He is handsome, well-spoken, rather charming—what people up north call well-bred."

Bentley nodded. "It's a term we southerners use also. Did he do or say anything that seemed odd or out of place?"

"No. Not at all."

"You appear to like him, perhaps even trust him?"

"Yes, and I am certain my father does. Should we not?"

"I am asking for your impressions, not mine."

"He is consistently courteous and kind, yet..."

"Yes?"

"I was just thinking of something I recently wrote a friend. You are not the only person, since the soiree, who has suggested Mr. Kiker intends to court me. While I am flattered and have considered the possibility, I do not believe it."

"Why? You are of a certain age and have many qualities to recommend you."

Phoebe tucked her head down modestly. "It's hard to explain. While we lived in Princeton, I sensed interest from a student or two whom Papa invited to tea. Mr. Kiker acts nothing like them.

Although he is charming and attentive, he rarely talks about himself or his aspirations for the future."

Mr. Bentley paused as if considering his next question. "Has Hugh indicated what he *does* desire?"

"No. He moves quickly from pleasantries to questions that make me feel…"

Mr. Bentley raised an eyebrow, though he leaned in a little closer.

"…quizzed. I don't know how else to put it. You are quizzing me, but this was what we agreed upon. Mr. Kiker asks after Papa's habits or Foster's, or the comings and goings of people around the parsonage. All are observations outside myself. He has never appeared to be interested in anything that takes place within."

"Intriguing…and perhaps helpful. Any idea *why* he is asking?"

How was she to answer truthfully without mentioning Birdie? "Oh—I forgot our attic."

"Your attic? Odd indeed. How do you account for that?"

"I've been hearing inexplicable noises, mostly when everyone has retired for the night. Clara Kiker said a former pastor's child heard them also, and her brother gallantly offered to help me investigate."

"What did the two of you find?"

"We were not able to look. On the occasion he visited, we did not have a chaperone, so we talked on this bench."

"Very judicious. Do you hear them every night? These sounds, I mean."

"I can't say every. I'm often so tired, I immediately fall asleep."

"What about last night?"

Phoebe ran through the minutes she lay quiet in bed, thinking over the day and praying. "You may think me silly: I thought I heard footsteps."

"Footsteps? Might they have been your father's? Perhaps your brother walking in his sleep?"

"I had not thought of that, though it makes better sense than false panels or hidden attic doors. Anyway, Mr. Simmons assures me there are none."

"Charles Simmons? What has he to do with it?"

"He happened by yesterday while Augie and I were speaking about the noises and one thing led to another. All three of us searched the attic thoroughly and found nothing except unused furniture. Besides, the staircase to it is off of our upstairs hall, near our bedrooms. No one outside my family could have gained access."

As he twisted to examine the parsonage, Phoebe wondered if he was losing interest.

"And what," he asked, turning back to her, "are your impressions of Charles?"

"Truthfully? He makes me…ill at ease. It is nothing he has done, exactly. It's the way he examines my…features. When I met him by the river with Mr. Kiker, the contrast in their conduct toward me was marked. To be fair, though, I suspect Mr. Kiker guessed I was the new pastor's daughter. People often treat the clergy and their families more politely than they do others."

"Has he since acted consistently with your first impression?"

For some moments, Phoebe did not answer. She was searching her memory for evidence to support or rebut her feelings. "Yes. Again, Mr. Simmons has *done* nothing to warrant my distrust. It's only the look in his eyes or tension I sense underlying his words. Or it may be my imagination."

"Tension? What sort of tension?"

"I'm not sure. Perhaps thinly veiled anger or resentment, particularly toward the younger Mr. Kiker—less than agreeable glances cast at him while he is looking elsewhere or a tone that belies Mr. Simmons' actual words."

"And he is also this way toward you?"

"No, he is altogether different. His demeanor, even the proximity in which he stands, feels too… personal for our acquaintance."

Mr. Bentley silently looked out over the river for a moment, his head tilted to one side. "What are your thoughts about Foster?"

"Foster?" Phoebe brightened. "Once I got used to his off-kilter eyes, I have found him extraordinarily kind and helpful, every bit as gentlemanly in his way as the two Mr. Kikers. I do not know how we would manage without him."

"I take it you think him trustworthy?"

"Entirely. I would be shocked to find him otherwise."

"What of Charles Simmons' mother, Mahala?"

Again, Phoebe thought before answering. "You are certain my observations will help? I do not wish to supply speculation and gossip."

"More than you realize, and what you tell me will go no further. If we speak of someone I arrest and bring to trial, the facts will then speak for themselves."

"I have an impression her husband was not...kind. No one, not even his widow, has mentioned grieving his loss; and after his funeral, I overheard a...servant...telling her sister he was cruel. Jeremiah said his father beat the Kiker's slaves with a whip." Flicking Mr. Bentley a glance, she was disappointed to find no answering censure and wondered if few southerners thought such behavior shocking. "They expect 'Mr. Charles' will treat them more fairly."

"I sincerely hope he will. What else have you learned?"

As Phoebe tucked her lower lip between her teeth, the lawman's gently searching gaze both encouraged and demanded she continue.

"One woman implied Asa Kiker was Charles Simmons' father, a rumor I have heard alluded to several times during the past few weeks."

When she blushed, Bentley laid a fatherly hand on her shoulder. "I have heard the rumor also. It's of long-standing, so please do not hesitate. For all you or I know, it holds the key to the murderer's motive. What other observations have you made?"

"I've wondered how fond Charles Simmons was of the...victim. If he had heard the rumor, he might have believed it true."

"Wouldn't he resent his mother rather than his father?"

Phoebe looked unconvinced. "If his father was as harsh as I believe him to have been, he might have preferred Asa Kiker were..."

"Ah, I see your point."

"It is only speculation. He appears genuinely fond and protective of his mother."

"Those are just the astute sort of observations that may be important. Can you tell me anything else?"

At first, she shook her head and tucked it down; then she quickly popped it up again. "Yes. I gave it scant notice, but when Mrs. Simmons and her daughters visited, she expressed an interest in seeing a four-poster stowed in our attic. It held memories of her youth spent with a former pastor's daughter. The two had carved hearts in the back with their initials interwoven with the men they hoped to marry. The girls exclaimed excitedly over their mother's, as they were woven with some other man's."

Mr. Bentley raised his eyebrows. "Again, very interesting. Often in these country hamlets, women marry young and begin families. Do you know which initials they were?"

"No." She frowned. "To be candid, I was growing tired of the visit and hoped to return to a book I had started. If you wish, we can go up to the attic and you can see them for yourself."

"Yes. I would like to, however, let's wait until your father can join us. Will he be coming for supper sometime soon?"

"He should be." Phoebe looked behind her shoulder at the sun still hovering fairly high above the roof. "I need to start preparing it soon. Would you care to join us?"

"If it's not an imposition. I enjoy your father. Will your brother object? The circumstances of our last meeting were extraordinarily unpleasant."

Phoebe sighed. "I will be happy to relinquish Augie to my mother's care."

"Asa says he's quite a little imp. Speaking of Asa, what are your opinions of him and Lavinia?"

"I would imagine, as a guest in their home, you know them far better than I do. They have been gracious to my whole family, extending us welcome and offering Augie a darling Chesapeake Bay Retriever pup. Other than topics such as slavery and the components of whiskey making, we have spoken only of the ordinary. On Sunday, Mrs. Kiker offered me a position as her secretary and companion."

"Do you plan to accept it?"

"It depends on my mother's wishes. She arrives tomorrow."

"Oh, excellent. I am looking forward to meeting her. I notice you have only mentioned Clara in passing. I would have thought her a desirable connection."

"I barely know her. Since the Simmonses have been in mourning, she feels the loss of their company, and she's one of the persons who raised questions about Charles' parentage. That is all I can say."

Matthew Bentley studied her intently. "Can or will? I get the impression you are holding something back."

Phoebe breathed in deeply. "It's nothing to the point: I suspect Miss Kiker does not like me, or perhaps she is simply unhappy.

Lavinia alluded to as much, saying she hoped my employment at The Lilacs might also benefit her daughter. How, I do not know."

"I am certain you will be an asset to them both. Would you like to tell me more? You have begun picking at your fingernails."

"I was just..." Phoebe started and stopped. "I recalled something she said about the younger Mr. Kiker and Mr. Simmons."

"Hugh and Charles?"

"Yes. It may be the reason for some of the impressions I offered earlier. Everyone seems to think they are close friends; even Mr...even Hugh told me they grew up seeing each other most days. Yet, she told us the late Mr. Simmons had given her brother a puppy Charles Simmons desired badly and implied it was a source of friction. I'm not sure whether it was over the dog itself or Edward Simmons' attention, and, said aloud, I'm not sure it squares with my other theory."

"Emotions are peculiar things. A boy whose father treats him harshly may cling to him all the more in hope of winning his approval. You said Clara told 'us'. Who else was present?"

"Allison Wilson, Lisa White, Mary Nelson, and her granddaughter Emily."

He wrote the names with a graphite pencil on a small pad he pulled from his breast-pocket. "Do you remember any other particulars?"

"Mr. Kiker did not want the pup if I recall correctly, but his father insisted he take it."

"Odd. Hugh loves his dogs and is an excellent master."

"Miss Kiker implied he had an aversion to the giver. Why, she did not say. It surely cannot bear on your case. Her brother and Charles Simmons were just lads, and I may be reading more into the conversation than existed."

"Still, it *is* interesting. I will follow up with the others you mentioned. If you can bear one more question, I'll let you go about your supper preparations. A young slave woman went missing from The Lilacs on precisely the same day Ed Simmons was killed. What do you know, if anything, about her?"

Phoebe's eyes widened. "Why...how could I know anything? We arrived the day afterward."

"I thought perhaps, especially if you have abolitionist leanings, you might have been enlisted to help conceal…"

"No. No one has asked me anything of the sort. I have met only one young woman who is dark of skin, but she is a freed-man, not a slave."

"May I inquire how and where you…"

Before he finished, he uttered a muffled cry, and Phoebe was engulfed in darkness.

Chapter 19

WHEN PHOEBE HEARD a loud grunt, she could not tell whether it had come from Matthew Bentley or her assailant. She had kicked something less-than-solid, but it might have been the old bench cushion. Struggling to twist free, she tried to scream but instead sucked in a mouthful of fabric and began sputtering to expulse it. The scent reminded her of laundry day, maybe even her handmade soap.

God, help us!

Her captor swiftly pinned her to the grass, winding a cord around the thick fabric with surprising care before tying it about her calves. Then, he hoisted her over a bony shoulder as if she were one of Foster's sacks.

He carried her across level ground, for his pace was steady and lacked the lurching and downward listing she would have expected on the slope. What had happened to Mr. Bentley, she could only guess; she no longer heard any protests. Indeed, she heard nothing except puffs of breath until the feet beneath her crunched over the herb garden's graveled path. They were headed directly away from the church.

When the crunching stopped, Phoebe guessed her assailant had veered onto grass; and within moments she felt an unsteady gait and sway. It announced they were heading down the hill, far beyond the willow and all hope, if Birdie was about, she might run for help.

A cold chill went down Phoebe's spine. Listening intently, she began to wonder if only *she* had been taken. The grass might soften a second assailant's footsteps, but she no longer heard any grunts. Why would anyone take her and leave him? Had the murderer overheard something she had said—something that confirmed his guilt to Mr. Bentley? As she thought of what they might have done to him, she began to feel queasy.

When Phoebe heard a gentle swishing of water and felt the ground level off, she knew they had reached the river. Presently, she heard something sloshing toward them through the ripples and afterward felt herself being lowered onto a firm surface. She was relieved. The man who carried her never faltered beneath her weight, but his shoulder had been pressing into her ribcage.

As he stretched her out lengthwise, he carefully set her head atop a pillow. No—it was not a pillow. Though it was soft, it was also warm. The surface beneath her began to rock, and hands—small, not tiny—protectively cradled her skull. The undulating motion declared they were on some sort of water-craft and the current was slowly floating them down the river. Holding herself still, Phoebe listened for sounds that might betray the identity of her captors or indicate where they were heading. Smelling anything within the thick quilt was impossible.

After a time, they thumped against their destination; but as she struggled to raise herself, the hands cradling her head drew her shoulders back downward. The conveyance began pitching so unsteadily, she knew she had been mistaken. They had not arrived. They were taking on an additional person, and the hands gently restraining her continued their stroking.

At last, they bumped against a bank. Someone must have leaped forward to tie the craft firmly, for the motion changed from severe rocking to placid swaying from side to side. As it dipped back and forth in quick succession, Phoebe assumed her captors were disembarking, and she soon felt herself being lifted. Two people now carried her—one by the arms and the other by the feet—though neither set of hands was small enough to belong to her guardian. No sooner had they rested her on grass than the man who had initially toted her picked her up again. Her ribs recognized his boney shoulder.

As branches frequently skimmed the quilt, she supposed he was thrashing through a forest. Birds took flight, calling out warnings, and water rippled swiftly over rocks or steeply downstream, for its song was more pronounced than the gently flowing river they had left behind.

Several sets of feet thumped up wooden treads, announcing they had reached their destination; and at long last, her porter came to a halt. A hinge rasped as if made of leather, as her captor paused then moved forward, and she heard the familiar scrape of chair legs before feeling herself being lowered onto a seat.

From within the folds of fabric, she called to her captors. "Who are you? Why have you taken me?"

While no one answered, she was sure they heard her muffled questions. One was taking great care to make her comfortable, loosening her bindings and propping her against the chair's high back. If they meant to ransom her, they would be sadly disappointed. Her father had nothing with which to pay, whether they returned her in perfect condition or ill.

After a few minutes, retreating footsteps, the squeaking hinge, and a door thumping securely against its frame led her to suspect she had been abandoned. Still, as she intently listened, she thought she heard breathing followed by deep moaning. Phoebe sighed with relief as she recognized Mr. Bentley's comforting baritone, which, in a short time, grew into surprisingly loud protests.

"PHOEBE, WHERE ARE you?" Pastor Farrell took the stairs to the bedrooms two at a time, puzzled by his daughter's absence. He pulled out his watch to check the time. "It's nearly six o'clock." Opening her door when she didn't answer, he scanned the empty room. The bed was made, as Augie's had been. Scratching his head, he mentally traced his steps. Her book and basket had been on the kitchen table, so she had returned to the house. "She must be in the herb garden or talking with Augie or Foster."

Tromping down to the foyer, he opened the front door and stuck his head outside. None of them was within sight. Going around to the far side of the parsonage, he peeked around the corner. They were not there.

"Phoebe!" He sprinted down to the river. "Augie! Foster!" Hurrying back to the church, he scanned the graveyard and went around the corner to the hitching post, nearly plowing into Asa Kiker. "Oh! Sorry, Asa. I didn't see you coming."

"Phoebe told Hugh your wife is returning tomorrow. I've brought a few things Lavinia sent in welcome. Granny Bett tucked in a jar of her best marmalade." As Mr. Kiker handed over the basket,

147

he took better stock of Reverend Farrell. His hair was disheveled and beads of perspiration dotted his brow. "Are you alright?"

The pastor glanced past him at The Pike. "It's Phoebe. She seems to have vanished into thin air, along with Augie and Foster."

"That can't be."

"No, it can't." Reverend Farrell felt uncharacteristically impatient. "Look, I do not intend to be rude, but with this rash of murders…" He handed back the basket. "I appreciate you coming all this way, Asa. Please thank Lavinia and Granny Bett, however, if you don't mind, just put this in the kitchen. The door is open."

"Could she be chasing Augie? He is full of energy."

"She could well be. Now, if you will excuse me…"

"Of course. I'll put this in the kitchen and help you search."

Reverend Farrell was not sure he wanted the help, though he could not very well refuse it. He felt foolish for kicking up such a fuss. "Thanks. You are probably right. It's not at all like her. She usually has dinner on the table before now, but she hasn't even started it. I don't care that I'm hungry; it's just not her pattern."

After Asa dispatched with the basket, he bent over to replace the bench cushion he saw laying on the grass. "Ernest! Over here."

When the reverend trotted over, he found Asa plumping up the crown of a black straw top hat.

"I found this squashed beneath the cushion." He jutted his chin toward the bench. "It's Matthew Bentley's. Only man around these parts gentrified enough to wear one. Not much use in the fields."

"How odd. I didn't know he was here. He surely wouldn't have taken her in for questioning."

"Not without your permission. They appear to have been drinking tea."

Reverend Farrell stared at the tumblers lying on the grass. "I didn't think anything of them—just Augie and Phoebe being careless. If Bentley was here, why didn't he pop in to the office?"

"No idea." Asa shrugged. "We have found him a bit secretive. Maybe necessary in his line of work. Still, I hardly think he would have left his hat."

Raking a hand through his hair, the reverend glanced about. "Clearly, something's not right."

"I noticed nothing unusual when he left the house." Asa curved the hat's damaged brim. "I'll run up to the Simmons' and send Charles and William with their hounds before I fetch Hugh and our hunters. Nelson's closest, but he doesn't own dogs."

The reverend merely nodded, grim-faced, and walked down the slope. "Lord," he muttered as Asa rode off. "I have no idea what to do. Where can they possibly be?" He looked upstream and down. "You never promised our lives would be free of trouble, but please not this. Don't let anyone hurt either of them. I just don't know what I'd do if..."

He could not finish his sentence. Dropping down to his knees, he could think only of Silas Rugger slumped over a desk, a knife plunged in his back.

"Lord, if not for me, for Amelia. She didn't want to move here any more than the children, yet Your will in the matter seemed so clear. Was I mistaken? Were you not in this? Oh, what have I gotten us into?"

From somewhere inside, words once forgotten bubbled up in his memory: *I will instruct thee and teach thee the way which thou shalt go. I will guide thee with mine eye.*

"Alright, Lord. I am counting on you. If I have erred in my judgment or veered off course, please correct me as only You can. Please have mercy on my little ones, and also Matthew Bentley."

"MR. BENTLEY, IS that you?" Trapped in the thick fabric folds, Phoebe could see nothing.

"Miss Farrell? What happened?"

"I don't know. While we were talking, someone put a blanket over my head and tied me inside it. From its scent, I'm guessing it's one of the parsonage's quilts."

"They did the same to me, only someone hit me in the head when I didn't comply. Are you hurt?"

"No, only uncomfortable."

"My head is throbbing. I'm completely encased and hot as blazes."

"I'm the same. My arms are pinned to my sides."

"Can you see anything?"

"A little. The man loosened the quilt around my head, but the edge is too tall to peer over. I can make out the ceiling."

"What is it made of?"

"Wood only rounder, maybe logs, though that may be a trick of the light. It's not quite dark yet."

"Are you seated or lying on the ground?"

"Sitting on a chair with a high back. My shoulders are tied to it."

"Same here. You said it's not quite dark. Any idea what time? The blow knocked me out."

Phoebe paused to think. "It was about five when I asked you to supper, and we talked a while afterward. Between six-thirty and seven?"

"So they did not take us far. What sort of conveyance?"

"A boney shoulder to the river, a boat or raft, and the same shoulder through trees."

Mr. Bentley softly laughed. "I said you have the makings of a fine detective. Anything else you can tell me?"

"They were surprisingly gentle, taking several measures to make me comfortable."

"I wish I could say the same. Wait." He lowered his voice to a whisper. "Do you hear something?"

Phoebe remained quiet, listening until she heard it, too. From the direction of the hinge came soft footsteps. They made her think of occasions her brother had tried to sneak up on her. The door began to rattle.

"Ow!"

"Augie?" Phoebe had never been happier to hear his voice.

"Sh-sh." He whispered. "They might still be in earshot."

As she silently waited, Phoebe noticed the light had almost disappeared. "What are you doing?"

"What do you think I'm doing?" he hissed. "I'm trying to cut through the rope."

"What rope?"

"Tying the door shut."

"Son," called Matthew Bentley. "Can you find a window?"

"Maybe."

The two captives listened while Augie jumped from the wooden porch, ran along the side of the building, and thrashed into the forest.

In a matter of seconds, they heard repetitive pounding and banging until a shutter clanged open.

Huffing and puffing, and with a great many grunts, Augie scrambled up over the sill to drop onto the wooden floor. "Finally. I thought I'd never bust through." Phoebe felt her quilt being folded down like a collar. "Hi."

"I'm so glad to see you. How did you find us?"

"Hold on. Let me at least pull down Mr. Bentley's quilt. Hey, isn't it the one you accused me of taking?"

"I can't see to say. Free Mr. Bentley first."

"Alright." Although Augie pulled out his penknife and sawed against the ropes, the sun had almost set before he managed to cut through the first.

"Thanks, son." Mr. Bentley rubbed his arms to circulate the blood. "If you will let me use that, I might be able to make faster progress."

Taking the knife, he sawed through the rope binding his legs, reached into his pocket, and pulled out another knife. "Here, Augie, use this one. It's longer and considerably sharper. While you tackle the rope around your sister's shoulders, I'll free her feet. Be careful. Don't cut towards her but away."

"Yes sir. This knife's a beauty."

"Keep it. You've certainly earned it."

"Wow—thanks!"

Once they'd freed Phoebe, her legs were so stiff she almost stumbled while rising from the chair. She grabbed her brother, hugged him hard, and planted a big kiss on his cheek. "Augie, you're wet."

"I know. Don't break my ribs!" Extricating himself from her embrace, he looked at Matthew Bentley, or at least at the place he had been. It was pitch black now. He corrected his direction when he heard the door shaking.

"As I suspect you discovered, Augie, we can't get out through this way. It's fastened tight. What's on the other side of the window?"

Augie shrugged. "Just the side of the cabin and a bunch of trees."

Mr. Bentley stuck his head out a square of night sky that contrasted slightly with the cabin's blackness. "Must be deep within the woods. I don't see any stars."

Both Phoebe and Augie answered.

"One at a time. I didn't understand either of you. You first, Miss Farrell."

"I felt branches brushing against me once we left the boat."

"Yep," added Augie. "We're in the forest beyond the South Branch, past the parsonage's park."

"Any idea how much further?" asked Matthew Bentley. "About the same width again as the Park's frontage along the river or further?"

"About double."

"How far is the drop from this window?"

"I had to pull a log-round over to stand on, but I kicked it over when I was trying to climb in."

Matthew let out a puff of frustration. "Then I'm afraid we'd best stay here tonight."

"We can't." Phoebe fretted. "Our father will be so worried, and our mother…"

"That's right," cried Augie. "Mama's coming on the early train."

"I don't like it any better than you two. We've no choice. Even if we all manage to climb out safely, we might lose our way in the woods. Better to wait until daybreak."

"But what if they come back?"

"If my suspicions are correct, they won't. Miss Farrell, you have already told me what you heard. Augie, if you will, please describe your journey here in as much detail as you can remember."

"I tracked them until they started getting into a boat they'd hid in a cove."

"So you saw them?"

"I was up in that big old willow when they grabbed you from the bench."

"Did you go for help?"

"Didn't have time. When they cut across the park, I was afraid I'd lose sight of you."

"You're probably right. How many were there?"

"Four. One toting Phoebe, one toting you, and another walking behind. The fourth one got on downriver. I couldn't get a real good look at any of them. They were too far off."

"Take your time and tell it just as it happened."

"I trailed them until they got in the boat, and then I didn't know what to do. We never lived around much water except an old swimming hole."

"So what did you do?"

"I snuck alongside the river, keeping to the bushes until I saw them heading to the other side."

"What then, son?"

"I just waded out into the shallows, keeping my eyes on them, and when it got too deep, I just plunged in."

"Augie, you were so brave!" cried his sister. "No wonder you're so wet. Take off those wet clothes and wrap up in my quilt!"

Augie grinned, though in the dark they didn't see him. "Already did. I don't need yours. They left extras."

"Your sister is right. You showed a lot of courage."

"I was too scared to stop. At one point, I thought I was a goner. I gulped in a mouthful of water and went to sputtering."

"Oh Augie, you could have drowned. What did you do?"

He knew the face Phoebe was making, even in the dark. "What could I do? I kept swimming as straight as I could until I bumped my head into a tree root."

"Were you hurt?"

"Nah."

"I'm glad to hear it, son. What happened next? Take it slow and try to picture each detail."

"Just righted myself and scrambled up the bank. I feared I'd lost them, but I heard branches breaking up ahead and spotted the color of your bundles."

"What bundles?"

"The quilts. They looked like long, colorful bundles."

"You said you couldn't get a good glimpse of their faces. Can you tell us anything about them?"

"Well...the leader was real tall and huge—like Goliath. He was toting you as if you weighed nothing but a twig. He made me scared of what might happen if I caught up."

"So what did you do?"

"I prayed—like Papa taught us, and thanked God for keeping away the cottonmouths. Then I did what David did and searched for some rocks."[xi]

Mr. Bentley chuckled. "Did you find any?"

"Nah. Just a couple of pinecones. Anyway, I didn't have a sling."

"What else did you notice—about the tall man? Did he remind you of anyone?"

"Yeah, now that you mention it. He reminded me of a slave I met in the Kikers' kitchen."

"He was dark?"

"It's hard to say. The sun was setting, and they all wore hats like Foster's. The one he wears when he's gardening, to keep from getting burnt."

"See, Augie? You are remembering more and more. What of the others—who do they remind you of?"

"Well, the scrawny one reminded me of Silas Rugger."

"Couldn't be Rugger; he's dead. You think it might have *been* Foster?"

"Nah, no way. He likes Phoebe; I'm sure of it. Besides, why snatch her while she's talking with a lawman? Every day since we've been there would have been more convenient. Could've been Lyin' John. Mr. Kiker said he was the man I saw running away from the office."

"I do indeed, and you've confirmed a suspicion. What about the other two?"

"The man they took on was sort of medium all around: not too tall or short or fat or thin. While I was peering through the trees, trying to make out their faces, I thought the one who'd been sitting in the boat might not be a man at all. He was wearing a blue fro......"

Phoebe jabbed him in the ribs, or tried to, as several puzzling pieces began to fit together. "Augie, this is no time to be fanciful. Many men wear blue. Anyway, you were trailing a good distance behind them."

"Oh...uh...right. It might have been a shirt. I followed them here and waited until they left."

"Augie, your father and mother should be proud of you. Indeed, they have good reason to be proud of you both."

"You are very kind, Mr. Bentley," answered Phoebe. "Do you think whoever they are gone?"

"I do, indeed, Miss Farrell. I doubt any of us will see them again—at least not as kidnappers."

Chapter 20

AUGIE SHOOK HIS sister awake. "Come on, Phebes. Get up. It's getting light outside."

With effort, Phoebe pulled her eyelids open, surprised at first by the sights awaiting her. "I must have fallen asleep." She took in the log walls, the plank floor, the splintered shutter hanging from the window, and the quilt her brother had shed. It *was* the one missing from her room.

"Mr. Bentley, it's morning." She tentatively jiggled a jacketed arm lying across the many-colored quilt she once had noticed hanging from the parsonage clothesline.

Springing to a seated position, the lawman shook his head as if ridding it of cobwebs. "What time is it?" Without waiting for an answer, he jumped up, thrust his head out the window frame, and pulled it back in. "Good morning, Miss Farrell, Augie." He smiled. "Did you sleep alright?"

Phoebe was stretching her shoulders. "Barely a wink."

"I slept like a log." Augie dragged over one of the chairs and stuck half his body out the opening.

"Careful!" Phoebe grasped hold of the back of his britches. Glancing over her shoulder, she saw Mr. Bentley by the door, digging Augie's knife into the wood around its hinges.

"Stand back." He sent both children a stern look and thrust his weight against it. With a loud thud, it burst open, leaving a swath of sunshine in its place.

Augie flung his arms into the air. "We're free!"

Following him outside, Phoebe located Mr. Bentley. "Any sight of them?"

"No." He was peeking around the other side of the structure. "But they left us food and water." As he nodded to a sack on the porch, Augie dropped down and thrust his hand into its mouth.

"Corn muffins!"

When Bentley returned from circling the cabin, he found Phoebe unplugging the top of a leather flask. "Don't drink too much. We should ration the water. We don't yet know how far we are from the parsonage."

Impressed with his calm, she took a much-needed draw. "You don't think they might return for us?"

"Highly unlikely. The fastenings on the door gave way far too easily, as if they had no intention of keeping us." He slid his eyes toward the cabin and nodded to Augie, who was still holding the sack. "Even less of causing us any real harm. I suspected they just wanted us out of the way."

Phoebe thought for a moment. "That would explain…"

Augie interrupted, but his mouth was so stuffed with cornbread, his words were garbled.

"Swallow first."

He did. "Why?"

"So you don't choke."

Augie tossed his gaze to the treetops. "I know that! Why would someone want you two out of the way?"

Mr. Bentley stepped from the porch. "Excellent question, though I'm afraid I don't yet have an answer, unless…" As both children cocked their heads inquisitively, he looked piercingly at Phoebe. "What were we talking about just before they threw those quilts over our heads?"

"So many things." She shrugged. "Mostly Mr. Simmons' murder. Do you think we'll get home in time to pick up our Mother?"

"We'll try." He peered down one trail and then the other. "Augie, do you know which of these two paths you took?"

"That one—it led me straight to the porch."

"Very good."

Putting his arm through the flasks' leather strap, he took the sack of muffins from Augie, handed it to Phoebe, and set off down the sun spattered path. The morning was already growing brighter, and in remarkably little time, they reached the edge of the woods.

As Phoebe picked her way through the weeds on the bank, she glanced down at her skirt and considered the layers of petticoats it covered. "How are we to cross, Mr. Bentley?"

Staring upriver, he broke into a wide grin. "In a boat as sound as any I have ever come across."

Following his gaze, she spotted a skiff in the distance, carrying a man as black as the forest's shadows. He was kneeling in the bow, searching the trees as he shaded his brow from the eastern light. Before Augie could grab Mr. Bentley's arm, the agent called out loudly. "Kitch! Over here!"

Augie glanced at his sister, his brow full of fretful wrinkles until he heard a voice that smoothed them away.

"Augie! Phoebe!" A second boat had rounded a bend, transporting a man waving so wildly he threatened to overturn it. Flanking him were Asa Kiker and Colonel Nelson, followed by eleven or twelve smaller boats and rafts.

"Papa! Papa!" Both children cried with glee as a dark-skinned pilot guided him to the bank.

Leaping to the shore, their father pulled them into a crushing embrace. "I've never been so scared in my life." He glanced over their heads at Matthew Bentley, his eyes shining with gratitude.

"Papa," said Phoebe. "How did you know where to find us?" While she smiled up at their father, Augie noticed the lawman eyeing Kitch.

"We didn't, Kitten. We've been up all night, scouring the park and adjacent properties; and when we couldn't find you, Foster suggested we search the woods opposite."

Turning toward the caretaker, seated just behind Asa Kiker and Colonel Nelson, Bentley saw he was both pleased and relieved to see the children. As several searchers began lobbing well-intended questions, Matthew gestured for everyone's attention. "When we land at the church, I'll fill in all the details. The Farrells have a train to meet."

His two charges hugged him with such gusto, he had to brace himself to keep from stumbling backward. Rejoining their father, they boarded the boat, assisted by a beaming Foster, who debarked to give them room.

Matthew Bentley, watching the caretaker board the forward skiff, spoke in a low voice to Asa Kiker. "When, exactly, did Foster join the search?"

Mr. Kiker considered a moment before responding. "I can't say. I first remember seeing him in the wee hours. I left to rouse a tracking party as soon as we discovered the children were missing."

Gary Nelson, who had obviously heard, leaned closer. "Foster came to fetch me first. He knew I'd be eager to help."

When they arrived on the bank of the church's park, Phoebe scanned the womenfolk scurrying down the hill. Lavinia Kiker looked as if she had endured a long night of worrying. Mary and Emily beamed with relief. Even Ruby and Mitilde hung close to the crowd's edges with expressions Phoebe labeled well-wishing. She might have even called it budding affection.

Mahala Simmons all but clucked as she separated the Farrells from the crowd. "Let them go get cleaned up. Bless their little hearts. They need to hurry if they are to meet their mother's train. Go on into the parsonage, children, and get out of those soiled clothes. My girls are heating water on the stove and we'll bring up your pitchers as soon as it's warm."

Phoebe was grateful. She felt self-conscious about her state of disarray and did not know how to answer their baskets-full of questions. Though their concern touched her heart, she yearned to see her mother.

AUGIE PACED BACK and forth on parsonage walkway, waiting for his father to pull the wagon up the lane. "You don't need to guard me, Foster, honest."

"Not guardin'. Just makin' sure you're alright. Yer Pa raised quite a ruckus. Must o' raised half the county."

"'Quite?' You've been hanging around Phoebe too much."

"Wouldn't hurt none if I picked up some o' your sister's habits, but I 'spect I'm too old fer refining."

"Is everyone gone?"

"No, they's still in the church, talkin' with the gov'ner's agent."

Phoebe ambled over from the peony bushes with a basket full of fresh-cut blooms.

Augie wrinkled his nose. "Who needs refining? I don't know why Mrs. Simmons insisted we wash up. We're going to get dusty again riding up The Pike. Phoebe, you better hurry. Papa's almost finished hitching up Esmerelda."

"I'll just run in and stick these in a vase."

After a second or two, Augie ducked into the front door and called to her. "Come on. We're ready to go."

"I'm coming." Phoebe hurried out, pulling the door shut, and climbed up next to her father on the wagon seat. "Don't get your clothes dirty back there, Augie."

"I'm not. Papa, can we stop at The Lilacs on the way back? I want to see Sparkles."

"Well son, you've just had an exhausting adventure and your mother may be equally tired. No doubt, she'd prefer to meet the Kikers appearing her best."

"Mama always looks beautiful."

Reverend Farrell smiled. "Augie, I agree with you. I often think she is her prettiest when her hair is tied up and her cheeks are pink from cooking and cleaning, but if I know your mother, she will assume she appears as worn out as she will feel."

"I can't wait to see her—and Lucy. I wonder if she'll look the same."

Phoebe pulled her brows together, thinking his question decidedly silly.

"We'll just have to see, son. Babies do change quickly at her age."

"You think she'll be walking?"

"I doubt it. It's been less than a month, and she wasn't even crawling when they left."

The trip up to Winchester seemed far longer than Phoebe had remembered, perhaps because she was fighting to keep her eyes open. Between alarm and uncomfortable surroundings, she had slept only on and off during the night. The scenery also held less interest, as much of it was no longer new. "I hope Mama will like the way I've arranged everything."

"She'll think you a wonder, Kitten." Her father put his arm around her and gave her an affectionate squeeze. "I know I do."

Phoebe leaned against him. Since she had finished most of the harder work, she had begun enjoying their new home, though the events of yesterday had raised a multitude of alarms. Why had Spry been tracking Birdie? The girl had claimed she was free. He claimed the role of the local law. Did he suspect she had murdered Simmons? Impossible.

As she wandered back over his questions, she found them nearly identical to Hugh's. However, she surmised, or at least hoped, Hugh's sprang from different motives. What had he meant by confiding 'Birdie was one of his mother's favorites'? Favorite *what?* It was certainly hard to imagine the two of them sharing tea.

Thinking of Lavinia's proposal, she began to grow uneasy. Her salary would likely derive from income earned by slaves. When she recalled Hugh's opinion on the offer, her cheeks began to warm. He was easily the most handsome man she had ever met, but she certainly did not share his assessment of her appearance. She thought it rather ordinary.

"I hear the train." Reverend Farrell could not hide his excitement. "We'll need to hurry if we are going to be on the platform before your mother steps off. Augie, jump down and run there ahead of us."

The boy did as he was asked while his father lifted down his older sister. "Mama! Lucy!" He trotted alongside the compartment as the engine came to a halt, waving as they pressed their faces against the glass. "Hurry, Phebes! They're getting up."

Phoebe and Papa climbed the step up to the platform, making their way as fast as they could through the rush of disembarking passengers.

"Ah, Amelia—you are a joy to behold."

"Oh, Ernest. Three weeks is far too long." As they swiftly embraced, she gazed over his shoulder at her two eldest and teared up. "Look at the two of you." She handed off Lucy to her husband and encompassed Augie and Phoebe in her warm, possessive arms. "I do believe you've both grown, though I hardly think that's possible. I'd almost swear you are taller, Augie, and, Phoebe, you have gained such an air of maturity."

Phoebe glowed. She had not allowed herself to wallow in pining, but once she laid eyes on her mother, all the days of missing her came rushing to the fore.

"Boy," cried Augie, "do we have a lot to tell you." When he glanced at his father, however, he saw the quick shake of his head. "I've got two frogs, and Mr. Kiker is giving me a puppy, if you give me permission to accept him, that is. Can I keep him, Mama, can I?"

161

"Hold your horses, son. Your mother hasn't been off the train for two minutes and the pup is still at The Lilacs. Here, Amelia, take Lucy. She has grown so accustomed to possessing all of you, she's starting to fuss. She acts like she no longer knows me."

"Ernest, do not take it to heart." Taking the baby, she gazed up at him tenderly. "For one so young, it's been a very long time. She'll soon grow accustomed to you all. And of course, you can keep your puppy, Augie." Mama appeared as if she would say yes to anything at the moment. "As long as you are willing to care for him yourself. As you can see, my hands are full."

"I will! Mr. Kiker and Hugh are teaching me how to train him."

"Hugh? Is he the caretaker Deacon Nelson wrote to us about?"

"No," her husband replied. "His name is Foster. Hugh is Asa and Lavinia Kiker's son. And Augie, you are to call him Mr. Kiker. He seems to have taken a shine to our daughter."

Arching an eyebrow, Amelia turned to Phoebe. "You have a new beau?"

"He's just a friend."

"Ah. 'Just a friend'? That's what I said about your father."

Augie appeared as if the notion had never occurred to him. "What would Hugh—Mr. Kiker—want with Phoebe? I mean, she's alright and all as a sister, but he's rich."

"Well, son," replied the reverend, "not every rich man desires only money. Your sister has charms of which you are unaware." He glanced reassuringly at his oldest, who in turn looked as if she would prefer to be invisible.

"She certainly does." Her mother caressed her cheek. "Any man would be fortunate to win her heart, though I'd thought it might be previously engaged. Speaking of Samuel, he asked me to give you this."

She took a letter out of her reticule as her husband and son retrieved her luggage.

"It's not post-marked. When did you see him?"

"Just before I boarded the train." Seeing her daughter's surprise, she explained. "He was in Baltimore meeting his father's train from Washington, and you will never believe who was with him."

"Who, Mama?"

162

"That sweet boy and girl who lived down the block from us—the rather timid ones with the auburn hair."

"Philip and Hannah?"

"Yes. You would not believe how tall he is, and she's grown into a beauty."

"What were they doing in Baltimore?"

"As I recall, Samuel promised to introduce Philip to his father. He is a Senator now, you know. Something about West Point."

"Oh." Phoebe slipped the letter into her reticule, feeling uncomfortably uncertain. Reaching out for Lucy, she began cooing. "Look at you. You *have* changed. Come on, come to sissy. Don't you remember me?"

Lucy recoiled, tucking her head beneath her mother's chin. "She's been a little less friendly since we went to my parents'—all the new surroundings and unfamiliar people vying to handle her every day. I'm afraid she's become a Mama's girl, but so were you, and I am so proud of how you turned out."

Contenting herself with stroking her sister's soft hair, Phoebe dimpled. "I'll always want you, Mama. I've missed you terribly."

"I will always want you, too. I love having you as a friend now that you are so grown. When you do marry, I hope the Lord sees fit to keep you close to me. I would hate for your husband to take you far away. Samuel said his sister has moved across the country—Oregon Territory."

"I don't think you'll have to worry about that."

"Oh? Is there something to what your father was implying?"

Phoebe turned as red as the roses growing along the train station's split-rail fence. "No. I meant now since you are home, I don't wish to leave."

"And Augie? Has he been much trouble?"

Making a mental inventory of the past few weeks, Phoebe landed on his recent heroics. "No. He has been in some ways, quite wonderful."

"I'm glad. One of my fondest hopes is for my children to grow up loving each other."

"How is Grandmother?"

"Let's save that for a discussion at home. Your father and brother will no doubt want to hear, and it is painful to repeat it over and over."

While her husband helped her and Lucy up onto the wagon seat, he tossed Phoebe a grateful smile. She was already climbing into the back with her brother so they could sit comfortably side by side.

"Mama," called Augie, unable to keep quiet any longer. "There's been another murder."

"Another?"

"Son, your mother will no doubt hear all the unpleasant details as she visits people from our congregation, so you needn't mention them now. Amelia, I am afraid your first visit must be to Mahala Simmons. She's the widow of the man we first heard was murdered and a member of our congregation."

"Oh, Ernest. What sort of place is this?"

"Aw Papa, can't we take Mama up to The Lilacs first? Mrs. Kiker will be eager to meet her too. I heard her tell Phoebe she is."

"All in due time, son, but for now, let's get your mother—and you and your sister—home."

Chapter 21

PHOEBE KNOCKED ON her parents' bedroom door the next morning before sticking her head inside. "May I come in?"

"Of course." Her mother put aside the shawl she was folding and wrapped her daughter in a snug embrace. "It's so good to be home, although I woke up wondering exactly *which* home I was in."

"I'm glad you are here."

Smiling tenderly, Amelia brushed a stray lock of hair from her daughter's face. "It sounds like you have been through quite an ordeal. You must have been so frightened."

"I was, but I don't think they meant to hurt me. Once they lifted me onto the boat, someone…" Phoebe stopped, unsure how much she might safely divulge. "They made sure I was unharmed and comfortable."

"I simply do not understand. Why kidnap someone without asking a ransom?"

Phoebe snuggled back against her mother, afraid of what her face might betray. The further she had considered Mr. Bentley's conclusions, the more deeply she felt convinced of their motive. "I suppose we may never precisely know."

"I am just glad to have you safe and sound. In one way, I am glad I wasn't here. I would have been beside myself with worry, which is the last thing your father would have needed."

"Mama, Augie was so courageous. He swam across the river to save me."

"That's what your father said. Thank you, by the way, for taking such good care of them." Disengaging, she nodded to the wardrobe. "You have done everything excellently."

"I wanted to make your homecoming as easy as I could. I meant to make you a fine breakfast."

"I would much rather have had you sleep. Come and sit down."

As she patted the bed, Phoebe scrambled onto it, tucking her feet under her nightdress.

"Do you mind if I continue unpacking my bag?"

"No. Go ahead."

"The Nelsons dropped by last night. They seem like a fine family. They were all sorry to miss you and Augie, but they understood why you both went to bed so early."

"I like them very much."

"You look like something else is weighing on your mind."

"It's about Mrs. Kiker. She offered to employ me as her secretary-companion and, now that you are home, I can't put her off any longer."

"What sort of woman is she?"

"Intimidating, but she is also gracious and warm—very much the *grande dame* of the neighborhood."

"Your father intimated her son—Harrold or Howard—fancies you."

"His name is Hugh. There is nothing in that, honestly. You know how fathers are. They love their little girls and assume everyone else does."

"Well, any man's interest in you would not surprise me the least. His mother is another story. Offering you a position sends the opposite message."

"I hadn't thought."

"So if it's not a matter of Mrs. Kiker's son, why are you hesitant to work for her?"

Phoebe looked down at her hands. "They own slaves, Mama. While we lived in New Jersey—or even during our discussion on the train—I found it distasteful. Since I've become...acquainted with some, I've begun to care more deeply."

"Is there something you aren't telling me? You're squeezing your fingers so tightly your knuckles are turning white."

Phoebe glanced up and quickly down again. "Yes. I've been keeping a secret, but it isn't mine to divulge, even to you. Mostly, I do not wish to be paid out of profits from slave labor."

"Ah. I understand. It's something your father and I discussed and prayed over when he was considering this pastorate. Inevitably, some of the revenues in the church coffers will come from the Kikers and others like them."

"Oh. I never gave it a thought."

"We can't tell them they cannot give, especially if they see nothing wrong with what they are doing. Like most issues, this one has many sides."

Phoebe rolled her eyes. "I know. Everywhere we have gone with Papa, the subject has come up."

"It is bound to, but if only pastors who agree with slavery fill southern pulpits, those views will hold sway over the people's hearts. Besides, if you will not work for someone with whom you disagree, for whom *will* you work? Few people, even pastors, hold precisely the same convictions. If they did, we would not have so many church denominations."

"Mama, I believe it is a sin."

"So do I. Still, as your father explained on the train, only changed hearts will lastingly change habits. I'm glad to see you approach this so seriously, but perhaps you should ask a different question: How may you best serve the Kikers' slaves?"

When a gentle knock drew their attention to Reverend Farrell, his wife crossed to the doorway and placed a warm kiss on his cheek. "I am so happy to be home with all of you. Phoebe and I were discussing the position Mrs. Kiker offered."

"I heard." He looked straight at Phoebe. "I didn't wish to barge in, Kitten, if you wanted to speak with your mother privately."

"No, please join us. I would like your opinion."

"I agree with your mama. I'm hard-pressed to see how you can love our new neighbors while holding yourself apart from them."

"Would Jesus want me to accept money gained through sin? Wouldn't that make me a participant?"

"An excellent question. What of Daniel? He and his three friends all derived their livelihood from a proud pagan emperor. It's clear God placed them in their positions."

"They had no choice, Papa. I do. What if Molly, the girl who lived above the tavern, wanted me to keep track of which men had paid her?"

Her mother's mouth fell open. "How do you know anything about those sorts of things?"

167

"I asked Samuel why a number of his fellow students came out of her door so early in the morning."

"And he explained what she did?"

"Not exactly." Phoebe dimpled when she spied her father studying his feet. "He turned bright red and began stammering, but between his embarrassment and the little he said, I understood the gist."

Her father cleared his throat. "I see your point, and I can also see all those hours spent debating with my theology students has paid off. What if she were ill and needed care? Would you be willing to give it?"

"Yes, but I would not help her carry out her business pursuits. Would you allow me to care for her?"

"I would hope so. Do you think you might come up with a similar compromise—not of your convictions but of how you might carry them out? Hugh said she has been beset by debilitating headaches. Perhaps you could demonstrate your care for her by helping her catch up with her correspondence. I doubt she sends letters promoting slavery."

"But Papa, I don't want to help someone who keeps slaves."

"I see. You think she is undeserving of it."

Phoebe winced.

"What of Levi, the tax collector? He was likely an inveterate cheat. Did Jesus hold him at a distance until he repented?"[xii]

"No, but I am not Jesus. I don't have His ability to see into a person's heart."

"That's the point, Kitten. I understand your feelings. I struggled with them myself until I read an uncomfortably similar question Jesus posed to Simon the Pharisee."[xiii]

Phoebe's cheeks went hot. She knew exactly what question Simon asked. Her father had preached about it last Sunday.

"The truth is, my lovely daughter, none of us know what goes on in another person's heart, and if we did, we wouldn't find anyone fit for God's Kingdom. If I kept Asa at arms-length because I consider him less righteous than I am, what would that reveal about me?"

"You think you are more deserving of God's approval."

"And what's wrong with that?" He flung up his palms. "Most folks deem themselves superior to *someone*. In fact, some men think they are so far superior to particular others, they feel entitled to *own* them."

Phoebe's hands flew to her mouth.

Father nodded. "Superiority is a very ugly sin and one to which we are all prone one way or another—especially those of us who ardently desire to obey Jesus—and we have the least excuse."

"Oh Papa, I feel ashamed. I know I am as deeply in need of God's grace as the Kikers."

"As am I. Jesus' first sermon began, 'Blessed are the poor in spirit,'[xiv]—those fully aware they cannot atone for their sin. To them belongs the Kingdom of Heaven."

AUGIE JUMPED DOWN the last two stairs leading to the foyer. "Hey, Phebes, what were you talking about with Mama and Papa?"

"Whether or not I should work for Mrs. Kiker."

"Will you?"

"Yes. Papa is going to drive me up there today."

"I want to go. I can play with Sparkles. Mama said I can keep him."

"I heard. I'm sure they expect you to since Mama is coming. On our way, we're stopping by the Simmons'." Her eyes twinkled. "You can tell Jeremiah all about your adventure."

Augie grinned from ear to ear. "Papa." Their father had just stuck his head through the front door. "Phebes says we're visiting the Simmonses and the Kikers."

"Yes. I didn't tell you? Why don't you two get into the wagon? Mama and I will be there shortly. Amelia, are you ready?"

"I'm coming." Amelia swished down the path, and Ernest lifted her into place. "Remind me of their names?"

"Mrs. Simmons is named Mahala. Her late husband was Edward. Her oldest son is Charles, followed closely by William. We have not seen much of him. She has three daughters, though I'm afraid I've forgotten what they are called."

"Virginia, Megan, and Sarah," replied Phoebe. "Virginia is my age. Megan is a couple of years younger, and Sarah is nine or ten. Jeremiah is the baby."

"Nuh-uh." Augie pulled a face. "He's not a baby. He's as old as me."

"Don't correct your sister, dear." Amelia twisted backward and ruffled her son's hair. "She only meant he is the youngest, and we all know you are not a baby. Look how brave you were while rescuing Phoebe."

"Very brave, indeed, son." His father smiled. "Matthew Bentley told me all about you knocking through the shutters. He said you 'showed method' every step of the way."

Amelia's face crumpled as she shifted Lucy to her other shoulder. "Oh, how did you all manage?"

"It was nothing." Augie shrugged. "Almost fun."

"You wouldn't call it fun if you were inside one of the quilts. I thought I'd pass out."

As they turned into the Simmons' lane, Reverend Farrell pointed to a black horse tied to a fence post. "Speaking of Mr. Bentley, look. I wonder if he's discovered anything about the bootlegger."

Augie screwed up his face as if he was thinking hard. "I think he—not Silas Rugger, the other—might have been one of Phoebe's kidnappers. Do you remember when we spotted him running? One of the four I followed looked just like him, or at least as much as I could tell."

Charles came out of the barn, brushed off his britches, and ambled over to the wagon. "Morning, Pastor. Is this Mrs. Farrell? I'm Charles." He held out his hand to Amelia.

"It's a pleasure to meet you, ma'am."

"Miss Farrell." Charles extended a hand to help Phoebe climb down from the wagon as Augie jumped.

"Where's Jeremiah?"

"He's just inside the door there." Tilting his head toward the barn, Charles let go of Phoebe's waist.

"Is this a good time to call?" Pastor Farrell squinted in the sun. "I hoped to introduce your mother to my wife, but I notice she has a visitor."

"She'd shoot me if I said 'no.' Besides, Mr. Bentley mentioned he was planning to stop at your place next to check on the *children.*" He winked at Phoebe.

"Is that Reverend Farrell?" Mrs. Simmons sashayed through the door. "And this must be Amelia?"

"Yes. The prodigal bride has returned."

"Come in. I'd hardly think taking care of her mother qualifies her as prodigal."

"You are quite right, Mahala." The pastor smiled at his wife. "I stand corrected."

Once they went inside and included Mr. Bentley in the pleasantries, the agent addressed Mrs. Simmons. "Would it be alright with you, Mahala, if I borrowed Charles and the reverend for a private conversation?"

"Of course. Virginia and Megan, why don't you take Phoebe to your room?"

Glancing at Phoebe, he cleared his throat. "If you do not mind, I would like to keep Miss Farrell with us. I have some questions that may pertain to her."

Charles looked pleased with the prospect despite his sisters' disappointment. "We can use Pa's office."

As he opened the door, Phoebe was hit by the reek of cigars and whiskey. A nearly empty bottle of it behind the desk. It was odd, she thought, that Asa Kiker's study did not smell the same way. Both held similar objects. Perhaps Mr. Simmons indulged more frequently or perhaps it was a product of his general cleanliness. This office was so strewn with papers and other paraphernalia, she needed to wait until Charles cleaned off the window seat so she could sit down.

A braided whip, coiled around a hook near the door, gave Phoebe a chill. Edward Simmons had evidently earned his reputation. Hanging next to the whip was the wide-brimmed hat—or one very like it—she had seen Charles wear on occasion. She felt relieved when her father took the seat closest to her.

While Charles sat down behind the desk, Matthew Bentley pulled up the chair adjacent to it. "Charles, I've learned something recently about the bootlegger your little brother and Augie saw in your barn. He is the same man the Farrells spotted running from The Lilacs' business office."

Charles flicked his eyes to Phoebe.

"She saw him too and was waiting in the wagon when Ernest discovered the second murder. The doctor confirmed the cause of death, though it was a mere formality, and his identity: one Silas Rugger. Several witnesses have claimed he was a *friend* of your father's."

"Pa knew everyone in this valley."

"Are you aware he was stealing The Lilacs' whiskey for the two Rugger brothers to sell on the side?"

Pressing his lips into a tight line, Charles looked down at the desk, though Phoebe could not tell if he was chagrinned or embarrassed. He was not surprised. "I reckon so." He raked a hand through the dark waves on the back of his head. "I didn't want to believe it, but I came across this on Tuesday." He handed Bentley a small, well-worn notebook, sized to fit in a man's coat pocket.

"Mind if I keep it?" Bentley flipped through the pages.

"No, go ahead. Do you think this has anything to do with his death?"

"Your father's? I did. I thought the Rugger brothers got greedy, however, it doesn't fit the evidence or actually make much sense. Your father had easy access to the brewery. Now, all they've been able to do is try to cover their tracks—and not very well." He glanced significantly at Reverend Farrell. "Mr. Greer, the owner of the tavern, sent for me early this morning. It seems Lying John was in his cups last evening. Confessed the entire incident to one of Greer's barmaids before he passed out. The brothers did indeed try to alter Kiker's accounts. Then they began arguing over something—I can't say what. Lying John was not exactly coherent when we hauled him in. One thing led to another as they fought." Beyond his shoulder, he heard Phoebe inhale sharply.

"He stabbed his brother and just left him there?"

Matthew nodded. "The barmaid reports he was horrified by what he had done, but he knew by the amount of..." His eyes slid to Phoebe. "He knew by the amount of obvious evidence, his brother was beyond a doctor's care. Besides, what was he to say about where they found him?"

Reverend Farrell shook his head. "A sorry business. What about Charles' father?" He offered the young man a sympathetic look. "Have you discovered any connection?"

"None. Neither Rugger was at The Lilacs at the time. Three witnesses swear both were with them hunting squirrel."

"And Phoebe's—and your—kidnapping? You implied something had turned up."

"Two things: John Rugger claims he was not the man Augie saw."

"Why do you think he's called Lying John?" sneered Charles. "Can't believe a word from his mouth—least not when he's sober."

"And the second thing?" asked Ernest Farrell.

"I conducted a thorough examination of the cabin yesterday and can now assure Miss Farrell our kidnappers will not repeat the incident. Whoever imprisoned us meant no real harm. In our haste to be away, we didn't notice they even left us this." He held up an old compass.

"Then…why?" The confusion in Phoebe's voice was palpable.

"I cannot answer precisely. My guess is they wanted to keep us out of the way for a short time. Whether I posed an immediate threat or you did, we can only speculate."

The pastor's eyebrows shot up. "Phoebe, a threat? Impossible."

"I suspect she knows more than she thinks she knows, and someone who was listening to our conversation was afraid she might reveal it."

The reverend stared at him incredulously. "About Simmons' murder?"

"Or something connected to it." Matthew shifted his eyes toward Phoebe.

"Who could have been listening? No one at all was around."

"We already know that's not entirely true. Augie was just down the hill, but he was hidden so well, we were unaware of him."

"Are you implying Augie had something to do with it? He could not have heard us from that distance. Ask him."

"No need to, Miss Farrell. He was not involved, but his presence raises possibilities. Ernest, did you see anyone skulking about in the church's park?"

Smoothing his mustache, Reverend Farrell ran through his memory of that day. "Augie saw Avery Spry and his hunting dog down by the river. You might ask Foster. He was gardening a good portion of the day, but I doubt he saw anything. He was readying the fronts of the church and parsonage for Amelia's arrival. Besides Spry, I only know of Asa Kiker. He was tying up his horse when I came out of the church."

173

Bentley nodded, glanced at the wide-brimmed hat, and turned to Charles. "Where were you yesterday?"

"Let me see." Charles put his fingertips together. "I was working in the barn and then the lower field until I rode up to The Lilacs. About the time the sun was going down, Asa Kiker galloped in as if a bear were chasing him. Told me to get Hugh and Kitch and any other men on hand, especially ones who could man a boat, and paddle down to the church. Said he feared the Farrell children had fallen into the river." He stopped when they heard a knock on the door. "Come in."

"Massa Charles," began Ruby. "Missus Mahala asked if you'd like me to bring tea."

Before Charles could answer, Bentley rose from his chair. "Not for me." When he picked up his hat, Phoebe noticed it looked quite new. "I was just about to leave. I've taken up enough of everyone's time and have learned what I came for. I'll just see myself out." Doffing his hat to the house servant, he exited the room.

"What about y'all, Massa Charles?"

Phoebe noted the title she gave him. Even worse, he took it in stride, as if it were his due.

Rising, he looked from Ernest to Phoebe. "We'll come out now and join Ma and my sisters."

"I'm afraid we'd best be going." The reverend waited with him while Phoebe passed through the door. "We are on our way to The Lilacs but thought we'd stop by so Amelia could meet your family."

"Well." Charles watched his sisters surrounding Phoebe. "I wish you could stay, though I understand. You have a fine young daughter, there, Reverend Farrell. She has significantly improved the neighborhood."

As Charles grinned, the pastor considered in what ways his daughter might be affecting the local social balance. "We think so, and hope everyone will think just as highly of her mother."

"No doubt we will." A smile played about Charles' lips as he continued to watch Phoebe. "You know what they say: like mother, like daughter."

Chapter 22

AS THE FARRELLS pulled into the long lane leading to The Lilacs, Amelia turned to her daughter. "What did Samuel have to say, Phoebe?

"We've been so busy today, I haven't yet read his letter."

"He gave me a note to pass on to Allison Wilson, his sister's mother-in-law. Ernest, do you think we will be staying at the Kikers' for long? I would like to drop the letter off today if it isn't far. With all I've had on my mind, if we don't, I'm afraid I might forget."

Though Augie appeared disappointed at the prospect, Phoebe leaned closer to the wagon seat. "Mama, you will enjoy both Allison and John Wilson. Of all the younger women I've met, my favorites are Emily and the Wilsons' daughter, Lisa White. I hope she and her family will be visiting them also. They are very close, and I'd like you to meet them."

The reverend patted his wife's hand. "If you are not too tired after meeting the Kikers, but let's not stay long. I'm looking forward to getting you all to myself."

"Ugh." Augie pulled a face as he whispered to Phoebe. "I wish they'd keep all their mushy stuff to themselves."

While his sister laughed, his mother sucked in her breath.

"What a magnificent home. It's huge—like one of the halls at the college. Can you imagine cleaning so many bedrooms, Phoebe?"

Before Phoebe answered, her mother was in rapture over the island of lilac trees.

"Darling, if you look to your right, you will see Hugh Kiker, Asa and Lavinia's son, exiting the stable."

"Oh, Ernest, he is handsome indeed—and grinning at Phoebe. No wonder there are rumors."

"That was Asa Kiker, The Lilacs' owner, coming out of the stable on Hugh's heels." While Pastor Farrell pulled the wagon to a halt, he waved at the two Mr. Kikers. "Been riding?"

"Yes," answered Asa. "We were checking a fence Kitch said needed mending." He nodded off in the distance toward a pasture where a huge bull was grazing. "I'm surprised to see you all out and about. I'd have thought the children would've slept all day."

"They were so exhausted after we collected Amelia yesterday, they dozed off before sundown."

Hugh lifted his eyebrows to Phoebe as he lifted her onto the gravel.

"It's a lovely day, Mr. Kiker. I didn't want to miss it."

"Neither you nor Augie appear to have suffered harm."

"We are both fine. Mr. Bentley's presence made it much less harrowing. Still, I don't think I will ever be able to sit on that bench without constantly glancing behind me. Thank you for your part in the search. I'd like you to meet my mother."

As introductions were made all around, Lavinia Kiker swept down the stairs. "My goodness, Asa. Why are you keeping our guests out in the sun? Oh, what a charming baby. Her eyes are huge, and look at those dimples—just like her sister's."

"We cannot stay long, Lavinia, but Amelia was eager to meet you before we drive on to the Wilsons'."

"I've been equally eager to meet you, Amelia. Come up onto the porch and we'll all have something cool to drink."

Seated in wicker chairs between the columns, the Farrells sampled an array of refreshments. The sun had drifted past its midpoint, casting them into the deep shade beneath the porch roof.

"You poor things." Lavinia fussed over Phoebe and Augie. "When we heard you were missing, we were frantic with worry. I can only imagine how terrified you felt, though I'm still confused about one thing. Matthew told us only he and Phoebe were kidnapped. How did you end up with them, Augie?"

As he recounted his part, Phoebe was not at all amazed certain details had grown larger. Her only surprise was Mrs. Kiker. She had supposed Lavinia would be eager to concentrate on Mama, but she instead demanded every detail. Clara, who had come out to join them, seemed bored beyond tears. Barely after Augie finished, Lucy began fussing, signaling to everyone it was time for her family to go.

Lavinia slipped her arm through Phoebe's. "Amelia, Ernest, would you mind terribly if we keep Phoebe with us a while longer? Hugh can drive her home in the trap."

"By herself?" Amelia glanced from Lavinia to Hugh, giving Phoebe hope she might refuse. "While I am sure you are a fine young man, the two of you can't go out riding alone. What would it suggest if you were seen?"

Lavinia was about to answer when Hugh cleared his throat. "I was hoping Augie could stay also. Father and I are taking the hounds out, and I thought he might like to come along."

"Yes, if you don't mind, Augie." Asa ruffled the boy's hair. "I'm sure Sparkles would welcome the chance to play with you. The more the dog comes to know the boy, Amelia, the easier his transition will be to your home."

"Can I, Mama?"

"May I, Augie. You are certainly able, and yes, you have our permission. Don't stay too long." Her gaze took in both of her children. I haven't had my fill of you, and I don't want you wearing out your welcome. Phoebe, this might be a good time to tell Lavinia your good news."

All heads spun in her daughter's direction.

"If you would still like for me to act as your secretary, Mrs. Kiker, my parents have given me their permission on a voluntary basis."

"Wonderful." Clapping her hands together, Lavinia offered Phoebe and her parents her most gracious smile. "Though it *is* a paid position."

"We would prefer, Lavinia," replied the reverend, "for Phoebe to help out for a while first. This way, we can see if her work suits you and if her mother can spare her the time."

"For now." Lavinia tightened the arm looped with Phoebe's, squeezing her closer to her side. "I haven't an iota of doubt her work will please me."

"Then, it's all settled." Reverend Farrell lifted the baby. "That is, darling, if you have no further objections."

As if Lucy thought he was talking to her, her fussing turned into wailing.

"Oh, dear." Amelia held out her hands to her youngest. "She didn't have her morning nap. I'm afraid we will have to leave the Wilsons for another day."

Since all was decided, each party headed in their respective directions. The eldest and youngest Farrells waved from their wagon, Augie and the Kiker men ambled to the barn, and Lavinia swept Phoebe and her daughter into the house.

In the foyer, Clara said her farewells and retreated up the stairs while Lavinia conducted Phoebe into her small study.

"This is where you will work every day, and I must admit your visit is timely. I have several important pieces of correspondence that must go out immediately." She retrieved a handful of paper from a drawer and positioned it, her inkwell, and blotter where Phoebe would find them most comfortable to use. "The first is to the station master in Winchester. Head it with today's date.

May 10, 1843

"Dear Mr. Franklin,

I am writing to you concerning a parcel you should have received from me yesterday. In addition, I am sending a letter for you to include with the said parcel. You already know the destination, as this particular stockholder is a constant correspondent of mine. Please see both the parcel and letter arrive at the next station at the earliest possible time, as both are quite important to me. I am personally in your debt and will remunerate you well for any costs to you.

Please forgive any inconvenience the urgent nature of this missive causes.

Yours truly,
Mrs. Lavinia Kiker

P.S. I am hoping to send you another load of potatoes at the beginning of next month.

"Very good. Your penmanship is excellent. The next letter is much like the other, except for the name and address of the recipient, of course."

Dear Mrs. Auger,

This letter is to introduce you to Bea Kiker and recommend her for the position we discussed in our last correspondence. The local ticket agent assures me she is on her way to you. She is a ready learner who will work very hard at whatever task you assign her. Her birth certificate and other papers are enclosed with this letter; please make certain they are returned to her, as she may need them in the future.

She is most precious to me, and I could not spare her were it not for her greater benefit.

Yours truly,
Lavinia Kiker

"Once you have finished copying them, just throw the first draft away and call Kitch. This parcel goes with him also—and make sure you place it in his hands. No one else's—not Asa's, not Hugh's, and certainly not one of our other slaves or employees. And of course..." She drew herself up into her most imperious posture. "I trust *anything* you hear or write within this room will *never* be repeated to *anyone*, no matter how official or how demanding."

As her conversation with Matthew Bentley began whirring in her head, she looked away. She could not remember mentioning anything about the Kikers beyond their kindness. "Yes, Ma'am. You have my promise."

"Very good. I would expect no less from our pastor's daughter."

"Where shall I tell him to take them?"

"He knows. I send all my correspondence by special courier."

"They are ready now, Ma'am."

Lavinia's surprise showed clearly on her face. "Excellent. I stand confirmed in my belief you were the correct choice for this position. After you find Kitch, come back here. I have a large stack of letters to go out, including some invitations to issue. They will likely be quite dull to copy, and you needn't finish them all today."

As she turned her attention to other matters, Phoebe did exactly as she was told. When she entered the hallway, however, she realized she did not know where she might find Kitch. Stepping into the kitchen, she spotted Mitilde. "Ma'am, would you please tell me where I may find Kitch? I have some correspondence from Mrs. Kiker to give him."

The dark-skinned cook cast her an amused glance. "Mm-mm. You best not get used to calling me 'ma'am.' Titles is reserved for Missus Kiker an' the like. I's just Mitilde, and you is Miss Farrell, ain't you?"

"I am, though you are welcome to call me Phoebe."

Mitilde shook her head. "What'd I just tell you? You is Miss Farrell to me, an' if you isn't wantin' trouble from Massa Kiker or to make trouble for me, you best be rememberin'."

Granny Bett shuffled into the kitchen. "I best be rememberin' what? I's rememberin' jus' fine. Don't know why y'all is tryin' convince folks I'm crazy."

"Never mind all that," muttered Mitilde, although Phoebe was not sure to which of them she was speaking. "Miss Farrell, you go back to the dining room an' wait a spell. I'll find Kitch and send 'im in."

As Phoebe waited, she grew restless. Moving over to the western window, she gazed at the pastures beyond the barn when she noticed a rich blue color from the corner of her eye. The bushes right in front of her housed a bird's nest, empty except for a broken shell.

Turning when she heard the kitchen door, she saw Granny Bett coming toward her, shakily holding out a glass of lemonade.

"This's fer you, Missy." The old woman peered into Phoebe's face, her expression a mixture of concern and sympathy.

Phoebe tilted up the edges of her mouth. "Thank you."

"You is smilin' at me, Missy, but I sees yer eyes is sad."

"I'm...I'm missing a friend whom I fear I'll never again see."

The aging eyes filled with mischief. "Don't you worry none. She be fine. Come 'ere." Granny Bett grabbed Phoebe's arm with her claw-like fingers and guided her back to the window. "You see that big ole cat over yonder?"

Phoebe nodded. He was a sizable gray tabby who wore a canny expression.

"Massa Kiker done fetch 'im from a friend's farm when Missus Kiker found herself a mouse—an' not a little one. More like a big ol' nasty rat." As she chuckled, her wrinkles nearly swallowed her eyes. "That ole prowler gotta keen eye on 'im. While he's searchin' for that big ol' rat, he spots this here little birdy." She angled her head toward the broken shell. "That Missus Kiker's special birdy. She been watchin' over her 'fore that egg was hatched, and she's not about to let that big tom catch her."

"What did she do?"

"Called Kitch and the caretaker. The two of them crept up on that big ole tabby and caught it in a sack, just like that." She acted out the motions with the words. "Tied it up real good 'fore they locked it away. But they gots themselves a...what do you white folks call it?" She paused to search her memory. "A dilemma. See, a sweet little kitten had sidled up to that ole prowler. So when they snatched 'im, they got no choice but to snatch 'er. Ain't nobody wantin' to hurt either one of 'em. Just gotta get that tom out o' the way 'til the little birdy can fly."

As the old shoulders shook with mirth, Phoebe began to grasp her meaning. "Did she—the birdy, I mean—fly away safely?"

"She done flied so high that ole gray cat ain't never gonna nab 'er."

When the door burst open, Kitch hurried over, his wide-brimmed hat in his hand. "What is you telling Missy Farrell, Granny?"

"Just showin' her that there little egg, and tellin' her the birdy flew away."

Kitch looked doubtfully from his great grandmother to Phoebe. "Don't pay Granny no mind, Missy Farrell. Her mind goes to wandering sumpthin' fierce. I hope she hasn't been botherin' you."

"No." Phoebe dimpled so deeply she could not will her cheeks to flatten. "I understood her perfectly, and she's not bothering me at all."

Chapter 23

EMILY SMILED AT her grandmother. "May Phoebe and I be excused from the table?"

"Certainly." Mary Nelson cleared the dessert plates. "Why don't the two of you go visit in your room? While Augie is finishing his pie, the four of us grown-ups will finish our tea."

Phoebe flashed her a quick smile. "Thank you for the delicious dinner."

"You are quite welcome. Amelia, your daughter is just a delight. I couldn't be happier Emily and she are becoming friends."

As Phoebe followed Emily down a hall, she felt a bit reticent. Emily had acted piqued on the way home from the Wilsons' tea and scarcely friendlier when her family last dined with the Nelsons. At the soiree, she had been her formerly affable self. "What a sweetly appointed room."

Emily tilted her lips up shyly. "Rose is my favorite color. You seemed rather far away during dinner. Are you concerned about your grandmother?"

"Yes, but she is progressing well. I'm so glad to have Mama back from Baltimore."

"Are you still suffering from your...abduction?"

Phoebe flicked a glance toward the door, though she had heard Emily close it. "No, I received this letter from a...friend... and have just read it as we rode here." She pulled it from her pocket. "He's the young man Mrs. Wilson and I were discussing during the tea in her home. His sister, Abigail, is married to Mrs. Wilson's son."

"Oh, I've met them both. When Joshua brought Abigail home, the Wilsons' held a reception. The wedding took place out West. She was beautiful and he—your friend—seemed nice when my grandparents introduced us. Has he written something upsetting?" Her petite features filled with concern.

"Not exactly. Here. Read it for yourself and tell me what you make of it."

Dear Phoebe,

I hope this note finds you well. I'm sending it along with your mother as the post takes so long.

A murder? In the Shenandoah Valley? It struck me as a peaceful spot during our travels to Abigail's in-laws.

Although I have only a few seconds to write, I am eager to tell you something I hope you will regard as good news: I'm coming for a visit later in the year. The Wilsons have given me leave to stay with them as soon as an opportunity arises. I will be pleased to renew my acquaintance with them and look forward to spending time with you—and your family, of course. I have been mulling over many things I would like to share, if time permitted, but perhaps they are better kept until I see you in person.

Your friend,
Samuel

"Are the two of you…close? He clearly expects you to welcome his visit." While Phoebe considered how much she wanted to divulge, Emily broke into such rapid speech, Phoebe suspected she had needed the pause to muster her courage.

"I am eager to hear your answer, but first I wish to ask for your forgiveness. If I ask you afterward, I will seem only to be expressing my relief; or if you tell me your heart belongs to another, I may lose my nerve. You see, though you have been kind to me, I've been growing so jealous I've entertained some uncharitable thoughts."

"Because of the attention Hugh Kiker has paid me?"

Emily dropped her gaze and nodded. "I have no right. He has expressed nothing toward me beyond a fondness for a younger sister."

"Of course, I forgive you, though you do not need to be jealous. Admittedly, he is very handsome, but I am certain he is not interested in *me*."

"If you are mistaken and something more…promising…develops between you, I am determined to be happy—genuinely happy—for you both. Have you shown this note to your parents?"

"No. I will if they ask to read it, but I would feel foolish admitting to the hopes it raised. It expresses nothing beyond a wish to share thoughts he finds difficult to pen. Lisa and her mother already look at me in a…particular way…when we speak of him. Papa has only recently noticed I am no longer a little girl."

"I know the look well—from Clara Kiker. Did you enjoy working for her mother? Grandpapa mentioned she'd offered you a position."

"I am just helping her out for a while, but the afternoon was pleasant."

"You do not want the position?"

Phoebe picked up a pillow laying against the sill and hugged it to her stomach. "It's not that. I have some…qualms."

"About what?"

"They own people."

Emily remained quiet for so long, Phoebe feared she felt offended. "Slavery is so common in Virginia and so readily accepted—even by some of our former pastors—I did not give that thought. If you feel uncomfortable, why did you agree to help?"

"My parents made me realize they—the Kikers—are also slaves. They just serve an invisible master."

"May I take the liberty of offering a piece of advice?"

"Yes, of course."

"God alone knows the secrets in each man's heart. People are not always as they seem. Do not form your opinion of Mrs. Kiker before you have time to know her."

LAVINIA SPOTTED THE Farrell children as she walked out onto the elevated porch. "Good morning, Phoebe, Augie. Hugh's with the new calves, just beyond the barn."

Augie jumped from his seat and took off running.

"I'm glad to see you have learned to drive the church's wagon. It's an important skill to master in the country. I reckon you all could walk most places in Princeton."

"Yes, ma'am. Our home was adjacent to the school, and people set up shops all around it—the school, I mean—to accommodate the students' needs and inclinations." While she ascended the steps, Phoebe removed her straw bonnet.

"Come in. I have a great deal for us to do. After luncheon, I will ask Hugh to let you drive the phaeton."

"I don't wish to be a bother."

"No bother at all." She smiled indulgently. "Men enjoy exhibiting their skills, particularly to pretty young women."

Phoebe tucked her chin down, pleased but shy with the compliment. If Lavinia noticed her discomfort, she was too polite to comment. Instead, she simply ushered Phoebe into her study and took her seat behind the desk.

After dictating a considerably large pile of letters, Lavinia noticed the time. "Why don't we take our lunch on the porch? It will be cooler." Once she had swept through the front door, she pulled out a chair for herself and another for Phoebe. "I simply love to see the lilacs in bloom. We should have them for a few more weeks. If we are lucky, they may return briefly in the summer. That deep purple one is my favorite, though I like this one, too, on your right. The variation in shade from lavender to blue is particularly charming."

"I had no idea lilacs grew so tall."

"Those are especially old, planted by Asa's grandmother." She pointed to the central group, which were more like trees than bushes. "They are lovely at first blossom. As the weather turns warmer, they quickly turn from white to cream and then a rather ugly brown. The lavender and purple blooms hold their color longer."

Mitilde pushed the screen door open with her hip, balancing a tray of sandwiches in one hand and tumblers in the other. "I's glad to find both of you together." She burst into a generous smile. "My niece and her man done jumped the broom a few days past. She said to be sure I tells each o' you special. She was might beautiful in her light blue frock."

Phoebe dimpled irrepressibly. As Mitilde retreated into the house, she glanced shyly at Lavinia. "You...know? About Mitilde's niece?"

Lavinia smiled graciously, unfolding her napkin before laying it across her lap. "Know her? I helped Granny Bett bring her into the world."

"She was born here?"

"Now, there's no use in getting bogged down in details, is there? Let's keep Mitilde's happy tidings to ourselves. There isn't anyone around here who'd desire to know them anyway, at least no one who hasn't already heard."

Phoebe's jaw dropped. "But..." She had so many questions, she could not think of how to frame one of them.

"Now, close that pink little mouth of yours before a bug flies in. If I hadn't already learned—on good authority—you are excellent at keeping confidences, I would never have offered you this position."

"How? Who could have..."

"How and who are best left unsaid, as is most everything, and look." She patted Phoebe's hand. "Here come Hugh and Augie."

Phoebe followed Lavinia's gaze to see them crossing the stable-yard.

"Mother. Miss Farrell." Hugh doffed his broad-brimmed hat as he lay his foot to the first step. "Mind if Augie and I join you?"

Augie assumed a polite expression until he spied the sandwiches. His eyes lit like a couple of fireflies.

"I'd like nothing better, and young master Farrell appears to be famished. Do you mind, Phoebe?"

As they reached the table, Mitilde was bringing out more plates and tumblers.

"It would be my pleasure, Mr. Kiker. This is an exceptionally happy day."

Though her brother cast her a quizzical eye, the cook slid her a subtle smile.

"How about your father and Charles, Hugh? Are they ready for lunch?"

"Yes, Ma'am. Both should arrive shortly."

"Then Mitilde, would you mind bringing out a few more place settings?"

"Yes'm, Missus Lavinia. I be right back an' I best be fetchin' a pitcher full o' tea. If you be needin' to speak to the new housemaid, she's upstairs, fixin' to clean your bedroom."

186

"Tell her I will be there presently. Phoebe, since you have the men to keep you company, would you mind if I just go up now? I've been developing a sick headache all morning."

Phoebe flicked her a concerned glance. They had been together all morning, and not once had she sensed anything amiss. "Certainly, Ma'am. Shall I recopy and post the letters you dictated?"

"That would be perfect. I will just go and lie down. I'm sorry Clara is not here to entertain you."

"It's all right. I'm used to being surrounded by men." As the words left her mouth, she heard how they sounded and felt her ears growing hot. "I mean since Mama has been away…"

Slapping through the screen with Asa on his heels, Charles shot her his widest grin. "You're like a treed coon surrounded by a pack of hounds."

Lavinia slid her husband a sharp glare as she passed him in the entry.

"Charles." Asa Kiker cleared his throat. "Miss Phoebe is…well, not exactly a guest, only she didn't grow up around you like your sisters or Clara."

"What? Can't I tease her a bit?" He plunked an amber glass on the table, sloshing the contents up against the rim.

As Asa set his down with more decorum, he took the seat his wife had vacated. "Don't mind Mr. Simmons, Miss Phoebe. He's had a rough morning. Here, Charles. You'd better eat a sandwich. Hugh, where'd your mother go?"

When Hugh tossed her a questioning look, Phoebe answered for him. "She's speaking with a new housemaid and then lying down."

"A new one? As soon as your mother trains them, they seem to disappear. It's getting to the point I don't want to send her another. We'll need all the hands we can muster in the fields this summer. The rainy weather is pushing up a great crop of rye."

Before his son could reply, Mitilde came onto the porch again.

"Massa Hugh, your mother's wantin' you to learn Miss Phoebe to drive the phaeton."

"Thank you, Mitilde." He turned his most charming smile on Phoebe. "I'd be delighted."

"I'll aks Kitch to hitch it up."

Augie glanced from one to the other. "Why? Girls are no fun at all."

"Heck," said Charles, sliding into a more lopsided grin. "That's the point. Her being a girl and all, not the 'no fun' part. If you're too busy, Hugh, I'll be happy to take your place."

Asa placed a hand on Charles' shoulder. "I need you to go out to the rye field and estimate how soon it'll be ready."

"Course, Asa. Wouldn't do for me to take Hugh's place, would it?"

"That's enough, son."

"Alright, *Pa.*"

Asa pushed back his seat so sharply, it banged against the gray stone. "Let's go. I'll check it with you. We can take a couple of sandwiches with us. Leave the glass."

Charles stood also, offering Phoebe an elaborate bow until Asa gripped his elbow. As the remaining diners watched them navigate the tall steps, Augie knit his eyebrows together.

"What's wrong with him? He was bowing to Phoebe like she's some princess."

Hugh twisted his lips into a grim smile. "He's not…feeling himself today."

"Why'd he call your father 'Pa'?"

Phoebe gave Augie a quick pinch.

"Ow! Cut it out, Phebes."

"Then stop asking so many questions."

Chapter 24

HUGH GLANCED FROM Augie to Phoebe and down at their now empty plates. "Charles is grieving today over the loss of his father. Are you ready, Miss Farrell? Now's as good a time as any. Augie, a phaeton seats only two. Would you like to play with Sparkles by yourself for a bit?"

"Sure!" Scraping his chair away from the table, he scampered toward the barn while Hugh led Phoebe to the buggy.

"You will find this a smoother and more facile ride than your wagon."

Grasping the reins, she began to circle the lilac trees before heading down the lane. "It's so light. Why is it called a phaeton?"

"It was named for the son of Helios who almost set the earth on fire as he tried to drive his chariot into the sun. Because of its weight, and spring action, some men are disposed to drive it recklessly."

"Do you enjoy Greek Myths?"

"As literature. And you?"

"Yes. I find the stories fascinating, and, as you have implied, they offer warnings about our hidden inclinations."

"Speaking of things hidden, Miss Farrell, I was glad Mother suggested this driving lesson. It gives me a chance to discuss something with you privately."

Phoebe held her breath, afraid she had been woefully naïve about his intentions.

"My mother is an excellent judge of character, so I suspect this goes without saying, but I trust you will keep anything you hear in her service confidential."

Lavinia had offered her a similar warning, and while she felt relieved this was all he wished to mention, she felt puzzled by his mother's need for secrecy. Her correspondence had fallen into only three categories: issuing or responding to social invitations, inquiries about parcels, and offers of condolence. Admittedly, she had a surprising number of friends who had recently—in her vernacular—reached the promised land or who were about to cross the river Jordan. The only Jordan River Phoebe knew was in the Bible, an ocean away from the Shenandoah Valley.

"You can depend on me, Mr. Kiker."

"I am glad. Mother is not well."

"Nothing serious, I hope."

"Honestly, I'm not sure. Today's headache is just one in a recurrent pattern of late. I don't remember when they began, but I suspect an emotional component and am trying to protect her from further strain."

"One kept her from Mr. Simmons' funeral and another prevented her from remaining at the Wilsons' tea."

"Yes, since you mention it, they seemed to have started with Simmons' murder. Initially, I blamed the sedative Dr. Stillwell had administered. She found the body, you know, and went into absolute hysterics. It took all of us to calm her down sufficiently to guide her to her room, and she didn't come out for several days."

"That's completely understandable. I would have been hysterical also."

Seeing her pinched brow, Hugh frowned. "I am sorry to burden you, Miss Farrell."

"Not at all. I greatly admire your mother."

"Thank you. So do I. She is a woman of strength and courage, if not by nature, then because she has had to be."

Phoebe was not sure of what he meant. Lavinia's life had seemed one of privilege. Nonetheless, she genuinely wished to be of service in any way she could. As she noted Hugh's discomfort—perhaps he felt he had confided too much—she decided to change the subject.

"Do you remember all the strange noises I was hearing?"

"Yes, and I must apologize. I haven't followed up on exploring your attic."

"There's no longer a need."

"Charles mentioned he and Augie explored it with you.

"He did, and we found nothing whatsoever to raise alarm. Since that day, they have altogether stopped."

"That seems odd, though you're probably growing used to your surroundings."

Phoebe looked down at the reins. "You mean, you think I imagined them?"

"No, just misattributed their cause. You look unconvinced."

She looked away as warmth crept into her cheeks. When her father suspected Augie was embellishing a story, he used the same tone.

"What has changed between now and the last noises you heard?"

Furrowing her brow, she traced the past days in her memory, when all at once she brightened.

"Well?" Hugh grinned. "Don't keep me in suspense."

"I've heard nothing since the day I was kidnapped."

"Hmm… That *is* peculiar. Wasn't that the day your mother arrived? Did she shift around the furniture?"

"Not that I can tell, but do you remember the limb Augie climbed down? Foster sawed it off. He feared a good wind would drive it through the dormer window."

"So there you have it. That limb must have been scraping against the side of the house." His tone was light, yet when she glanced his way, he was narrowing his eyes while toying with his lip. As an idea of her own began shifting into place, she was amazed she had not already thought of it. Afraid it might occur to him, she quickly changed the subject.

"Am I keeping the reins well-enough in hand?"

"Wh-what? Oh. Yes, you are driving admirably. If you will, pull over by the barn. I see Charles sitting up on the porch and intend to talk with him."

"Thank you for the lesson, Mr. Kiker. I'll just see if your mother has any more correspondence she needs to dictate."

PHOEBE FOUND LAVINIA resting, so she stepped into the kitchen for some tea. "Mitilde, Mrs. Kiker has one of her headaches. I think I'll go out on the porch and sit a spell. Please call me when she awakens."

"Yes'm, Missy Farrell. I be sure to let you know."

As Phoebe pushed the screen door open, she spotted Hugh and Charles sitting at the wicker table where they had all eaten lunch. Augie was kneeling beside Otto, Hugh's oldest Chesapeake Bay Retriever, while Charles was pulling the stopper from an amber filled cut-glass decanter.

"You've had enough." Hugh took the decanter from his grip.

"Growing greedy with your liquor? You always did keep the best of everything." Hearing the door swing shut, he craned his neck around. "Speaking of the devil, or maybe I should say an angel, here's Phoebe now. We better watch out. She may be coming to make sure we're not bad influences on her little brother."

As she reached the table, Hugh nudged Augie and whispered, "Stand up. A lady is present."

"Phoebe? She's not a lady. She's my sister." Rolling his eyes as his hero arose, he stood also.

Charles wobbled, bracing himself against the table, but he snatched the decanter to pour himself another drink. "Don't worry, Miss Farrell." He raised his glass in salute. "The boy is only drinking tea."

Hugh offered her a slight bow. "Would you care to join us?"

Charles pulled out the chair between him and Augie. "Sit next to me. Hugh's becoming as stingy with your company as he is with…well, everything. First Charlotte Wimpler. Oh, you do not know her—a girl we met while at Virginia Military Institute. Sweet thing, a lot like little Emily, another of his conquests. Looks like Hugh has now set his sights on northern territory."

"Please excuse him, Miss Farrell. He is not himself, and Charles, get a hold of yourself."

"Of course, Hugh always does get his pick of everything—even dogs. You know, Miss Farrell, Otto was supposed to be mine. Picked him out before he opened his eyes. What kind of stupid name is Otto anyway?" Charles bent down to pat the dog's head.

"I like it," squeaked Augie, running his hand down the retriever's spine. "And he does too, don't you boy? See—he's smiling."

"Careful." Hugh patted his hand against his leg. "Come, Otto. He's not smiling, Augie. He's beginning to bare his fangs." Fastening the dog's collar to a chain, Hugh turned to his friend. "You know I would have given him to you if I'd been allowed, so drop it."

"Yes, Massa. Anything you say, Massa. Why, you not only get your pick of women and dogs, you got your pick of fathers."

"I didn't make that choice and you know it. Since you can't control yourself in the presence of a lady..." Flicking Phoebe an apologetic glance, he grasped Charles by the shoulders, hauled him down the steps, and shoved him toward the barn. "Go sleep it off."

As Otto began growling and straining against his chain, Augie darted to the rail. "Look out, Hugh!"

Charles had struggled to his feet and was taking a run at him.

"Augie." Phoebe sprung up beside him. "Go fetch Kitch. He's in the stable."

"And miss the fight? No way!"

Phoebe hurried down the stairs, looking for someone—anyone—she might call for help. They were wailing away at each other like a couple of schoolboys.

"You're the only son who mattered." Charles wiped the blood from his lip. "Heck, even my 'pa' liked you best—licking at your hand like a blasted dog!"

As he was taking another swing, Hugh caught him by the arm and pinned him to the ground. "Have you had enough?"

Growing oddly still, Charles narrowed his eyes. "It was *you!* All this time I've been thinking..."

"What was me?" Hugh got up and brushed the grass from his shirt. "I don't know what you are talking about."

Charles staggered upright, cradling his head in his hands. "She came running at me out of nowhere, hollering like the house was on fire..."

"Who?"

"Birdie...sobbing something fierce. 'Massa Kiker, Massa Kiker—'e done kilt 'im.' I thought she was..."

"Was what?"

Charles stared at Hugh as if seeing him for the first time. "You think I don't know, don't hear what even the slaves mutter? All this time I've been searching for her, afraid she'd bring the law down on Asa...but *you* killed him!"

"Me? I was..."

Making a guttural rumble, Charles rushed forward, knocking into Hugh with such force he stumbled backward. Charles was panting so erratically Phoebe thought he might be crying, and Hugh lay so still even Augie looked afraid. Stumbling forward, Charles grabbed Hugh's shirt collar and dragged him toward the lilacs.

"Stop!" called Augie. "You'll hurt him."

While Charles flipped Hugh face downward, Augie fell silent. A bright patch of red was widening through Hugh's black hair.

"Get away, boy," snarled Charles, sliding Augie a menacing glare. Ripping Hugh's shirt, hem to yoke, he tore off a sleeve, bound the unresisting wrists to a slender trunk, and gripped the whip on his belt. "He killed my pa, and now he's gonna pay."

Phoebe and Augie locked eyes, each recalling vividly what their father had said he would do. "No!" mouthed Augie, his lips quivering as she threw herself in the way of the lash, then he began crying at the top of his lungs. "God, help Phoebe! Give her courage! Give her courage—and quick!"

Otto started barking and howling.

"Mitilde!" Mrs. Kiker called from inside the house. "What's that boy doing to the dog? Tell him to stop his caterwauling! Oh, I'm beginning to rue the day..." Flinging the screen wide open, she halted so abruptly Mitilde stumbled into her back. "Charles Simmons! What on earth do you think you are doing?" Snatching up her skirts, she ran down the steps as Charles was flinging Phoebe aside. As he raised the whip to bring it down, Lavinia seized his arm.

"Step aside, Miss Lavinia." He shook her off. "You've been nothing but good to me. This here is between me and Hugh."

As Phoebe rose, Augie wrapped his arms around her waist and held her fast. Mitilde, an arm's length behind them, bent over, her chest heaving from the unexpected sprint. Hearing all the commotion, Kitch had come running from the stable and was looking anxiously from his mistress to the foreman, and Granny Bett was slowly hobbling down the steps.

"Let me go, Augie." Dropping down beside Hugh, Phoebe placed her fingers against the base of his neck.

"Is he breathing?"

She nodded, turning from her brother to Lavinia. "I think he's coming to."

Faint with relief, Lavinia pulled herself up to her full height and calmly took a stand where the whip would strike her face if Charles dared to bring it down. "I do not know what you think you have discovered..."

"It was Hugh, Miss Lavinia. *He* killed my pa. Birdie smacked right into me that day, all hysterical-like, fighting me like a wild thing an' bawling his name."

"Oh, Charles. I've prayed this day would never come. Hugh didn't kill your father. *I* did."

The gasp Phoebe heard might have come from her own lips or Mitilde's or even Augie's. His eyes had grown as round as moons.

"You?"

"Yes, Charles. It was me. Hugh was nowhere about. Birdie was calling his name because she was desperate to *find* him."

As they all stared in stunned silence, Lavinia pressed her hands to her face, as if trying to shield herself from the memory.

"I had been searching for Kitch. That morning, I purchased a new kind of bean from Mr. Schrag and wanted him to plant it in the garden. I was approaching his cabin when I heard an unearthly shrieking and what I *thought* must be cat whimpering. So I picked up the hoe Kitch had leaned against his cabin, set on defending the poor creature, never imagining..."

As she glanced from Kitch to Mitilde, she struggled to subdue her emotions. "When I snuck around the corner, I saw Birdie on the grass, trying to keep herself covered up while she was frantically scrambling backward. I will *never* forget that moment. She looked like a cornered animal who knew perfectly well what was bound to happen: trembling all over, crying and begging your father to leave her be. He just...laughed."

Charles glanced away, too ashamed to reply or even hold her gaze, and spotted Asa Kiker rushing toward them with Mr. Bentley.

Lavinia squared her shoulders and set her jaw. "I was not about to let Edward do to Birdie what he'd...what he'd done to me."

Asa stopped abruptly, the blood draining from his face.

"Charles, have you never wondered *why* your father paid Hugh so much attention?"

"I...I thought he..." Charles glanced again at Asa, who clinched his jaw so tightly, he could not speak. "I thought he hated me because of what Asa and my mother had..."

"Oh, Charles. You are the spitting image of Edward. The differences between Hugh and you are all me—my father's nose and jaw, my mother's shape of eyes. Think for a minute. You know Hugh's grandparents and all his uncles. Is there a dark-eyed Kiker among them?"

Asa shot Charles a look that nearly dropped him to his knees. "If your father wasn't dead already, I'd kill him myself. Go get your things and clear out."

Spinning toward his voice, Lavinia laid a gentle hand against his cheek. "The boy has suffered enough under Edward's cruelty."

"Oh, my sweet Lavinia." He wrapped her in his arms. "Why did you insist I keep the man on?"

She pressed her forehead against his chest, tears she had been straining to keep back flowing freely. "He...he threatened to tell you he was Hugh's father."

"*You* could have told me." Sweeping his hand over her hair, he caressed the back of her neck, and encouraged by his tenderness, she raised her face.

"Could I, Asa? If you had discovered I was with child, would you have fulfilled our engagement? By the time our parents finished the arrangements, I was thoroughly in love with you. I couldn't have born for you to...to..." She tucked her head down, unable to sustain his gaze. "I...I felt so...*dirty*. And when Hugh was born, you were so delighted. The two of you were inseparable. How could I destroy..."

While Asa held her close, he searched for Hugh, and his eyes filled with clear relief as Phoebe helped him stand upright. Matthew Bentley stepped forward, but Granny Bett blocked his way.

"Now don't you go touching my Missy Lavinia." Raising a knotted finger, she poked the lawman's chest. "I done told you already, but you wouldna listen. I killt him. She only think she done it."

"Now, Granny Bett." Bentley stepped back a pace. "We have been through this before."

"Don't I know it? Nobody believes an old slave woman. Y'all think I done lost my senses. Well, I got sense enough. When I heard that nasty ol' polecat moanin' and seed him raisin' his ugly head, I took my foot and pushed it right back into the dirt where it belonged. Wasn't nothin' to it. Birdie'd run off, an' everybody else was tryin' to calm down Missy Lavinia. I just held my foot there until the varmint

196

quit his wrigglin', then walked off." She brushed one palm against the other.

"Matthew." Asa shook his head. "You can't arrest her. She wouldn't make it to trial, and even if she did, you can't prove anything. It's just her word, but they'd string her up on the spot."

Mr. Bentley thrust a hand through the back of his hair, looking down at the ground as he considered how to answer. "I certainly don't desire that, but she just confessed to killing a man. Am I to simply let her go?" He glanced from Asa to Lavinia.

"You can't charge Mother either." Hugh pressed his fingers to the throbbing spot where his blood had matted. "You have a witness who will swear she didn't do it and another—if we can find her—who will swear Mother struck him in her defense."

As Phoebe held him steady, she noticed the tender look he was giving Lavinia and understood his constant probing.

Mr. Bentley was not so easily satisfied. "So you're saying they *would* believe Granny?"

"You know they would," Asa answered, "if her testimony saved a white woman—and this county's most prominent one at that. You also know how that confession would end. We have come full circle to a lynching, not that Granny's old neck would take much to crack."

"What about you, Hugh?" asked Matthew. "Do you intend to press charges against Charles? It's well within my bounds to arrest him for assault."

"No." Hugh shook his head, peering a little uncertainly at Asa. Charles had dropped to all fours and, from the shaking of his shoulders, seemed to be weeping. "If I thought he'd killed *my* father, I'd have done the same."

"Come on then, son. Are you able to walk?" Asa glanced questioningly at Phoebe, who disengaged Hugh's arm. "Let's take you inside and clean up your head. It's a good thing it's as hard as your mother's."

Standing on his own, Hugh noticed Phoebe's torn frock. "What happened?"

"Why," answered his mother, recollecting what the girl had done, "she threw herself right over you, Hugh, to protect you from Charles' whip. Phoebe, are you alright?"

197

"I'm fine, Mrs. Kiker." Phoebe hugged her little brother, who had squeezed into Hugh's vacated place. "Charles pulled up on the whip when he saw he might hit me."

"Come inside the both of you, and we'll have Mitilde mend that tear. We can't have you going home to your mother looking like that. She'll never let you come back. You are one brave young woman whom I hope to keep around for a very long time. And by the way, my friends call me Lavinia."

"HOLD ON, PHOEBE." As Matthew Bentley saw her driving the church wagon out of The Lilacs' drive, he urged his horse to a trot. "I'd like to accompany the two of you home if you don't mind. The sun is beginning to go down, and I'm going your direction anyway."

"We don't mind at all, do we, Augie?"

Augie offered Mr. Bentley a ready grin. "Where are you headed?"

"Richmond. My job here is finished, but I would like to speak to your mother and father." He laughed when he saw the look on Augie's face. "No, you are not in trouble, son. I want to say goodbye and commend them for raising a pair of very fine children. Mitilde told me what you did, Miss Farrell."

"It was only what my father told us he would do in a similar situation."

"Are you alright? That must have been quite an ordeal, especially on top of our kidnapping, even for a daughter of Ernest Farrell."

"Now, you are teasing me." Phoebe dimpled deeply but they quickly faded. "I am concerned about Granny Bett."

"As am I. I dare not take her to Richmond for the reasons Asa already cited."

"You do not look entirely happy."

Bentley nodded soberly. "I am a lawman. She may have been defending Birdie in her own mind as much as Lavinia did, or if not Birdie, then all those like her, whether in Simmons' past or the future. You are too keen not to have noticed their coffee-colored footman. Nevertheless, by taking justice into her own hands she acted no differently than the vigilantes might if I attempted to bring her in."

"What will you do?"

"With Granny Bett? I see little point in doing anything. I have yet to figure out if her mind is going or if she's exceedingly clever. Either way, I suspect she's not long for this earth. She was so overwrought, Mitilde had to guide her to her bed and is worried she may never arise from it."

"What if Mitilde, not Lavinia, had swung the weapon?"

"If I had a satisfactory answer to that question, I would run for Congress, although I doubt I'd be elected. To quote your father, 'Changed hearts change habits.' Justice needs to be meted out fairly, but while the current constituency is run by fear rather than fairness, I don't see much chance of that."

"I'm not sure I understand."

"Fear comes in many forms, Miss Farrell. Nate Turner's rebellion is still fresh in most slave owner's minds.[xv] Asa Kiker is not one of them, but he has the livelihood of his family to consider. Without slave labor, he might not be able to support them, certainly not in the manner in which they've become accustomed. Then he has Hugh's future to think about, and Clara's. As I'm sure you are aware, a sizable dowry makes a woman more appealing than she might be otherwise. It's one thing for a man to give up his wealth and quite another to deprive those he loves."

Phoebe looked down, at a loss to provide even a theoretical solution, but Augie cut in. "I still don't get why Birdie was so upset she went bawling to Mr. Charles, and why has she been living in our…"

His sister pinched his thigh, though she hoped, perched atop his horse, their escort could not see.

Bentley only cocked his head and grinned. "Augie, your sister has just convinced me she knows the answer to your questions. However, I'd prefer, Miss Farrell, if you were to forget *everything* you learned today. Were any of it revealed, it could cause a great deal of damage."

Augie flicked him a doubtful look. "No chance of that. Papa says she's as sharp as a…as a… Phoebe, what is it he says?"

Mr. Bentley chuckled. "A steel trap. I'm inclined to agree with him, but there's forgetting by accident and forgetting on purpose. It's the latter type of forgetting I'm trusting your sister will do."

"I will happily oblige you, sir, but what about Charles Simmons?"

"He can say nothing without recounting his part and Lavinia's motives. Both would hurt his whole family deeply if they became known."

"Poor Lavinia. I can only imagine how she feels."

"Yes, and she will need your help now even more than before—and not just your friendship."

As Phoebe spun her head in his direction, she found his eyes crinkling at their corners.

"Yes." He smiled. "I am aware of Lavinia's endeavors, or at least I had strong suspicions. You have just confirmed them. If you truly wish to be an asset, you had best school your face to remain as silent as your voice. Avery Spry is not as witless as he looks."

Blushing profusely, Phoebe could not think of a reply.

"I hope you decide to permanently accept the position. You are perfectly placed."

"You have been talking with my father."

"Indeed, I have."

"Are you encouraging me to…"

"Love your *neighbors* whenever opportunities present themselves."

"But…if I understand you correctly…your beliefs set you against the very laws you are sworn to uphold."

Compressing his lips together, he reflected for a moment before answering. "I've often been pondering that very thing of late. As I see it, I am faced with three choices: enforcing the law as it is written, deciding to take it into my own hands—which would bring me full circle to the beginning of our discussion, or moving to a place where the law is just. Only one of those is tenable."

"You are leaving Virginia?"

"I am. I've been offered a position in a small industrial town named for the late Chief Justice Allen of the colonial supreme court. I wrote my letter of resignation the evening after our kidnapping and will be turning it in to Governor McDowell tomorrow."

Augie scrunched up his face. "I don't get what you are talking about. I mean…I understand most of your words, but half the time it's like you are speaking in some sort of code."

"Ask your sister when you are a little older, or if she is like my sister and refuses to tell, come and see me when you have gained your majority. My home, wherever it may be, will always open to either one of you."

Epilogue

WHEN ALLISON WILSON spotted a wagon rolling up the lane, she hurried to her home's heavy door. "John, the pastor and his family are here."

John Wilson slipped up to tower behind her. "Come in, Ernest. Amelia, children. We were glad to meet you at church this morning. Phoebe, I wish we knew you were coming. We would have invited Lisa and Jordan. "

"Amelia, I almost feel I already know you, and this must be Lucy." The warmth in Allison's voice was unmistakable, and when she held out her arms to the baby, Lucy surprised everyone by leaning into them. "How was your trip, and how is your mother?"

"She is doing better than the doctors first expected, and the trip itself was uneventful. It's all that's happened since I've arrived that has thrown me into a bit of a dither."

Allison, who had been making faces to engage Lucy, returned the whole of her attention to the baby's mother. "Why, what has happened?"

Ernest's eyebrows arched up. "You haven't heard?"

"No," answered John. "This far north, we are at a disadvantage. Please come in. Allison and I would be interested in hearing about it."

"Well, first," began the reverend, "I'd like to ask you to please excuse our delay in coming to visit you. We were on our way Thursday, but we turned back. Lucy was over-tired from all the excitement. She seems quite taken with you, Allison. She's not too sure anymore about me."

John smiled at his wife as he ushered them all into the parlor. "Allison has a way with babies. Don't worry. Joshua acted like that when I returned from an extended trip to Washington. He was just about Lucy's age. I think he had become accustomed to having only women about, and my deeper voice alarmed him."

While they were choosing seats, a maid brought in a tea tray with the Sally Lunn bread Phoebe remembered Lavinia liking.

"Thank you, Dahlia." Allison handed Lucy to Phoebe while she poured. "So, tell us what has happened."

Amelia looked at her husband. "Ernest, you are so much better at telling stories than I am, and it all happened before I arrived. Do you mind?"

"Not at all, though I'm not sure where to begin."

"I can tell it," offered Augie.

Amelia rumpled his hair. "Let your father, then you can fill in details along the way."

"I guess," began the reverend, "we haven't spoken much with the two of you since the Kikers' soiree. The evening before Amelia was to arrive, the children went missing, and Foster was nowhere to be found. Fortunately, Asa Kiker happened by so he called out the Simmons boys and a handful of folks from The Lilacs to form a search party."

"Oh, my stars," said Allison. "You must have been beside yourself."

"I was. To make a tediously long story short, someone had snatched both Phoebe and Matthew Bentley, who—unbeknownst to me—had been visiting that day."

John Wilson sat up straight. "Snatched? What do you mean?"

"It was a very strange business, and I must admit I still do not understand it. While Bentley assures us we need not fear a repeat, he does not explain his reasoning well."

Phoebe absorbed herself in amusing her sister.

"Well, where was Augie?" asked Allison. "You said he was missing too."

"He was trailing them. It's largely due to him they escaped."

John gave Augie a look full of surprise and congratulations. "How many kidnappers were there?"

"Four." The boy's eyes gleamed. "One of them was as tall as you are and another looked an awful lot like the man Papa found stabbed in the Kiker's office."

"Wait—what?" Allison sat forward while the pastor sipped his tea.

"I didn't get to that part yet. The man's name was Silas Rugger. His brother and he were altering The Lilacs' distillery log and got into an argument. One thing led to another, and the brother—a man called Lying John—pulled out a knife."

"How horrible." Allison set down her cup. "Do you know them, John?"

"I know of them. Why were they in the distillery?"

"Edward Simmons had been selling Kiker's barrels on the black market."

Mrs. Wilson poured everyone another round of tea. "So, was Silas Rugger's murder connected to Edward Simmons'?"

"Not according to Bentley."

"Then who did kill Edward?"

"I'm very short of details. I thought the guilty party confessed, but Bentley said there weren't any charges to bring. In fact, he returned to Richmond yesterday."

John Wilson sat back in his chair. "Maybe a case of self-defense. The Kikers must be relieved."

"I confess I am," admitted Amelia. "I'd begun to wonder what sort of place Ernest had brought us to."

"Here, Phoebe." Allison held out her hands. "I'll take Lucy again if she'll come to me. Honestly, Amelia, I can't remember anything like this in all the years I've lived here."

"I thought you'd been raised in this valley."

"I moved here after marrying John. I grew up in a small town north of Philadelphia. I lent your daughter a book written by my closest childhood friend. Are you enjoying it, Phoebe?"

"Yes, when I've found time to read. I'm at the part where Alcy's future husband proposes, but I don't want to spoil it for Mama. She'd like to read it after Emily if that's alright with you."

"Of course, and speaking of Alcy, we've had some exciting news. Samuel's mother wrote to me recently. The whole family is coming for a visit."

"Oh, that reminds me." Amelia reached into her reticule. "As we waited for my train, Samuel gave me this to give to you."

"Well, let's see what he has to say." Allison read the brief note. "John, we need to begin refurbishing the guest rooms."

"I can't imagine Samuel caring what they look like."

"It's not from him; it's from Anna Mary." She glanced from her husband to Amelia and Phoebe. "Our Joshua's mother-in-law. They've accepted our invitation and will be here for Christmas."

Meet the Author

Sydney Tooman Betts resides with her husband near the extensive cavern system that inspired the setting for several chapters in her series The People of the Book.

While single, Ms. Betts (B.S. Bible/Missiology, M.Ed) took part in a variety of cross-cultural adventures in North and Central America. After marrying, she and her husband lived in Europe and the Middle East where he served in various mission-support capacities. Her teaching experiences span preschool to guest lecturing at the graduate level.

Before penning her first novel, *A River too Deep,* she ghost-wrote several stories for an adult literacy program.

For My Readers

By now, you have likely guessed that at least one if not several characters in this book were part of the Underground Railroad. Perhaps you became suspicious when you read of the quilt hanging on the parsonage line. The multiple box pattern announced it was time to pack up and be ready to leave, in this case, because a new family was moving into the parsonage. Had I hung a bear paw pattern from the line, it would have advised passengers to travel via the mountains.

Since members of the Underground Railroad did not document the use of quilts, some historians cast doubt on the tradition. Ozella McDaniel Williams, however, asserts her family handed down these signals for generations.[xvi] Geese patterns pointed north, a bow tie declared a change of clothing was essential, and a monkey wrench said tools were necessary for the journey. Whether this information is true or false is unprovable, though it served my purpose for this story.

All names employed throughout the book are historically accurate, whether the character is enslaved or free, but *Phoebe's Secret* is wholly a work of fiction. I loosely based The Lilacs on an extant plantation in the Shenandoah Valley, and in 1843, James McDowell was Virginia's governor. Beyond him, each character is a product of my imagination except for a few portrayals, by name and with permission, of beloved friends.

I would like to thank Alan Dyer, a criminal detective who graciously took the time to answer my questions. I plan to use his name and the name of another detective friend as characters in subsequent mysteries. Fellow author, Nadine Keels, not only read my manuscript but she also tirelessly made herself available to answer my questions or advise me concerning sensitive issues that I, as a pink person with brown spots (rather than her deeper, richer hues) might have otherwise missed. We have never met each other in person, but I consider her a friend.

Writing is far easier for me than letting readers know my books exist, so please consider leaving a rating on Goodreads or an honest review on the site where you purchased this novel. I am deeply grateful for any help. Reviews make a huge difference.

Lastly, you have been getting to know me through these pages. I would enjoy getting to know you. If you like this idea or would like to know more about following Jesus, please send a message to my Facebook author page, Sydney Tooman Betts, or visit my website: https://toomantales.weebly.com.

To my readers who have become friends and my friends who have become readers: I am sincerely grateful for your constant love and support. You know who you are. You have kept my head up when it was drooping and have pushed me to become a better writer. Your friendship is a true reward!

Endnotes

---

[i] I Samuel 28:12
[ii] Genesis 9:25
[iii] Luke 6:31
[iv] John 1:1-5
[v] Genesis 1:1-2
[vi] Philippians 2:6-8
[vii] Isaiah 49:15
[viii] Romans 13:9-10
[ix] I Corinthians 8:13
[x] Judges 17:6, 21:25
[xi] I Samuel 17:40
[xii] Luke 5:27
[xiii] Luke 7:36-50
[xiv] Matthew 5:3
[xv] Nate Turner's rebellion, 1831
[xvi] Dobard and Tobin, *Hidden in Plain View*, 1999

Made in the USA
Monee, IL
01 August 2020